Dear Reader,

Christmas, while lovely, can be quite stressful. There are so many demands on a very small amount of time. There are the cards (we've designed our own for years and years but sometimes I yearn to just buy them!) the presents, the wrapping, the shopping, the cooking, and all those trillion other little and big things that need to be attended to.

So not much time for reading, I hear to you say! Well, the point of *A Christmas Feast* is that it's full of little treats – stories you might have time to read while you're waiting for the mince pies to brown or for the bath to run.

Most of the stories have appeared before in magazines, but unless you've read every magazine ever printed there's bound to be something you haven't read yet.

There are a couple of longer stories that have only appeared digitally before and one brand-new story, written especially – *A Christmas Feast* – in honour of the collection's title.

So there should be something for everyone and with luck, you might find a little time to find out!

Here is my Christmas gift to you, with love and Happy Christmas.

Katie Fforde
2014

About Katie

'I live in the beautiful Cotswold countryside with my family, and I'm a true country girl at heart.

I first started writing when my mother gave me a writing kit for Christmas, and once I started I just couldn't stop. *Living Dangerously* was my first novel and since then, I haven't looked back.

Ideas for books are everywhere, and I'm constantly inspired by the people and places around me. From watching TV (yes, it is research) to overhearing conversations, I love how my writing gives me the chance to taste other people's lives and try all the jobs I've never had.

Each of my books explores a different profession or background and my research has helped me bring these to life. I've been a porter in an auction house, tried my hand at pottery, refurbished furniture, delved behind the scenes of a dating website, and I've even been on a Ray Mears survival course.

I love being a writer; to me there isn't a more satisfying and pleasing thing to do. I particularly enjoy writing love stories. I believe falling in love is the best thing in the world, and I want all my characters to experience it, and my readers to share their stories.'

Also by Katie Fforde

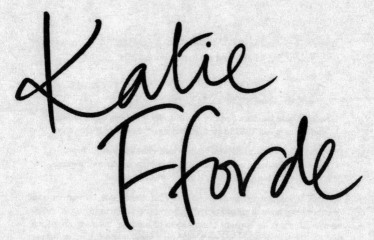

Katie Fforde

A Christmas
Feast
And other stories

arrow books

Published by Arrow Books 2014

2 4 6 8 10 9 7 5 3

First published in Great Britain in 2014 by Arrow Books

Arrow Books
Penguin Random House
20 Vauxhall Bridge Road,
London SW1V 2SA

www.randomhouse.co.uk

Addresses for companies within The Random House Group Limited can be found at: www.randomhouse.co.uk/offices.htm

The Random House Group Limited Reg. No. 954009

A CIP catalogue record for this book is available from the British Library

ISBN 9781784750398

Typeset in 12pt Palatino by SX Composing DTP, Rayleigh, Essex
Printed and bound by CPI Group (UK) Ltd, Croydon, CR0 4YY

MIX
Paper from
responsible sources
FSC
www.fsc.org   FSC® C018179

Penguin Random House is committed to a sustainable future for our business, our readers and our planet. This book is made from Forest Stewardship Council® certified paper.

Contents

A Christmas
Feast
And other stories

Champagne and canapés

Christmas Shopping

Evie's overloaded trolley slid slowly but unstoppably into the trolley next to her. She'd been wishing all the way round that she'd tested it for wonkiness before she set off and should have changed it the moment she realised it wouldn't steer. Now it paid her back for her inefficiency by crashing into a trolley that seemed a dream – a perfect dinner for two: a packet of pheasant breasts, a bottle of champagne and some potted shrimps. Evie was very fond of potted shrimps. She looked up at the lucky shopper, who apparently didn't need enough food to feed a small country, just because it was Christmas. Of course, because Evie was showing the strain of the festive season in every line, wrinkle and pore, he was extremely good-looking. He had greying black hair, strong eyebrows, and beneath them dark eyes that crinkled attractively at the corners. Evie was aware her hair needed cutting, she hadn't bothered with make-up that morning and was wearing clothes she did housework in. She smiled, hoping to distract him from her looks.

'So sorry. Can't control this wretched thing. I should have changed it, but you don't quite have the heart, do you?' Then she looked at the contents of his trolley again and wished she'd just said 'sorry'. Those choice items did not indicate a man who'd appreciate small talk about shopping trolleys.

But he smiled. 'They're not very well designed, are they?' It was only to make her feel better but she was grateful – and he had a lovely voice.

She sighed. 'No.' Then she frowned. 'I'm looking for agar agar. I've got the family for Christmas and I don't cook much as a rule.'

He glanced down at her load which she now had under control. 'You wouldn't guess that from the amount you've packed in there.'

She laughed. 'Panic buying. My sister-in-law is a vegetarian and I can't decide what to cook for her. I thought agar agar would be useful.'

'I'm sure you must have the ingredients for several recipes – a whole book, possibly.' His gaze roamed over the disparate ingredients – quinoa, bulgur wheat, various forms of tofu, and some mushrooms she'd have sworn were poisonous if they hadn't been for sale in an upmarket shop.

'That's what I thought! But as I can't decide I think I'd better have—'

'Here you are.' He put the packet on top of the other things.

'Thanks. I wish I liked cooking more. It's my turn to have them all and I dread it. Some of them are such foodies.' The pheasants and champagne caught her eye. 'Oh, you probably are too.'

'Well, I do cook, but I have no one to cook for this year. My parents are on a cruise. I'm living in the family home, looking after the cat.'

'I expect you're looking forward to a quiet Christmas. I know I would be.'

'Mm, yes, sort of. It'll be different, anyway.'

Evie looked up at him, and on impulse she said, 'Would you think I was absolutely mad if I invited you round for Christmas dinner?' Aware of his astonishment she went on. 'Of course, say no. I don't expect you to accept, but I wouldn't feel right about myself if I didn't ask you.'

He laughed. 'Why ever not?'

She hesitated. 'Lots of reasons. The most important

to me is, if Christmas is about anything it's about welcoming strangers into your home.' Too late she wished that she'd said something different – anything but the truth really. She tried to explain further – which would probably make it worse – but what the hell. 'I'm rubbish at cooking, and cleaning and decorating the house stylishly. I never get the Christmas cards out in time and I mostly buy people things from Marks and Spencer so they can take them back. But I do feel strongly about being welcoming.' She was blushing so hard now she was challenging the cardboard Santa's that swayed above her head. 'Now you've confirmed I'm completely batty, you can move on and finish your shopping.'

He laughed again but kindly. 'Actually, I was going to offer to come round and make you a vegetarian dish. I haven't got much cooking to do at all and I like it. And you obviously have a lot.'

'Would you do that?' Gratitude almost made Evie fling her arms round his neck. Fortunately middle-class restraint saved her from herself.

'Of course. It would be a pleasure. Where do you live?'

She gulped, suddenly aware that she'd invited a complete stranger into her home. She didn't know anything about him. He could be targeting her – he could have seen her neediness and deliberately got talking to her. Then she allowed common sense into her panic-stricken brain. She would be surrounded by people on Christmas Day; she'd be perfectly safe.

'I live at the top of Stoke's Hill. One of the big houses up there.'

'Oh yes, I know. Do you live in all of it? Or has it been divided into flats?'

She smiled to hide an unexpected sigh. 'No, all of it.' It wouldn't be for long. Once everything else had been sorted out after her parents' death, the house would go on the market. It was why everyone decided there needed to be one more family Christmas in the old home. Then it *would* be divided into flats, no doubt.

She gave him the rest of the address and they exchanged names and contact numbers. Then she finished her shopping, adding two boxes of crackers to the pile, just because they were reduced to half price. Still, crackers were always good fun even if she was the only member of the family who thought so.

She didn't tell her family that she'd invited Edward for Christmas. She hadn't really meant to lie to them, but she didn't work hard enough at finding an opportunity to do it. They were all so busy, preoccupied with deciding who should have what from the house.

Evie had two brothers, Bill and Derek, both married. Donna, the vegetarian who was causing Evie such food-stress, was married to Bill. Derek's wife was much more practical but she always made Evie feel like a bit of an idiot. It was probably because Sarah never saw Evie in her working environment, running a team of sales staff, but only when she was being domestic, and not making a good job of it.

Evie's own sister was the eldest of the family. Diane was married to a lovely man called William who always reminded Evie of a Labrador, friendly and always trying to be helpful – not always succeeding. Diana nagged him horribly, Evie felt. But then Diane nagged everyone, especially Evie.

They all had two children each, and Evie always called them the wrong names, which caused huge offence although Evie had no idea why. She always got people's names wrong – as had their mother before her.

Christmas Eve went well, Evie felt. She had bought things to add to the children's stockings and had even bought stripy socks and filled them for the adults. This had kept everyone in bed for a bit longer than usual on Christmas morning, giving Evie time to defrost croissants and make Buck's Fizz. Her sister would disapprove of champagne at breakfast, even if it was mixed with orange juice. Donna would sweetly but firmly refuse all the organic, wheat-free, stone-ground, air-dried, free-range cereals that Evie had bought on spec, and eat half a banana and some wheatgerm, produced from her own bag of healthy supplies. The men would probably demand eggs and bacon and there was no telling what, if anything, the children would want for breakfast; they were probably full of chocolate already.

The present opening would go on after lunch so now, after breakfast, and with a huge effort, Evie managed to get them all to go for a walk. She didn't go with them, she wanted to fiddle with the vegetables and wonder what to cook for Donna. Donna had asked her what she was getting for Christmas dinner. Evie had said it was a surprise.

Annoyingly a fine rain descended and the walkers came back early. Evie had depended on them being out until at least midday giving her plenty of time to cook. Edward, she decided, was a figment of her imagination. She'd so wanted to meet a nice man who'd cook a vegetarian dish for her she'd created one in her head.

She didn't want sisterly help so she sent the women into the dining room to set the table and make it festive, the children into the den to watch telly – an illicit treat in daytime for those particular ones. The men she sent down to the cellar to sort out wine. They could spend a happy time there discussing what her parents had bought over the years and if any of it was still decent.

When she heard the doorbell ring she was surprised but delighted to find Edward on the doorstep, his arms full of carrier bags. Not that she'd thought about him all morning. She'd gone for quite long spells – as much as ten minutes at a time – without giving him a thought.

It was hard to decide if he was actually more attractive than she'd remembered him or if he just seemed more attractive because she thought she'd made him up anyway. In her head she'd just made him a keen cook and didn't allow him long legs or a quirky smile or anything else he seemed to have in reality.

'Hello! I didn't think you'd come!' she said, instantly aware it made her sound terribly needy.

'I didn't think you'd be here. I thought I'd find

the house empty and shuttered, or sold and half-converted.'

They laughed awkwardly. 'Come in,' said Evie. 'Happy Christmas.'

He put down the large number of carrier bags he had with him. 'Happy Christmas.' He bent and kissed her cheek.

Evie flushed, hoping he'd just think it was slaving over a hot stove that made her so pink, and very glad she had dressed carefully for Christmas Day and was looking OK.

'Come into the kitchen. Let me get you a drink.' She didn't say, 'come quickly before the family see you,' although she wanted to.

The kitchen was fairly tidy, in that the table was only partly covered in potatoes, carrots, parsnips and sprouts, some half-made stuffing and various attempts at vegetarian options.

'Oh, so you had a go yourself then,' said Edward, seeing the soaking bulgur wheat, and the tofu, still in its bag. A packet of alfalfa looked very like duck weed.

'I had to. In case.'

He didn't ask 'in case what?' 'Well, as I had the time I made a dish all ready. You just need to put it in the oven.'

Evie, who'd had her breakfast champagne without the sobering effects of orange juice, embraced him. 'You're an angel!'

Just then the eldest child came in. Luke was ten. 'Oh, Auntie Evie. Hey, everyone, Aunt Evie's got a man in the kitchen!'

Had he shouted 'fire' they would not have appeared as quickly, but as it was the kitchen was filled with people within seconds. And they were all staring. They were so used to Evie being single that the sight of her with a very attractive man in the family kitchen threw them completely.

Evie was aware she had to take charge. 'Everyone, this is Edward. I invited him for Christmas.'

'Why didn't you say anything about him coming?' asked her sister. 'Where did you meet?'

'In the supermarket,' said Edward. 'Evie was looking for agar agar.'

'What on earth is that?' asked Bill.

'A vegetarian setting agent,' murmured Donna, 'but I'm surprised you knew about it, Evie.'

'Anyway it turned out that Edward was going to be alone for Christmas Day so I invited him.'

'You'd better do the introductions,' said Diane, and Evie obliged, pleased with herself for getting all the children's names right for once.

'But which one is your husband?' asked Edward when the others had drifted away again, back to their tasks, wondering about their aunt or their sister, depending on age.

Evie was confused for a moment. 'Oh, I haven't got a husband. Those men are my brothers.'

'Your brothers? That is good news. I assumed you were married.'

'Did you? Why?'

'Single women don't usually have shopping trolleys they can hardly push,' he explained.

Evie bit her lip. 'I hope you don't mind that I'm single. I would hate you to think I was trying to entrap you or anything.'

'Mind? That's the best Christmas present I've had in years.' Edward put his arm round Evie and hugged her.

'I think I should tell you,' said Luke, who had come back for a second look, 'that my Auntie Evie is a rotten cook.'

'But I'm a brilliant one, so that's all right.' He looked at Evie. 'Did you say something about a drink?'

Run for Cover

Drops of water splattering on the shop counter caused Clare to look up, startled. There was a man standing there, very wet, very angry and not wearing many clothes.

He was wearing a pair of shorts, a rugby shirt and there was a laminated number tied to him: 124 Ambleton Half Marathon. His trainers squelched and he was extremely muddy. He was also the first customer she had had for hours. 'Can I help you?' she asked, moving her replies from Bettadates out of the way.

The pouring rain had kept people away from the local charity shop that Saturday, which was why Clare had been able to make progress with her letter writing.

While not exactly displeased to have a customer, she had been hoping to compose her reply to Ben of Ripley, dog lover, non-smoker, hobbies hang-gliding, opera and reading, before it was time to go home.

'Er, yes,' said the man. 'Those clothes in the window – can I try them on?'

Clare shook her head. The manageress of the shop was very strict on this point. Under no circumstances could clothes be taken out of the window unless they had been there for at least a week.

This time, however, the rule didn't annoy her quite so much, as she'd personally spent a happy morning arranging the displays, and was particularly pleased with both windows, having found some yellow plastic ducks to add to the one with the green Hunter wellies and umbrella. She had even flaunted superstition by opening the brolly. The other window housed a Barbour jacket and good quality corduroy trousers.

Clare wanted to prove to the manageress that she could price clothes and do window displays as well as anyone.

'I'm sorry,' she said breezily, as if she was not being at all unreasonable.

'I can put them aside till next week, but they've only just gone in the window. We're not allowed to disturb the display.'

It did sound rather petty. 'But I want to buy them! Surely you're not going to turn away such a good sale?'

'I'm sorry. Rules are rules.' She had a feeling that this man was used to having things his own way. 'I will make a note that you want to buy them, if you like.'

'But all the other clothes you have here are for sale, aren't they? I can take *them* away? I don't have to reserve *them* for six months' time, do I now?'

This was extremely unfair, she felt.

'You only have to wait a week. It's worth waiting for a bargain, isn't it?' His expression told her it wasn't. Perhaps this man wasn't familiar with charity shops.

'They're very good quality clothes.'

He held back a snarl with visible effort.

'Oh, never mind!' he snapped. 'I'll just find some other things to wear.'

He went through the stock very carefully, discarding quite nice shirts for more worn ones, hunting for jeans, not by condition or brand name, but by some other mysterious criteria, which seemed to be the stains on the knees or the state of the pockets.

He was lucky there'd been a suitcase full of lovely

stuff only that morning. Sometimes their stock of nice clothes was very low.

Clare went back to her letters. Ben of Ripley seemed a dating possibility, which meant that they had more than just one thing in common. In Ben's case it was not smoking and liking opera.

Clare actually didn't like a lot of opera, but she liked some and hoped her distaste for hang-gliding wouldn't make them entirely incompatible. The others were all fairly hopeless, but her friend had said you had to be prepared to wait a while.

She'd only just joined the dating agency. The right man was probably in there somewhere, he'd just take time to come to the surface. In the meantime, her bedraggled and disgruntled customer had accumulated quite an armful of clothing.

'Why not leave all that other stuff here?'

'No, it's all right. I might want to try all of them on, too.'

Clare decided against drawing his attention to the notice above the counter asking customers not to take more than three items into the changing room at a time. When he emerged he was wearing not the dinner jacket he'd said he'd wanted to try, but a whole lot of other things.

He looked really quite attractive in them, they certainly fitted extremely well, but it simply wouldn't do.

'I'm afraid if you want to buy those clothes, you'll have to take them all off.'

'Oh, why?' he asked archly.

'I don't know how much they cost.'

'Oh, don't worry, I pulled off all the labels.'

Clare flinched. She really needed clothes and labels together or it would take absolutely ages to ring them through the till.

'Don't tell me,' he sighed. 'It's against the rules to wear the clothes you want to buy, you can only carry them home in the required plastic bags.'

She ignored this slur – it wasn't her place to argue with the customers. 'Give me the tickets, and anything else you want to buy, I'll add it all up for you right now.'

Somewhat grudgingly he went back into the changing room and brought back a pile of labels. She took out the pad and started making notes on the clothes.

'That's fifty-five pounds,' she said, wanting to ask why he needed to buy so much at once. Customers were usually quite glad to chat, but not him.

'Fifty-five pounds? Good God! I won't have the DJ, then.'

'Then it's forty-five pounds. The dinner jacket is quite cheap because it's rather an old-fashioned style.'

He frowned, looking at the dinner jacket as if taking this disparaging comment personally. 'So I owe you forty-five pounds?'

'You do,' she told him.

She regarded him gravely. He was making no signs of paying. It was then she remembered he had been wearing shorts and a rugby shirt when he came in.

'You haven't got any money, have you?'

'No, I mean, I have some, well, forty-five quid anyway. Just not on me. I don't suppose you can trust me until Monday?'

Clare took a deep breath, but didn't speak. She just shook her head.

'Does that mean I have to take off all these clothes?' he asked after a few telling moments.

He glanced at the window. The rain had increased. Claire found herself softening towards him. It would be horrible to have to go back out in only shorts and a rugby shirt.

'No, I'll lend you the money for the clothes you're

wearing. You'll have to leave the others until Monday, I'm afraid.'

'But you can't do that! Why should you stand the loss if I don't pay?' he said quickly, more indignant than ever now she had offered to help him.

'It's a charity shop. I can't be charitable with their money, but surely I can choose to risk my own cash if I want to.'

'I really don't think you should do that—'

'The alternative is taking them all off again and going back out there.'

He shivered at the thought. 'Someone was supposed to give me a lift home, but they didn't turn up.'

'Where do you live?'

'Oh – not far. Littlethorpe.'

'Oh.' Littlethorpe was a charming little Cotswold village, but it was a good three miles from town.

'I really like walking,' he said.

'But you've just run a marathon—'

'Half marathon.'

She bit her lip. 'I'll give you a lift home. Then you can pay me back for the clothes.'

'No! You can't do that! You're a single woman. You don't know me!'

'How do you know I'm single?'

He picked up the pile of letters and the page of correspondence.

'You wouldn't join "Bettadates" if you weren't single. And I'm not sure it's a very good idea either.'

'Everyone does it these days. It's very well regulated and perfectly safe. And I may be single but I'm not a fool. I think I can spot an axe murderer at twenty paces.'

'No you can't! No one can. Anyone can be a psychopath these days.'

'So, are you?' she asked sweetly.

'No, as it happens,' he answered. 'But you're not to know that.'

She shrugged and smiled. 'Well, it's up to you. You can risk getting a lift from a single woman, or walk.' She glanced quickly across towards the window.

'I think the rain is turning to sleet.'

'Listen,' she went on. 'You're obviously one of the good guys, you've run a half marathon, for charity, I'm sure I'll be safe.'

'It's very kind of you,' he said meekly.

They walked up the hill towards the car park in silence. It was still pouring with rain and Clare thought about the umbrella in the window with regret.

If she'd been on her own she could have borrowed it, but having made such a fuss about not disturbing the window, she couldn't really do that.

'Littlethorpe is probably miles out of your way,' he answered.

'I knew where you lived when I offered you a lift,' she replied.

'So you haven't got a hot date courtesy of Bettadates?' It was his turn to tease.

She opened the driver's door wide and regarded him coolly.

'I may have, but I've still got time to give you a lift home. If you get in, that is.'

He folded himself into the passenger seat without another word.

He directed her up the drive of quite a large house. Either he only lived in part of it, or it was mortgaged to the hilt, otherwise he wouldn't need to shop in charity shops at all.

'Do come in while I find my wallet,' he said. 'Unless you'd rather wait in the car . . .'

She was far too curious to do that and followed him through an oak-panelled hall to a stone-flagged kitchen of the kind dreams are made of. An Aga the size of a car was against one wall.

Opposite that was a mirror-topped sideboard, and written in lipstick on the mirror was a message.

Note on table.

The man and Clare saw this at the same moment, and muttering angrily, he picked up the note. A moment later he handed it to her.

'You'd better read it.'

It said, *If you're so keen on doing things for charity, you should look to charity to find your clothes. You've more time for handicapped children than you have for me! Hope you enjoyed the walk home.*

Clare bit her lip, fighting laughter. 'Why didn't you tell me they were your clothes?'

'I wasn't sure they were at first, then I remembered she'd threatened to do this before. When I realised, I was too embarrassed to say.'

Clare turned away so he wouldn't see the smile that was breaking through her defences. 'There's nothing to be ashamed of.'

'You're laughing!'

'No, I'm not!'

'Yes, you are. It's not at all funny!'

Now she'd been caught out she didn't bother to hide her mirth.

'Yes it is! You must admit it's hysterical.' She

looked at him quizzically. 'Possibly you haven't got the required GSOH?'

A reluctant smile disturbed his mouth. 'I do usually have quite a good sense of humour. I lost it for a moment there. Here, let me give you the money.' He found his wallet and handed her some notes. 'I don't know your name.'

'Clare.'

'Grant. Clare?'

'Yes?'

'Can I prove to you that you don't need to join dating agencies to meet men? Have a drink with me in town tonight?'

She considered. At least he was local. Ben of Ripley lived miles away. 'Aren't you suffering from a broken heart, then?'

He shook his head slowly. 'I don't think my heart was ever really involved in that last relationship.' Then he smiled and suddenly his being local wasn't the only thing in his favour.

'OK then. The King's Head?'

'At eight.'

Clare drove away with a smile still lingering, thoughts of Ben in Ripley completely abandoned.

Love in the Afternoon

Olivia watched the handsome Italian chef teaching them how to make ravioli, wondering why she'd bothered. If it hadn't been her best friend's present – in lieu of a hen night, she wouldn't have gone near a cookery course, let alone one a fortnight long. Food held no interest for her. It was messy and unpredictable and she hated mess – stickiness was a particular aversion. She didn't much like sex for the same reasons.

But neither did she like being ignored or failing. Usually she avoided both. She made good choices and she worked hard. So why couldn't she get this young man to pay her any attention? She didn't want him to admire her as a woman, but as someone who'd followed instructions and was doing a good job.

She tried harder. She got hold of a list of menus

and dishes that they would be taught. In the afternoon, when Hannah, her best friend, and the other women on the course had siestas or went sightseeing or shopping, she went back into the empty kitchen and practised. She practised her knife skills so she could cut tomatoes, cucumber, peppers, courgettes, into tesserae hardly bigger than sugar crystals. She turned celery into translucent crescents, carrots into matchsticks, parsley into heaps of emerald dust. She practised chopping onions until she could turn one into the consistency of rock salt in seconds, ignoring the tears that poured down her cheeks as she did it.

Five days into the course she could bear it no longer. 'Why don't you ever say anything to me?' she demanded of the chef as he made to leave the kitchen. 'You don't praise me, you don't even criticise me!'

He was a demanding teacher, seeming sometimes to forget that people were there on holiday – that they weren't being trained to be master chefs. But when Olivia's pasta turned to glue he said nothing.

He looked at her, from her sleek, tied-back hair, make-up-free face, to her trainer-clad feet. 'You! You do not need to learn how to cook,' he said.

'You need to learn how to eat! I'm not sure you even know how to live!' Then he sidestepped her and left the kitchen.

She was incandescent! How dare he? She knew exactly how to live, exactly how to keep her life on track, her body in shape. Who was he, a cook, for God's sake, to tell her she didn't know how to live? Then, just for a moment, she wondered. Was she right? Had she got her life sorted or was it actually a bit arid? She batted away this disturbing doubt and she did what she always did when she was angry, she went for a run.

She never looked at the scenery when she was running even if now it was through stunning Tuscan scenery. Running wasn't for 'getting fresh air' or enjoying your surroundings, it was to get fit and keep fit. Her arms and legs moved perfectly together. She'd had lessons and her technique was perfect. Even though the area around the cooking school was hilly as well as beautiful, she didn't change her pace for the gradient. When she got back to her room she felt better. She had a shower and put on a dress that showed off her toned arms and her flat stomach, proving to everyone she had food in its proper place, way down the order of priorities.

*

'Hi!' said Hannah. 'You look well. What have you been up to? Apart from running, I mean. Why do you never come out with us? We've had a brilliant time.' There was a tiny reproachful pause. The reason Hannah had insisted that they go on this holiday was so they could have 'quality time' together. Apart from on the first evening they'd hardly spent any time socialising. Hannah declared they never saw each other in London because Olivia was either working, at the gym or engaged in some other form of self-improvement. She'd hoped that on this holiday things would be different.

Olivia considered lying but only for a moment. Hannah had known her for a very long time. She also owed her the truth. 'I can't bear that I can't do it,' she said. 'I have to practise.'

'But you can do it! You're brilliant! You're always brilliant!'

Olivia didn't deny this. It was too important for false modesty. 'So why does Claudio never praise me? Talk to me, even? It's driving me crazy.'

Hannah shrugged and sighed, possibly thinking that her friend's need for perfection already made her unbalanced.

*

Olivia continued to spend her afternoons practising, certain that one day Claudio would notice her, and one day he did. He came into the kitchen where she was making risotto, determined to make it as creamy and unctuous as his. It was two days before they were due to leave and this was their exam piece. She didn't hear him come up behind her.

'What are you doing?'

She jumped and screamed but couldn't think of an answer. He seemed angry, his dark brows lowered, his generous curving mouth tight.

'You are stirring something. What is it?' he demanded.

'Risotto.' She managed not to stammer but it was an effort.

'And what does it taste like?'

'I haven't tasted it. It should be delicious. It's nearly ready.'

'Then taste it.'

'I don't eat rice. It's a complex carbohydrate.'

The look he gave her made her feel that if she'd declared she ate babies he would have despised her less. 'You cannot cook if you do not taste! Would you paint a picture with your eyes shut?'

'But I know what's in the food,' she explained.

37

'I followed the recipe, measured everything carefully—'

'Eat it!' he roared.

Until that moment Olivia thought she wasn't frightened of anyone, but she was frightened of this ferocious chef. She fumbled for a fork, a plate, a napkin. He made a furious noise and thrust her wooden spoon into her hand.

'Taste!'

'The germs!' she said. 'I can't eat from that spoon, it'll—' She faltered as he took the spoon from her hand and plunged it into the risotto.

'Shut your eyes,' he ordered. 'Open your mouth!'

It took a huge effort of will but she did it, certain she would choke or gag. She felt the wooden spoon on her lips for a second and then he said, 'No, this is no way to do it. Clear up this mess and then come with me.' Then he tossed the dirty spoon onto the worktop.

While Olivia wiped and tidied, he threw things into a bag, apparently randomly, from the fridge one minute, from around the kitchen the next. A ripe melon from a bowl, some tomatoes, cheese, a knife, some bread, a bottle of wine, some oil, a pepper grinder, a paper of Palma ham, some mascarpone and some figs. 'Now, come!'

Olivia was not accustomed to being treated in this way. Her boyfriends, such as they were, respected her, knew she referred to herself as Ms and stood her round at the bar, knew that she never needed to have her bags carried and preferred to sleep alone. This cavalier treatment was a shock. It made her tremble and sweat. She tried to do some yoga breathing without him noticing. She was halfway through a calming Ujjayi breath, when he took hold of her wrist and practically dragged her out of the room.

She debated using her self-defence course to free herself but didn't want to risk failing. He wasn't hugely tall but he was very fit and she could see muscles under his T-shirt. One of the other women described him as 'sex on legs' and the others seemed to agree. Just now, Olivia didn't know what she thought, but it was certainly more to do with hormones and pheromones than considered opinion.

He stopped by the red Ferrari he drove up in every morning. Olivia had muttered something about it being a terrible cliché, driving such a car, but no one else seemed to agree with her. He pulled open the door, dropped his bag into the back and said, 'Get in.'

In London Olivia would no more have got into a car with a man like this than she would have swum the Thames. How could she trust herself to a virtual stranger? Worse, a stranger who was more than likely to drive dangerously? But if she'd refused he'd have seen it as weakness, proving his point that she didn't know how to live. She almost fell in and fumbled for her seat belt, feeling his eyes on her, knowing he thought her a wimp for bothering.

She kept her eyes shut for the entire drive, keeping her head turned away from him so he wouldn't see. When she got out her knees were shaking. She wiped her hands on her dress so he wouldn't take hold of one and find it sweaty.

'Follow me,' he ordered, taking the bag from the car and not looking to see if she was following or not. He had left the keys in the ignition. She could just get in and drive it back if she wanted. Not easy but possible. She didn't.

'Olivia.' He gave her name several more syllables that it usually had. 'You are going to learn to enjoy food. Sit.' He indicated the rug he had spread on the ground. They were next to a river and pine trees gave a pleasant shade. A quick glance round told her they were in an idyllic spot but she didn't take it in, she just sank to her knees onto the rug.

He dropped down next to her like a panther from a tree and pulled the bag towards him. 'Melon.' He extracted the knife, scythed into it and handed her a slice, juice dripping.

Automatically she wiped her hand on her dress before she took it gingerly.

'Now eat.'

'I haven't got a spoon—'

'Not with a spoon, with your teeth!' he roared.

'But I'll get it all over me—' Then thinking better of it she bit into the flesh of the melon and liquid heaven poured into her mouth, down her chin and all down her front.

'Close your eyes,' he said, quieter now she was doing as she was told. 'Is it good?'

She nodded, her eyes shut, taking more bites, the gloriousness of the taste making her ignore the stickiness.

'Good. Now cheese.'

Gorgonzola so ripe it was nearly liquid stuck to her fingers so she had to suck them, the flavour mingling with the melon juice.

It was as if she had never tasted food before. He handed her more cheese, ham, grapes, a ripe fig he had opened for her. When she stopped eating he kissed her.

'Are you sure you're not coming back with us?' Hannah sounded worried. 'It seems so unlike you!'

They were standing by the minibus and all the other women were inside, waiting to be taken to the airport.

'I will come back sometime, to sell my flat and things,' Olivia explained, 'but Claudio wants me to stay. And I don't see any point in going back to London immediately.'

'I can't believe it! Olivia! You're in love. I never thought you'd do anything so random!'

Olivia smiled, trying not to look smug.

'So—' She paused. 'Is it with Claudio or with food?'

Olivia shrugged. 'They sort of go together. I could just be in love with life.'

Hannah drew her friend to her in a long hug. 'I really hoped this course would make you loosen up a bit, but I never imagined you'd go this far.'

'Nor did I,' said Olivia, sighing expansively. 'But it made me realise how being so controlled all the time was just cutting me off from all the best things in life – love, food, sex, everything that's important really. I feel I've walked into the sun after a long time in the shadows.'

'I hope you'll still come to my wedding.'

'Of course I will! But I may have to have my dress altered. I don't think I'll still be a size zero in September.'

'You can be my fat bridesmaid instead of my skinny one.' Hannah laughed, aware how once this would have been Olivia's worst nightmare.

Similarly aware, Olivia joined in the laughter. 'I'd be honoured. Now do get in, you don't want to be late.'

Olivia watched the minibus drive away and then went back to where her lover was waiting.

You're the One

Lisa was on the point of abandoning Oxford Street and going home. Her toe had gone through her tights, which was painful enough, but her new shoes had also let her down and given her blisters. To top it off, she'd had a text from her friend, who had been going to help her buy an outfit for her cousin's wedding, saying she couldn't come. They'd planned a girly lunch and a film afterwards. Lisa didn't like shopping and needed a reward.

She was just checking out how far Boots was so she could get plasters and new tights when she saw him: Ben, her friend from university – more than a friend, really, someone she'd wondered about ever since.

Had he been 'the one'? Had he not asked her out because she'd been with someone else when they met? Had they missed their chance of happiness because he never saw her as a woman and treated her like a younger sister?

He was actually a bit of an obsession. She measured the men she went out with against him and she'd never managed to get him out of her system.

She didn't hesitate. She went towards him, reached up and kissed his chin – all she could get at – before wrapping her arms tightly round him.

There was only a second's hesitation before he returned the embrace, his arms came round her body and he laid his cheek on the top of her head. They stayed locked together for a few moments. Lisa was in heaven. Then he released her.

'I'm terribly sorry,' he said gently, 'but I'm not the man you think I am. Although I really wish I was.'

She looked up and of course now she was close enough to see properly, Lisa could see it wasn't Ben. His eyes were the same colour, but he had bushier eyebrows, was taller, a bit slighter and wore different aftershave. He was quite remarkably like him but nevertheless wasn't him.

She felt sick. Why on earth hadn't she looked at him for a bit longer and spotted her mistake? But she'd been so pleased to see him she hadn't thought.

'As the ground hasn't opened up and swallowed me,' she said eventually, having worked some moisture into her mouth, 'I might just die of embarrassment.'

'Oh, don't do that. Not when we've just met!' The man who wasn't Ben had eyes that were kind and gently twinkling so she didn't feel obliged to speed off down the street. Which was just as well, considering her blister was starting to throb and her tights were cutting painfully into her little toe.

She managed to return his smile. 'OK, I suppose I can see how that would make it all even worse for you, if I dropped dead now. There might be questions, a police inquiry or something.'

He nodded. 'It would be better to get a drink, or a coffee and do some retrospective getting to know each other.'

'Would that make the kiss all right? If we found out about where we work and live and stuff, so we would at least know each other in a regular way?'

He nodded again. 'That would work for me. I was so pleased when I saw you limping towards me at a rate of knots.'

'I've got blisters. But why were you pleased? Most men would be horrified if a strange woman flung themselves at them.'

'So would I be, normally, but apart from the fact that you're very attractive, I've just been dumped.' He paused. 'Your hug came at a very good moment.'

She thought he'd been looking more than a bit lost. 'So, how long ago did it happen?'

'Moments ago – by text.'

Lisa was appalled. What sort of woman would dump a lovely man like this, by text? 'Are you sure? You're not just reading it wrong?'

He pulled out his phone and read. 'Sorry, it's not going to work.'

'That could mean she's missed her train – anything! "It" means the date, not your whole relationship.'

He shook his head. 'No. She could just jump in a taxi to meet me here.'

'Taxis are expensive!'

'She's a taxi sort of girl.'

Lisa instantly wanted to comfort him. 'Maybe she just went off the idea of doing whatever you were going to do. Was it the London Eye? Does she suffer from vertigo?'

He shook his head, starting to laugh. 'We were going to go shopping and then have lunch. Which means I carry the bags and pay for lunch, and possibly for some of the shopping. What sort of woman doesn't want to do that?'

Lisa carried on trying to cheer him up. 'Me, for one, although that was what I was going to do if I hadn't been stood up, too.' Seeing concern cross his face she hurried on. 'My girlfriend. She can't come now. She was going to help me buy an outfit for a wedding. Then we were going to have lunch. I like that part of it.'

'But not the shopping?' He seemed to find this hard to grasp.

'I hate shopping for occasions,' Lisa explained. 'You always spend too much on something you'll never wear again.'

'I've got a good idea. Let's go and have a coffee or something first, then I'll stand in for your girl-friend, help you buy the outfit, and then you could return the favour and stand in for mine while we have lunch?'

Lisa bit her lip. 'I don't know. I don't think you have really been dumped. It would be wrong to have a sort of date if you're still seeing someone.'

'I don't think I'm seeing someone any more. I really do think that text was dumping me. It's the sort of thing she'd do, the way she'd do it.'

Hating to see the sadness in his eyes, Lisa relented. 'OK – it wouldn't be a date exactly. We'd just be two people helping each other out.'

He smiled. 'And we're nearly friends now. Any minute now and that kiss will be perfectly all right.'

Lisa frowned. 'I do wish you hadn't reminded me. I'm still so embarrassed.'

'And you still have blisters. Let's go and get plasters then we'll have coffee and you can tell me all about the man you were so pleased to see. By the time we've done all that we will really be friends.'

Lisa sipped her cappuccino. 'We never actually went out. We were just friends, but I always fancied him.'

'How did you meet?'

Lisa told her story, the details, the non-events. Eventually she finished. 'I've always wondered if he was "the one".'

'He wasn't the one,' said the man she now knew was called Tim.

'How can you ever know?' Lisa stared hard into the bottom of her coffee cup as if trying to divine the future, or maybe the past.

'Because Ben is my brother and I think he's started going out with my very-recently-ex-girlfriend.'

Lisa's jaw dropped open and he gently closed her mouth with his finger. 'I might be the one, though. Shall we find out?'

Starter

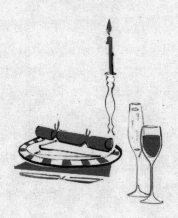

The Undercover Cook

Emily crouched over her heap of parsley hoping no one would notice her. From behind she'd look like anyone else working in the kitchen; in anonymous chef's whites – and hardly less anonymous from the front – no one knew who she was, after all. But because she knew she was there under false pretences she felt sick with guilt and fear of exposure.

She'd been in the kitchen for four days now but this was the first time the executive chef had come in. Apparently he always made sure he was around for the weekend and often cooked on Saturday or Sunday. If you wanted to eat at The Cornucopia at the weekend you had to book for months in advance.

Emily didn't dare look round as she heard his footsteps come up behind her. All she was doing was picking through the parsley, making sure there were no bits that were wilting or substandard in any other way.

'You all right there?' he said.

She had to turn round and face him. 'Yes, chef, thank you,' she said, looking at him for the first time.

She'd seen pictures of course, everyone locally had. He was the bright young thing of the area, but she hadn't ever seen him in the flesh.

At first he seemed quite ordinary-looking. Not particularly tall, pale, dark hair, a shadow of stubble, but when Emily forced herself to look into his eyes – and she felt she had to – she was startled by their brightness. They saw, she was certain, absolutely everything. It made him terrifying.

He picked up some parsley between finger and thumb and grunted. Then he moved on and she went back to her work. She sighed with relief.

When she'd finished picking the parsley over she would wash it, making sure not even an atom-sized speck of grit remained. Then she'd dry it and put it in the walk-in fridge. When not a drop of moisture remained she would chop it so there was a small emerald pile for the cooks to use.

She'd done this every day since she'd been there and liked the chopping part. She'd been taught how to fold and refold the parsley into a tight package so when her knife went through it, it would come out in tiny shards and she wouldn't have to go over it again and bruise it. She felt quite confident about her parsley chopping.

'So, who's the new stagier?' she heard Theo Milton ask Adam, the head chef who'd taken her on.

'Emily. She thinks she wants to be a chef and thought she ought to find out about professional kitchens before she trained.' That was her story and now she heard someone else tell it, it sounded quite convincing.

'Any good?'

'Yup. Quick to learn, doesn't complain. No skills though. We have to teach her everything.'

'Well, don't forget we're not here to babysit hobby chefs.'

Adam laughed. 'No. We don't have to babysit her and she is free labour.'

Emily heard Theo Milton give a short, cynical laugh. 'That's something I suppose.'

In her head Emily was demanding to know how top restaurants justified their prices when they didn't pay all of their staff. Why did people work – over fourteen-hour days sometimes, incredibly hard work too – for nothing? It was one of the things she was here to find out. The trouble was, she was just too exhausted when she finally staggered home; she could barely stand under the shower long enough to get wet. The thought of doing more than typing a few sentences on her laptop while she waited for the kettle to boil seemed beyond her.

Emily was a journalist, and the boss of the company she worked for – which produced several local papers and a couple of society magazines – had asked her editor to assign someone to dig the dirt on Theo Milton.

The job at the local paper was Emily's first, and the first time she'd been asked to do anything like this. Up to now most of her work had been very basic: reporting on local fêtes, giant vegetable competitions and local pantomimes. ('Don't leave out a single cast name,' her editor had urged her. 'If they're in the show, they're in the paper!')

But she had done a couple of interviews on local celebrities that had gone well, including one on a thriller writer who had a fearsome reputation. Emily knew no one had expected him even to see her, let alone spill his guts in the required manner.

Yet somehow, in time for the publication of his thirtieth novel, he had agreed to see Emily. While there hadn't been any gut spilling, Emily had managed to show a softer side to him and the piece had made the front page. Her colleagues had muttered that she'd only got him to see her because she was young and pretty. Incensed, Emily had implored her editor to let her prove this wasn't a fluke and that she could actually do the job. When this assignment had come up she had begged to be given the chance.

'Look,' she had told the meeting when they were informed the big boss wanted this done, 'please let me. I'd be perfect. It would be easier for me to pass myself off as a student chef.'

There was reluctant agreement. Not only was she young but she looked younger. She was constantly asked for ID in pubs and kept her driving licence at the ready at all times. She could easily pass as a school leaver on a working gap year.

'And I'm the only one here who has any interest in food – apart from eating it – at all!'

'I don't think being addicted to cookery programmes on television counts,' said one of her detractors.

'It's better than nothing. And you can learn a lot

from TV.' She didn't like to mention that she could at least cook a bit herself.

'But Emily,' said Bob, the editor, who had the final word. 'Mr Knutsford – who we all owe our jobs to, in case any of us is in danger of forgetting – wants a proper hatchet job.'

'Why?' asked someone else. 'The Cornucopia's got a great reputation.'

'I'm not sure of the details,' said Bob, 'but I think it's something to do with the prime location the restaurant's in. I think his daughter wanted to put a shop there, but I'm only surmising.'

Someone grunted. 'The power of the press, eh?'

'Doesn't sound like something young Emily should be involved in,' said a fatherly man who seriously irritated Emily a lot of the time.

'She's a bloody good cook,' said the most senior of the team.

'How do you know?' demanded everyone in various ways.

'She cooked a surprise meal for my wife for me. It was fantastic. My wife couldn't believe I hadn't got a real chef to cook it.'

'This one's for you then, Em,' said Bob. 'But take care. I know you have a way with bastards but this one might not be impressed with your youth and pretty face. He's a lot younger than that thriller writer.'

Emily was stung by this persistent assumption that she'd got that interview because of her looks and determined that she'd write a really scathing piece and no one would say it was because she was a natural blonde.

So, here she was, in the local hot new restaurant doing 'stage'. This term – which rhymed with 'large' – was what aspiring chefs did, working for nothing for the chance to watch masters of their craft and so learn their trade. Someone had explained it to Emily as being like how passing your driving test was only the beginning. You learned to drive afterwards. Training to be a chef at college was all very well but you didn't really know a thing about cooking until you'd worked in a professional kitchen. She'd smiled politely at the time but she wasn't quite convinced.

Emily had been lucky. When she went for the interview at The Cornucopia she'd been taken on because they were short staffed, and on being asked to make an omelette as a test it turned out perfectly. And they were a bit desperate. Someone had walked out halfway through service the night before. Emily decided she must find out why – it tied in with Theo Milton being impossible to work for.

She was grateful that he wasn't there when she started. It gave her a chance to settle in before her job became even more terrifying than it was already. Although she couldn't really find out why the kitchen porter had walked out. No one seemed willing to give Emily a reason. Phrases like 'couldn't take the pace' were bandied about but her journalist's intuition told her there was a bit more to it than that.

But now Theo was back the tension in the kitchen had gone up several notches.

She had produced her hillock of parsley and divided it between several bowls. She would normally have asked Adam what she should do next, but he was talking to Theo and she didn't like to disturb them. This feeling bothered her. She was a journalist, albeit a very junior one, she shouldn't have felt shy about interrupting people. That was her job. Would Jeremy Paxman have quailed at the thought of asking his boss what he should do next because he was talking to *his* boss? Of course not.

She excused herself this cowardice because she was undercover. She should behave like an aspiring chef and an aspiring chef might well have treated anyone with Michelin-star potential like a demi-god. She'd seen it on television and that particular demi-god had been benign and well meaning, not one who was known for his explosive temper.

But it was what she was here to investigate. Her boss wanted a hatchet job on Theo. Theo Milton had not yet displayed his kitchen-rage on television, but word had got out to the boss of the newspaper chain and as far as Emily could gather, he'd seen it as an opportunity to wear away at his reputation. In a recession a damning article might cause a restaurant to lose enough business for it to close. Then Mr Knutsford's daughter could have the space. Only Emily wasn't going to write that. She was going to convince people that eating there was akin to supporting slavery.

Now, pretty much a slave herself, she went to the sack of shallots and filled a bowl with them. Then she took them back to her space and started peeling them. Chopping would come later. She wanted Theo Milton to be well out of the way before she picked up a knife. She was convinced that if he saw her using one wrongly, he'd stab her with it, or maybe just cut off a finger.

She was just about to go back to the kitchen with

her peeled shallots when she heard shouting. Theo Milton was giving someone absolute hell.

'You ****ing imbecile!' he began and went on to throw every swear word Emily knew, and quite a lot of ones she didn't understand, at someone. Even though she wasn't being blasted from here to Eternity in language unfit for human – let alone female – ears, Emily still cringed horribly. It felt as if she was being physically assaulted. How the poor soul being berated felt, she could only imagine. 'Get out of my sight! You pathetic, incompetent, cack-handed, careless, slip-shod waste of oxygen!' he finished.

Instinct told Emily Theo would now storm out and she flattened herself against the wall, clutching her bowl for protection as he whistled past. She hadn't had time to breathe before he wheeled round and addressed her.

'You'd better go in there and do the amuse-bouches. That cretin is incapable.'

Then he strode into the restaurant.

As Emily crept back into the kitchen having dumped her shallots, she felt that 'mouth amuser' was the least appropriate name ever for anything made in that kitchen. Nothing could possibly be amused in that hell-hole.

'You'd better go home. Come back in a couple of days for your shift, and we'll see,' Adam was saying to Fred, the wretched boy who had been lambasted. 'Emily? I heard Theo say he wanted you on amuse-bouches. Find William and he'll tell you what to do.'

Emily felt awful, as if she'd put Fred out of a job personally. What on earth had he done to enrage Theo so? Supposing she did that? How would she react if he shouted at her, using that language? She wasn't a wimp but she wasn't sure she could withstand that sort of treatment.

Knowing that she didn't really work there only helped a bit. It would take several seconds to strip off her chef's whites, drop them on the floor and walk out – she'd have to walk, she wouldn't want to look as if she was running away. But she wouldn't be out of a job. Or would she? Maybe admitting she couldn't hack working for Theo Milton would get her sacked – they were always looking for opportunities to cut down on staff at the paper. She'd better not risk it.

'You're lucky,' said William. 'All I want you to do now is fill these shot glasses with vichyssoise. But they must all have exactly the same amount in them and you mustn't smear the glass whatever you do. Then drop a spot of chopped parsley in the middle. I'll do one for you to copy.'

'I'll never be able to do that,' she said, having watched him.

'Yes you will. If you smear the glass, wipe it very carefully with kitchen towel. If you pour in too much, pour the soup back into the bowl and start again. If you mess up the parsley you're snookered. I want twenty. Then you can do the prawn cocktails.'

'That's a bit retro isn't it?' Emily wouldn't have said this to Adam, let alone Theo, but William was a bit more approachable, probably because he wasn't as high up the chain of command.

'Yes. We serve it on spoons. You'll have to peel the prawns.'

Emily's back and legs were killing her but eventually she was able to pour exactly the right amount of soup into each glass. Although she knew completing this task would mean she'd have to spend the next few hours peeling prawns, she was still pleased with herself. There was a lot of satisfaction in producing restaurant-quality food, she had to admit that.

The next day she crept into work seemingly at dawn. Her feet still ached from the day before but she wanted to get a start on the day. If she was on the amuse-bouches again, she wanted as much time to do them as possible.

She wasn't the first. Theo and Adam were both there although it was only seven o'clock. They were drinking coffee and looked up as she came in.

Adam glanced at his watch. 'Your shift doesn't start until eight.'

'I know,' said Emily as boldly as she could, not mentioning that as she wasn't getting paid anyway she wasn't expecting overtime. 'I just wanted to get ahead. What do you want me to do?'

She didn't know if she should address this to Adam or Theo so spoke to the space in between them.

'Have a cup of coffee,' said Theo, 'and then back to the amuse-bouches. You did well yesterday.'

Emily beamed inwardly as she headed towards the coffee machine. Unlike almost everyone else in that kitchen who drank their coffee so strong it was almost solid and so hot it would take the skin off a normal person's mouth, she had milk and a lot of sugar in hers. She made it as quickly as possible, aware of the eyes of the men on her as she diluted it. She felt embarrassed and guilty; embarrassed because of the time making her coffee seemed to take and guilty because she felt she'd done poor Fred out of a job.

'What do you want as the amuse-bouches today then, chef?' asked Adam.

'Well, we've got a novice so we can't do anything too fancy. What about a pea and mint sorbet?'

Emily swallowed a mouthful of coffee, glad she'd put three spoons of sugar in it. It gave her courage and calories – one of the things she'd learned about professional kitchens was that you didn't always get to eat much.

'And tuiles to go with it,' said Theo.

Adam went with Emily to the cold station. 'You can start off here until William needs the space. Then move to the pass until we're nearly ready for service. William will tell you what to do.'

Emily felt she'd get on better if everyone spoke English but kitchens had a language of their own, some of it French but none of it understandable to the first timer. All those television programmes weren't really much use to her – they'd just made her get the assignment.

'You're in luck,' William said, 'we use frozen peas for the sorbet.'

Some tiny part of her did feel lucky, actually, however hellish it was. She was learning, with every second, and it was exciting.

'But start by doing the brunoise.'

Emily looked bemused. William smiled. 'Chopping those shallots?'

She was just going to get some carrots, which William had deigned also needed turning into tiny orange tesseri to match the shallots, when she overheard Theo talking to Adam. 'That girl – what's her name again?'

'Emily.' Adam sounded surprised at his interest.

'She's good. Keep an eye on her.'

Emily was insanely pleased. To get praise – even if not directed to her – from Theo Milton was unheard of. She felt like she was the heroine of the novel *The Girl with the Pearl Earring*, being plucked from the kitchen by Vermeer because of the way she colour-coded the vegetables. Curiosity kept her in the cold room risking hypothermia and overhearing something less pleasant.

'How old is she?' Theo asked.

'Not as young as she looks,' Adam said. (Emily hadn't dared lie about her age on an official form.) 'She's above the age of consent.'

Theo laughed. 'You've got a dirty mind, Adam.'

'So if you don't want to shag her, why do you ask? You never take any notice of stagiers.'

'I didn't say I didn't want to shag her,' said Theo, causing such a confusion of emotion in Emily she thought she might faint or wet herself. 'I just think she has promise as a chef. Now get your mind out of the gutter and back to business.'

When Emily staggered home that night her aching feet and back were not for once uppermost in her mind. How was she going to write a reputation-ripping exposé on a man who admitted to fancying her? Or indeed, a man who thought she had promise as a chef?

She was surprised to see Fred appear at eight o'clock the following morning. She would have left the country before she went back to the kitchen if she'd had that verbal battering.

She watched out of the corner of her eye as he came into the kitchen. Theo glared at him. 'None of that crap apology for cooking you gave us the other day.'

'No, chef,' said Fred in a whisper.

'Get to work then,' said Theo.

Emily selected another shallot wondering if she'd be demoted now Fred was back.

'Is that fucking knife sharp?' Theo demanded. He snatched it up from the bench and tested it against his thumb. Emily thanked every god in heaven and the patron saint of lowly kitchen workers that William had given her a lesson on knife sharpening and that her knife would cut silk. Theo's recognition was a grunt as he handed the knife back to her. Somehow it was enough.

During the night she had processed what she had overheard while in the cool room. Men fancied lots of people – it was how they were made. But it didn't mean much – anything really – and she shouldn't let herself feel flattered by it. The compliment about her cooking was harder to dismiss. That wasn't down to too much testosterone in a top chef, that really meant something. But a corner of her couldn't help being pleased he wanted to shag her. Theo wasn't as black as he painted himself, she concluded. Underneath the swearing and bullying he was a nice man.

She revised this opinion only an hour later, when the girl who had peeled several potatoes so finely the strips could be weaved into baskets dropped her knife. It turned out she was wearing the wrong shoes.

Emily was actually in the room this time when

fire and brimstone came down on the poor girl's head. She was not at all surprised that she burst into tears and ran out. Emily felt she might have actually thrown up as well as sobbed if she'd been shouted at like that.

In any other world Emily would have gone after her to see if she was all right. But she didn't dare. It wasn't just her job she had to guard but her cover. It might easily come out that she wasn't really learning to be a chef. Although she realised there were moments when she completely forgot about being a journalist and just wanted to be really good at what she was doing now.

Emily was back on the amuse-bouches when she happened to look out of the window into the yard beyond. Theo was talking to the girl. Then he handed her some money. He must be paying her off. But Emily knew Theo didn't deal with the wages. How odd. She must find out why – find out the name and address of the girl and interview her. And yet somehow getting a first-hand account didn't seem quite as interesting as getting her amuse-bouches absolutely perfect.

'Those look almost good enough to serve, Emily,' said Theo, regarding her tiny cucumber cubes that were to garnish an iced soup.

'Thank you, chef,' said Emily, and she looked directly at him for only the second time.

Her heart skipped and her head slapped it down. Her heart had imagined the electricity, the minute widening of his eyes, the fact that he seemed to hold her gaze for a nano-second longer than necessary.

Theo nodded and moved off. Emily's heart and head battle continued, causing her hands to shake a little as she formed those cubes. Get a grip she demanded of herself. He thinks you're a good worker – that is all!

A few days later, Emily was summoned to a meeting at the paper's head office. She was relieved to see Bob was there as well as Mr Knutsford. The meeting was the last thing Emily wanted. She was exhausted and desperately needed a shower and had to tell lies at the restaurant to explain why she had to leave before service. But at least the paper paid her. The restaurant didn't.

Emily felt she had to go through quite a lot of explaining as to why she was so sweaty and ill-looking, how chefs didn't get to see a lot of daylight and why her fingers sported a couple of blue plasters.

'So, how's the exposé coming along – er, Emily?' asked Mr Knutsford.

'I haven't really got enough material,' she began, although she wasn't being entirely honest. She'd found out quite a bit. The first was that Theo often tore the staff to shreds and yet, somehow, none of them really took it to heart. He hadn't shouted at her yet but she felt it was only a matter of time and it would have meant he'd accepted her as part of the team. Her head had won the battle – she may have had feelings for him but she had completely ruled out that these feelings were in any way reciprocated.

'Oh come on! You've had three weeks haven't you? Bob, are we sure Emily was the right person for this story?'

Bob nodded. 'She was the only one who looked like a student and knew anything about cooking.'

'I see. Well, Emily, don't let us down. Let us have something by the weekend. And make sure you show us Theo Milton as he really is.'

'Actually, I've found out that—'

'That's right. Lots of inside dirt. I want him out of business before the end of the year.'

'Why?' demanded Emily, forgetting how junior she was in the scheme of things and suddenly finding this grossly unfair. And she wanted to know if the rumours about why he was so keen to do a number on Theo Milton were true.

'My daughter wants that location,' said Mr Knutsford. 'If it's any of your business.'

Emily left feeling that while it wasn't her business it was Theo Milton's. And far from finding him a complete bastard, she'd discovered his ferocious exterior was a bit of a front. The money he'd given to the girl he'd torn apart had been for work shoes. This girl now worshipped the ground he walked on in his chef's clogs.

She took time to explain all this to Bob, after they'd left head office in the City and gone back to their own provincial headquarters. Bob had his own problems with the chairman of the board and listened with some sympathy.

'We can't put out a load of lies about him,' he said. 'However much His Knibs wants him out of business. I'll see what I can do.'

Emily went back to the restaurant, wondering how – or if – they'd managed without her. Over the three weeks she'd worked there – notwithstanding the horrendous hours and the backbreaking work – it seemed the place she belonged.

'OK, here's the deal,' said Bob on the phone to her the following day. 'You have to write a review of the restaurant and make it bad.'

'I can't,' said Emily, when she could speak. It would be like writing a character assassination of her mother, or something. 'I mean, I can't write anything that's not true.'

He sighed. 'You're too straightforward for this business. I'll compromise. It doesn't have to be a bad review, just honest. Say it like it is.'

Emily didn't bother to explain that wasn't the only reason she'd said she couldn't do the review. And really, it should have been obvious to Bob. How could she review a restaurant when they knew her? Reviewers should at least try to be anonymous.

Then she thought about the man who usually did reviewing for the paper and realised she had to do it. He knew nothing about food, seeming to judge a restaurant by portion sizes and 'good value' than by what the food tasted like. She had found this out the hard way, when she'd gone to one of his favourites as a birthday treat. Nothing seemed to have avoided the deep fat fryer. No, she'd rather go in disguise than let The Cornucopia suffer at his hands.

Although originally the thought of dressing up as a restaurant critic had been a sort of bizarre joke, now she thought about it harder she felt it was the only way forward. She would give the restaurant a fair review and if, as a customer, she had issues with it, she'd write them. Now she had to find someone she could go with.

A wig, short skirt, high heels and false eyelashes made Emily wonder if even her own mother would recognise her. Adding her most respectable platonic man-friend would make her disguise complete. He would pose as the reviewer, she would be the plus-one. He'd had the misfortune to go grey very early and develop a small paunch. It could easily look as if he'd eaten one too many restaurant meals.

They were going to be anonymous of course, but as Emily did want Mark to take notes, that she would dictate, she was prepared for them to be recognised as reviewers. But she was fairly sure that if Mark was doing the writing, no one would bother to look at her closely. And anyway, Bob had promised the review wouldn't be printed until she had finished her stint at the restaurant. She'd begged to be allowed to stay until the end of the following week because one of the KP's was leaving. They'd be very short handed if she left too.

'Where do your loyalties lie, Em? Don't forget who's paying your wages. You're getting emotionally involved in this assignment,' Bob warned. 'It's not professional.'

'I know,' said Emily, sighing. 'But I will leave when I say I will. There isn't a job for me anyway.'

'Emily? You're a journo not a chef!'

'So I am,' she said, wondering if this was really true. Would she have felt like this if she hadn't developed a little crush – OK a major one – on Theo Milton?

It was perfectly normal, she told herself. He was in a position of great power and was brilliant at what he did. A work-place crush was almost inevitable. The fact that he didn't really notice she was there most of the time was completely by the by.

Emily had to admit it had been fun putting on her best clothes and, aided by a friend, a wig and false eyelashes. She looked so unlike herself she wasn't even nervous about being recognised as she walked into the restaurant, clutching the arm of her escort rather tightly – her heels were high and borrowed and not what she was used to wearing.

It was very strange being on the public side of

the swing doors. And very useful. She was able to see how efficient the front of house was (extremely) and how the restaurant looked when the candles were lit and it was full of diners.

She managed not to make eye contact with any of the staff by giggling a lot and giving her companion orders out of the corner of her mouth.

The meal was sensational! The amuse-bouches weren't quite as neat as when she made them. There was vichyssoise on tonight and she couldn't help noticing that her parsley was chopped finer and would have been exactly in the centre of the little glass of soup.

But she couldn't find any other faults. She and her co-conspirator, Mark, chose as many dishes as they thought they could eat.

'I must say, you're awfully good at this acting lark,' she said to him, having accepted a forkful of his braised pigeon.

'You're not so bad yourself,' he said, retrieving his fork. 'You'd think you were made to be a restaurant critic. You can taste things I can't begin to recognise. I just think it's all delicious. I don't know why. You seem to be able to pick out the individual flavours.'

Emily found herself feeling proud. 'Maybe it's

because I've been working in the kitchen I can taste the ingredients better. I'd love to learn more, I must admit.'

'I thought your dream was to be a top journalist?'

Emily considered. 'I think I went into it because I was good at English and it seemed the perfect job. I'm not sure it was ever a passion.'

'But you were so pleased when you got that writer to be interviewed. You were well chuffed!'

'I was, wasn't I? I like to do a good job I suppose. Which is probably why I want to learn a lot while I'm working in the kitchen.'

'That's probably it,' said Mark, but he didn't look entirely convinced.

'Hey!' said Emily, who suddenly felt odd, as if something she thought was certain wasn't. Did she want to be a journalist? Or did she want to work with food?

'Yes?'

'I've just had a brilliant idea. Let's ask if we can have a menu? We can say it's a special occasion. It would be really useful when I write the review.'

'Better if you asked the chef to sign it,' Mark said. 'I think people do that with celebrity chefs.'

Emily looked at him in horror. 'Oh no. I'm not

getting up close and personal with Theo, even looking like this. Supposing he found out it was me? God knows what would happen.'

'You might get some good material for your hatchet job?' suggested Mark, smiling.

Emily shook her head. 'I don't have to do that any more. I won't risk being recognised.'

'Then I wouldn't risk asking for the menu either. It would look a little odd. I think I've already been spotted taking notes.'

'OK then. Time for pudding.'

'Do you always eat this much or is it only in the interests of research?' he asked.

'Research obviously, but I am really hungry.'

What it really was, she realised, was a desperate need to find out how as much as possible on the menu tasted.

Emily had never enjoyed a piece of writing as much as writing that review. Halfway through it she wondered if, really, she did want to be a food writer. It would combine her training with her new-found passion. She so loved the language, describing taste and texture so the reader would feel they'd eaten the meal and not just read about it.

Bob seemed pleased with the piece too. 'Not sure

His Knibs will like it. He wants the place closed down remember.'

'Frankly, when a restaurant's this good one bad review wouldn't affect it much anyway. I think you should just put it in and take the risk.'

'I will.'

'But not until the week after next's paper? I'm still working till then.'

'I think you've enjoyed yourself in that kitchen. Even if it has made you look as if you've been living under a stone.'

Emily sighed. 'It's been absolutely brilliant!' And she realised how desperately sorry she'd be to leave.

She'd had to put up with quite a lot of joshing in the kitchen about her weekend off when she went in on the Tuesday.

'For goodness sake! I don't know how you'd get a day off around here if you were actually paid,' she said, putting on her whites.

It was a couple of days later and still very early when she was making some brunoise. It was her default occupation which always seemed necessary. She was just noting how much faster and more neatly she now produced her perfect cubes when Theo came in.

Emily experienced the frisson his presence always created in her. It was half terror and half pleased excitement. She had got a bit more used to him now but his being there, early on a Thursday morning, was unusual. She slipped away to the store room on the pretence of finding cling film. She never felt quite in control of her emotions when he was around.

When she came back she found the kitchen in festive mood.

'Hey!' Adam and Theo were high-fiving each other. 'Way to go, bro.'

'Yeah! We rock.'

Emily assumed there was some private reason for their joviality and took no notice until she saw Adam with an edition of her paper.

She went hot and then cold and then wanted to be sick. For some reason her review had come out a week early and for some other reason, Theo had got an early edition.

She forced herself to keep calm. There was no reason for anyone to associate the review with the couple who were in the restaurant the previous Saturday. No one had noticed her at the time, they wouldn't notice her now. But her hands were shaking as she cling-filmed a bowl of chopped shallots.

Theo and Adam continued to read out bits of the review to each other. 'The flavour of the lightly salted beef cheek will be remembered with joy for years to come.'

Emily, who'd found some onions to chop now she'd done with the shallots, cringed. She could have put that better. It sounded a bit too enthusiastic. But as she remembered how well it had gone with the shavings of salad she decided she'd been right about it.

'The smoked trout mousse combined intense flavour with delicate, perfect texture,' read out Adam. 'I told you that would work.'

The two men just seemed to get higher and higher on the praise Emily had heaped on them. Had she known it would all go to their heads she'd have been more restrained, she decided.

Then came disaster. Theo had the paper open on the work surface. Had anyone else used this surface to read a paper on they would have been strung up on the batterie de cuisine to die slowly and painfully. He was studying the review for the zillionth time, possibly looking for phrases to use for publicity purposes when suddenly he said, 'Hey!'

Everyone jumped, from habit as much as anything. Then he roared, 'Emily!'

Emily could hardly make her legs move so she could go to him. 'Yes?'

His bright eyes bored into hers. 'Yes, chef!' he demanded.

'Yes, chef,' muttered Emily obediently.

'You wrote this review didn't you?'

Her eyes flicked to the paper he was holding. There was her photo, tiny and blurred but recognisable. There was no point in denying it was her. 'Yes, chef.'

'You're not a stagier at all, are you? You're a journalist?'

'Yes, chef.'

'You've been here under false pretences all this time?'

'Yes, chef.'

Theo's expression was unreadable. Possibly he didn't know how to react. She had been there under false pretences and yet it hadn't done him any harm. It had been free – good quality – labour and then a very good review. And yet he was obviously outraged. 'I think you'd better get out,' he said very, very quietly.

Emily realised that all the swearing and shouting was nothing. It was when he was quiet that he was really deadly. 'Yes, chef,' she whispered and undid her apron.

*

She was on the doorstep of the newspaper at nine o'clock, getting there before Bob with whom she had a massive bone to pick.

He came into his office the very picture of remorse. Emily couldn't bring herself to shout.

'Oh God, Em, I'm so sorry! It was nothing to do with me.'

'I had to leave, Bob!'

'You were going to leave anyway, it's only a bit earlier than it would have been. It's not as if it was your real job.'

'I know but—' Something in Bob's expression made her stop.

'There's worse, Em.'

'Worse?'

'I'm afraid you're out of your real job too.'

'Why?'

'You didn't write the hatchet job and you gave the restaurant a stunning review. I was bloody lucky not to be given the boot too.'

'But they can't sack me, can they? Wouldn't that be "constructive dismissal"?'

'Not sure.' He sighed deeply. 'I'm terribly sorry, Emily. I was leaned on to put the review in early so I did but the review was so bloody brilliant it's going to increase his trade, not put him out of business. That was the plan. Someone had to suffer.'

Emily tried to feel the devastation she was sure was appropriate. 'I'm not sure I was cut out to be a journalist anyway. I'm better with food.'

'Come on, let's go next door. I'll buy you breakfast. It might not be gourmet but when times are hard you can't beat a bacon butty.'

The greasy spoon, beloved of everyone who worked in the building, did a good bacon butty. Strong tea helped too and soon Emily felt able to get up from the table and face her future – even if it was a trip to the job centre. She hugged Bob, thanked him for all he had done.

Then she went home.

Sitting on the steps of her building, in his chef's whites, looking very fed up, was Theo Milton.

He had no power over her now. He was just a very, very attractive man she had once worked for. Now she no longer worked in his kitchen she allowed herself to admit just how attractive.

He got to his feet. 'You took your time getting here,' he said.

Emily shrugged. 'I had things to do.'

'Yes?' Theo Milton couldn't really accept that anyone had anything to do that didn't involve his restaurant.

'I'm out of a job,' she said.

Just for an instant she saw his pupils dilate as if with pleasure. 'No you're not,' he said and kissed her firmly but swiftly on the mouth. 'Come and work with me – if you think you can stand the pace . . .'

It was all Emily could do not to fling herself into his arms. She didn't know if it was the thought of working with Theo that was so thrilling or her new career as a kitchen slave.

'And in case you're worrying,' said Theo. 'There's no policy against relationships in the workplace.'

Emily blushed. She had been worrying about that particular thing. 'Oh?'

'But it doesn't mean I'll treat you any better than anyone else, if you go out with me.'

'No, chef,' said Emily, lowering her head so he wouldn't see her ecstatic smile.

Main course

From Scotland with Love

If Daisy's job hadn't been on the line she would never have set off for Scotland in that dark time between Christmas and New Year. Nothing would usually have taken her out of London then except perhaps a very good invite for Hogmanay with close friends. And the most difficult author in the known world certainly wasn't a friend. Still, she wasn't planning to stay long. If her plan worked she'd be in and out of his house in an hour and then be on her way back to England in plenty of time for New Year's Eve.

She hadn't terribly taken to Scotland so far. She really only liked scenery if it was on television, accompanied by Bear Grylls. All these snow-capped mountains were a bit too majestic for her. And the sky was so dark it was almost purple.

'Are we nearly there, yet?' she asked brightly,

hoping her driver, who'd hardly said a word, would realise she was being funny. Well, mildly amusing anyway.

'Aye. Another ten minutes should do it.'

'Jolly good!'

She looked out of the window, trying to distract herself from her nervousness and car sickness. It didn't matter how many Magic Trees he'd hung from the mirror, you could still tell this car belonged to a smoker.

'It's the wee cottage on the hill,' the driver said.

Daisy looked where he was pointing. 'It can't be,' she said. 'It's tiny.'

'That's the address and there aren't so many properties in the area I could get them muddled up,' he said. He sounded pleased with what he took to be her disappointment.

Daisy was actually surprised, not disappointed. Why would one of the most successful authors in the world live in such a tiny house when he could probably have bought Balmoral if he'd really fancied it?

'You'll have to walk from here, hen,' said the driver. 'It's up that wee track.'

'Can't you drive up there?'

'No.'

She considered arguing but didn't want to give him the satisfaction of telling her how bad the track was. 'OK!' She took out her Cath Kidston wallet. 'What do I owe you?' When she'd handed over quite a few of the strange-looking notes she'd got out of the cashpoint, she said, 'Can you come back in an hour?'

The driver hesitated. Daisy had given a generous tip. 'All right. Or maybe I'll send another driver.'

'Well, give me your card, just in case I need to get in touch with you,' said Daisy.

When he had done this, Daisy could put off facing the great outdoors no longer. 'Fine,' she said and got out of the car.

Her boots were leaking within two minutes of setting off from the car and her little case on wheels, bumping along behind her, kept catching in the chippings that covered the track and falling over. It was also really steep, zigzagging its way up what seemed to be a mountain. She couldn't see any other houses either. Not only was Rory McAllan the most difficult author ever, he lived in the most inaccessible house ever. By the time she got to the door she was freezing cold and her PR girl's positive attitude was stretched to its limit. Still, it would soon be over, she told herself as she rapped the stag's head knocker. As she waited for the door to be opened, she looked down the track and saw the taxi disappearing round the bend. She suddenly felt very alone. The driver hadn't been very friendly, or helpful but he was at least another human being. What would she do if Rory McAllan was away? Would she have to walk, in her leaking boots, all the way back to the nearest town? It was miles!

Just for a moment, Daisy wanted to cry, but she controlled herself. It wouldn't help. She was cold and it had been a long time since she'd eaten a sandwich at the bus stop; that was why she was feeling pathetic. She'd have to man up. She banged on the door again and it opened almost immediately. Rory McAllan stood glaring at her. Well, at least he was at home.

'Who the hell are you, and what do you want?'

Daisy, who was known for her charm, did her best. She smiled. 'Hi! I'm Daisy Allway. We have met. I work for—'

His brows came together as he stared down at her and then glowered even harder. 'The PR girl? The bloody PR girl, who wanted me to miss my flight so I could sign books?'

'I didn't want you to miss it, I just said there'd

be another—' She did feel guilty about this. She'd let herself get distracted by a boy with floppy hair and so failed to get the Star Author to sign books at the right time. Her boss, Venetia, had gone ballistic, no other word for it. The boy hadn't been all that interesting when she'd got to know him better, either. Which was why Daisy was going to such lengths to keep her job. Venetia didn't know she'd come up here – Daisy planned to give her the signed bookplates with a big 'Ta da!' when Venetia summoned her for the 'little talk' she'd promised after the Christmas break.

'What are you doing here? My address is a well-kept secret?' His voice was very low with a Scottish accent that sent some women crazy. Now it had overtones of fierce-dog-confronted-by-burglar and while it was effective, it was making Daisy want to run away, not jump into bed with him.

Daisy shook her head. 'Not that well kept, actually, as secrets go. My boss knows everything.' She smiled again, this time she hoped, appealingly. 'Could I possibly come in?'

He didn't move. His large frame filled the doorway. 'How did you get here?'

'Budget airline, bus and taxi,' she said. 'I spent the night in a budget hotel, too.' She laughed prettily. 'That was a first!' She paused, not telling him that she didn't usually pay for her own travelling expenses. He still wasn't letting her across the threshold. 'Could I come in? Just for a little bit? I'm not saying it's cold but I reckon Eskimos would feel right at home here.'

He thought about it for a worryingly long time and then he grunted. 'I suppose you'll have to.'

'You needn't look so anxious,' said Daisy. 'I won't be here long at all. My cab is coming back soon, I've booked him. I just want you to sign some book plates.'

Rory was not a handsome man but now, as he almost laughed, he developed a sort of craggy charm. 'I don't bloody believe it!'

Daisy nipped in through the open door while she had the chance. She pulled her case in behind her and once in, put it flat on the floor and then she opened it. 'OK, I've got the bookplates here, if we could just find somewhere where you could sign them . . .'

'You have absolutely no bloody idea, have you?'

'What about?' She looked up at him, holding the bookplates and his favourite Sharpie pen, wishing he'd turn a light on or something.

'That you've arrived just before the biggest storm

forecast for years?'

'I did think it was a bit dark but I put that down to being in Scotland,' she said breezily. 'Now, if we get these signed. As I said, my taxi's coming back soon. I don't want to keep him waiting.'

'You won't see your taxi again for days, weeks possibly,' said Rory.

'I'm sure I will. I gave him a massive tip. Anyway, he said if he didn't come he'd send another cab. I've got your favourite type of pen.'

He ignored the bookplates and pen that she was thrusting at him. 'Have you looked out of the window?'

'Not recently, no. I saw the view on the way up here.'

'I'm not talking about the view, I'm talking about the weather.'

Daisy turned to the window. It was suddenly very dark. It hadn't been bright before but now it had turned sort of yellow, the colour of a bad cold and just as dense. She saw that it had just started to snow. 'OK, it's snowing, but only a little and the flakes are tiny.' He did seem to be making a big fuss about a bit of snow.

'It's the tiny flakes that settle, not the great big goose feathers.'

God, he was irritating! Going on about the snow and not hurrying up and signing the bookplates so she could leave! 'Maybe we should get a move on, then? Get these signed? Then I can hop into my cab and be out of your hair. I'll just confirm he's coming.' She got out her phone, wishing now she'd just asked him to wait.

He shook his head. 'Too late. You won't be able to leave for days.'

'You are joking?' said Daisy cautiously. Just at that moment her phone was answered. 'Oh, hi! I've booked a cab to come in an hour. I was wondering if it could come immediately? To—' She gave the address, hoping she wasn't pronouncing it so wrong that Rory would laugh at her.

'Sorry, madam, there's no way any car is going up there today. There'd be no guarantee he'd be able to get back.'

'But I need to get to the airport—'

'You need to be there within the hour then. That'll be the last flight before it's all closed down. There'd be no way you could do that without a helicopter.'

'Oh. Thank you,' she said and disconnected.

'Let me guess,' said Rory. 'He won't send a car?'

She nodded. She was suddenly desperately

homesick. She'd been out of her comfort zone for too long. 'There must be some other way of getting to the airport—'

He shook his head. 'Nope. And even if we had the right sort of vehicle, it takes over an hour and a half when the roads are clear. And the roads close very quickly once the snow starts.'

Everyone who worked for Athene Publishing knew he was stubborn. His editor had to be incredibly tactful if she wanted to suggest a change, like putting in a full stop instead of a semicolon, for example. 'You're absolutely sure?' Daisy was fairly stubborn too.

He nodded. 'Yes.'

'Oh dear.' Daisy knew this didn't make her sound terribly intelligent but it was better than bursting into tears, which was what she felt like doing. She was stuck, a million miles from home, with enough clothes for one night only and wouldn't be able to get away for days, possibly. Missing the best party ever almost stopped being important, there were so many worse things she had to deal with. Spending time with Rory was hard work at the best of times, he was so bloody grumpy, and having her landed on him, like something out of some sentimental Christmas movie, was not going to make him any more fun. She shivered convulsively, the tears even nearer the surface now.

'You'd better come into the kitchen. It's warmer there.'

Daisy, somewhat reluctantly, put the pen and bookplates back in her case and tucked it to one side, out of the way.

The kitchen was a big improvement on the hallway. Here there were some indications that this Scottish equivalent of a mud hut actually belonged to a writer who must be a multi-millionaire, what with his stunning sales figures and most of his books being made into amazingly popular television dramas. There was a gorgeous red range cooker and a lot of pale wood worktops. This was a good kitchen. And it was warm.

'Would you like a drink?' Rory said.

'Yes please. A glass of white wine would be lovely. Or a Campari and soda if you haven't got wine.' She hadn't looked at her watch recently but she was certain it was past wine o'clock.

He gave a short laugh. 'I meant tea or coffee, but maybe you've got the right idea. He opened a cupboard and took out a bottle and two glasses. He poured large measures into both. Daisy opened her mouth to protest at the size of the drinks but then shut it again. She'd need alcohol if he was right about the storm and she was stranded. She recalled that Rory never drank anything alcoholic except neat whisky and that not very often. Famous Grouse. She remembered the brand now. Her boss would never have let a detail like that slip her mind. She took the glass he handed to her.

As he didn't seem to be making toasts, Daisy took a throat-burning sip. She didn't desperately like the taste but a few seconds in, she found she quite liked the effect. 'Do you have the internet? Or something? I ought to tell people where I am and that I might not be back when I said.'

'You'll have to be quick as it all might go in the storm, but we usually have fairly good reception. Over there is comfortable.'

She went to where he indicated an area where there was a table, a desk lamp and a chair, a sort of mini office. She pulled out her phone from her bag that was still slung round her neck. She'd tackle Venetia first. 'Hi! Hope you're having a good break. I'm at Rory McAllan's getting those bookplates signed. Unfortunately there's a bit of a storm on its way and I may not be back on Monday. I'll keep in touch. Daisy.'

To her mother she wrote, 'Oh God, Mum! Really done it this time! I'm here but there's a storm and I might be stranded with Mr Grumpy for days! Eek! He's got a lush kitchen though and I know I'll be safe. Love, Daisy xxxxxxxxx.' She didn't want her mother to worry about her being hit on by the famous author. She was absolutely confident that wasn't going to happen.

He'd finished his whisky while she was still only halfway through hers. 'I suppose you'll need feeding.'

Daisy nodded. 'Don't you eat, then?'

'Of course. And I can fend for myself well enough. I'm not used to guests.'

'As I'm not really a guest, maybe I could get us something?'

He looked at her questioningly. 'You can cook?'

'Yup.' She didn't add that her parents had sent her on a course, considering it a necessary life skill. She'd turned out to be good at it and really enjoyed it. She cooked for her parents and their friends' dinner parties, to make money when she was between jobs, which was often.

'You don't look as if you can do anything.'

'Really?' Daisy was appalled. She didn't think she looked too bad. 'Why?'

'Blonde hair, blue eyes, too much make-up, wrong clothes.'

She was annoyed. She took great pains to dress appropriately. Today she was wearing a kilt, thick tights and knee-length boots – and her coat, which was a bit thin and short. But how much more appropriate could she look? 'That's the most appalling stereotyping.'

'It's not. I'm speaking from experience. You're the girl who failed to get me to sign books when I was in London and nearly made me miss my flight. You are not good at your job.'

Daisy swallowed. She had been told this many times and had now come to accept it. 'Well, I admit that. But my clothes aren't wrong.'

'Aren't they? You'll freeze to death if you move too far from the range.'

'I'll be fine if I stay in the kitchen.' She wondered why this house had such a great kitchen – it didn't go with the rest of the 'Scottish simplicity' theme. She also wondered if there'd be other nice surprises, like a sauna, or a well-heated home cinema.

'You're only saying that because you're still wearing your coat.'

Defiant, if a bit reluctant, she took it off and hung it over the back of a chair. She was relieved to discover her cashmere sweater was almost, if not completely adequate. If only her feet weren't so wet and cold. She unzipped her boots and took them off. They were completely ruined, she noticed. 'You wouldn't have a pair of socks I could borrow?' she said bravely.

He grunted and left the room. He came back with a pair of the sort of socks you wore inside gumboots. She pulled them on. 'That's better! Now I'll make lunch.'

He still wasn't convinced by her lunch-making abilities, Daisy could tell.

'You won't be able to cook on that,' he said, indicating the range. 'Being a city girl.'

Daisy felt telling him that being a city girl with parents who had a large place in the country with a very similar range was unlikely to endear her to him. His working-class roots were famous and he would despise her even more if he realised quite how middle class she was. She just smiled. 'If I can't manage the range I'll use the conventional cooker next to it. So if you'd just show me what food you've got and I'll get on.'

He opened the fridge. 'There's quite a lot of ham. Eggs. Milk. Staples, really.' He closed the door and then crossed the room and opened another door.

'This is the larder. Vegetables, tins of things. A sack of spuds. All in here.'

'OK,' said Daisy. 'Why don't you leave me to it?'

He seemed reluctant, like trusting a toddler to cut up its own meat for the first time.

'Come on,' said Daisy. 'What harm could I do with a few potatoes and a carrot?'

He laughed. 'OK then. There's always a tin of soup we could open. I'd have done that anyway.'

'Give me an hour,' she said. 'Then come back.'

As Daisy familiarised herself with the kitchen, finding pans, knives, things she'd need, she speculated on Rory McAllan. Everyone at Athene tiptoed round him like he was a dangerous beast. He was grumpy, there was no escaping that, but he probably was human, deep down. The trouble was, at Athene, everyone was so conscious of him being such a star, of paying all their wages and keeping their elegant London offices in good decorative order. They couldn't afford to offend him. He wasn't the sort of writer who was burning to express himself; he always said he didn't much enjoy doing it, and could stop at any moment. This would be a disaster for Athene. They'd never find another 'book a year' author who was critically acclaimed and sold shedloads – they just didn't exist, normally.

But Daisy felt she had to treat him as if he was at least half human or she'd never survive being snowed in with him. As she sharpened a knife (Global, very nice) she realised she still hadn't got him to sign the bookplates. There was hardly any point in her asking him to do them now.

'This soup is really good!' Rory said.

'No need to be so surprised,' said Daisy. 'I'm not a complete ditz. Try the soda bread.'

She was being nonchalant but Daisy was pleased with herself. She'd made a thick and tasty broth which could just about be labelled 'Scotch' and some soda bread to go with it. There didn't seem to be any bread otherwise, and at least it was quick to make. Although she'd found a vast freezer in the larder, it didn't seem to have anything normal in it, like bread. Instead it seemed to be filled with anonymous plastic bags of meat which could have been anything. She'd ask a few pertinent questions before she messed with any of those bloody little packages.

They didn't speak while they ate but Daisy was thinking. She would have to stay the night. And she would have to keep herself occupied. She could cook, of course, if he wanted her to. Make ordinary bread if there wasn't any. She'd found a sack of locally milled flour in the larder. They wouldn't starve. But she was used to being busy. And keeping out of his way might be difficult unless he had a study to disappear into.

'So did you do a fancy cookery course to learn how to produce food like this?'

Daisy would like to have been able to say it was innate ability that made her able to produce a tasty soup but she was honest. 'Yes. It's one of the few courses where I actually excelled.'

'So why don't you do that for a living instead of being a crap PR girl?'

'I'm not a crap PR girl,' she said, although he had pretty much put his finger on it. 'And it's hard to get work as a cook if you don't want to work in a restaurant or in someone's private house. I do dinner-party cooking for friends but there's no money in it.'

'All anyone seems to think about is money,' said Rory.

Daisy glanced up from her soup. He sounded bitter, not just grumpy. 'Well, a girl's got to keep herself in shoes.' She wasn't quite sure why she wanted to reinforce his bad opinion of her. Maybe because she didn't think she'd ever convince him she wasn't just a silly girl. But she wanted to redeem herself this time, for this job. She'd majorly messed up when she'd failed to get Rory to sign the books and the subsequent telling off had been painful. And it was most painful because her boss had said, 'When I took you on, I thought you had something about you.' She had been surprised to hear this and now very much wanted to prove her boss right. She wanted to have 'something about her'.

'I have to go out,' he said.

'What? Go out? I thought we were stranded here!' She looked across and realised she could hardly see out of the window it was so dark, and nearer the house, she could see more incessant snowflakes hurling themselves into the glass making her feel dizzy.

'We are. I'm going on foot. I want to be back before the snow sets in properly.'

Daisy looked out of the window. 'It looks pretty well set in to me.'

'It'll get worse. Which is why I have to be off.'

A pang of real guilt stabbed Daisy. 'Did you delay because of me arriving?'

He studied her. 'I'd love to say yes, to make you feel bad, but actually, there are other reasons I couldn't go sooner.'

'So where are you going? If you don't mind my asking? I'm assuming there isn't an offy round the corner.'

He gave a short laugh. 'We're all right for whisky, if that's what's worrying you. No, I'm going to fetch a friend.'

'Lovely,' said Daisy.

Later, when she'd found dried yeast and was getting some bread going, she speculated on the friend. Another woman would be good. Another man might be OK. But a tiny part of her was disappointed. She'd rather enjoyed being alone with Rory. He was a challenge. She wanted to get to know him better and that might not happen if there was another person there.

She was waiting for her bread to rise when she checked her phone again. Constantly checking was part of her PR world. There was a text from Venetia. She was never out of touch, even if it was the Christmas/New Year break. 'Whatever you do, do not piss him off! We haven't got him on board for another book yet! Was total madness you going up there!!! V x'

Daisy was grateful for the x. It meant that Venetia hadn't completely lost it with her. Knowing her,

Venetia would appreciate Daisy's efforts to help, even if they were the wrong side of insane.

Her mother seemed fairy relaxed, which was good. She just said, 'Keep warm, darling! I used to love Scotland.'

Daisy looked out of the window again. Tiny little flakes were coming out of the sky in dizzying amounts. It suddenly occurred to her to worry about Rory. He and his friend were out in the snow. Would they be all right?

Daisy had decided there was no point in alerting the emergency services and was just wondering if she ought to defrost one of the unappealing packages when she heard Rory come home. The front door opened. 'There you are, lovely girl,' he said. No one replied. The lovely girl was probably too loved up to speak. Marvellous! thought Daisy. I'm snowed in with a couple who won't be able to keep their hands off each other. I'll have to sit with my fingers in my ears to avoid hearing them making love. Eugh!

She heard Rory approach the kitchen door. She was sitting at the table with an open cookery book and a cheerful expression pinned to her face.

'Come and meet Griselda,' he said. 'There's no

need to be frightened.'

Daisy got up from the table, wondering what sort of woman Griselda was that Rory had to reassure her about.

'Come on, girl,' he said fondly. And in walked a very large grey dog.

'A deerhound!' said Daisy delightedly. 'You've got a deerhound! And oh – is she—'

'Very pregnant? Yes. The pups are due any time now. Grizzie's been staying with my cleaner while I've been away. I couldn't pick her up until they'd all come back from her mother's.' This was a bit complicated but Daisy went with it. 'I just hope Hamish – he's the vet – will be able to get through when her time comes.'

Daisy went over to the dog. 'She's gorgeous! Hello, Grizzie!' she said softly and started rubbing her chest.

'I thought you'd be afraid of her,' he said.

Daisy, who was on her knees by the dog cuddling her, looked up. 'You wanted me to be afraid of her, didn't you?'

He almost smiled. 'Let us just say I expected you to be.'

Daisy smiled. She didn't mention her dog-filled childhood. He was unlikely to be interested.

'Er – Daisy—' He remembered her name with a struggle. 'You couldn't cook her something, could you?'

'That depends. What would Madam fancy? Some macaroons? Sour apple sorbet?'

'Venison stew, actually. Could you manage that? Do you do stews?'

'No,' said Daisy. 'I do daubes, ragus and maybe a casserole, if pushed.'

He frowned, not sure if he was being sent up or not.

'Of course I can do stews! Where's the meat?'

'In the freezer.'

'Aha!' she said. 'I wondered what all that was. Dog food.'

'Human food actually. It's culled venison. But she likes it.'

'And would she like that with garlic? Onions? A splash of red wine?'

'Just the basic kind. But we could have all that other stuff.' He frowned. 'I'm not used to women who cook.'

Daisy realised she felt flattered to be described as a woman, not a 'slip of a girl'. 'Well, someone cooks around here. It's a great kitchen.'

He harrumphed. 'I put it in for my ex-wife

who said it was her dream kitchen. She had all the gear and no idea, as the saying goes. She liked to play kitchens, not actually get her hands bloody.'

'Not keen on that either, actually. But I'll cope.'

While she was waiting for the meat to defrost in the microwave, Daisy checked her phone again. There was a text from Venetia. 'How's it going? You haven't pissed him off, have you?'

'Not at all!' Daisy texted back triumphantly. 'I'm cooking his dog a stew. He thinks I'm amazing for being able to cook at all!'

'Well, you are good at that,' said Venetia, who'd been to Daisy's little flat for supper. 'So if you get the chance, ask him if he's going to write another book!'

Daisy thought she probably wouldn't be doing that. It really wasn't her place to get top authors to agree to new contracts.

'So where will Griselda have her puppies?' she asked Rory a bit later, when he came into the kitchen for tea. She'd made scones, having decided that a kitchen full of lovely equipment and quite a good stock of provisions should be used. And she wanted to keep busy. It would make her feel less of a nuisance.

'I'm hoping Hamish will take her away before that happens. I'm a bit squeamish.'

'But the snow? If I can't get out, surely Hamish can't get in?'

He looked at her pityingly. 'He has a four-by-four and he lives very close by.'

'Oh,' said Daisy. 'That's OK then. But just in case—'

'My study. It's on the ground floor. I've converted it into somewhere Grizzie can be. My laptop is upstairs now.' He frowned. 'I suppose we'd better sort you out with somewhere to sleep.'

'Would be good,' said Daisy. She hadn't allowed herself to explore the house while Rory was out, expect for the little loo by the front door. She was longing to get upstairs.

Daisy grabbed her case and headed up the stairs behind Rory.

'You can sleep here,' he said, opening a door to a very comfortable-looking room with a double bed. It looked like the master bedroom to her. It had cushions on the bed. Men didn't put cushions on beds.

'Why don't you sleep here?' she said.

He shook his head. 'I don't want to sleep where my wife has slept. There are clothes in the cupboard if you need anything.'

Daisy wasn't really into second-hand clothes but she did realise she'd need something. She opened a cupboard and saw a pair of sheepskin slipper boots. Her feet were cold, in spite of the gumboot socks.

'There are sheets in the cupboard outside the bathroom.'

'What? Isn't there an en-suite?' It was the sort of bedroom that suggested the presence of a glamorous bathroom close by.

He shook his head. 'Never got round to it. We were just living here while we had work done on the main house.'

Daisy frowned. 'Why aren't you living in the main house?'

'I gave it to my ex-wife. I'm happy enough here.'

He hadn't given much detail but Daisy sensed there was a lot of sadness behind those simple words. She would have to find out more.

She had borrowed a cashmere cardigan and the sheepskin slippers and was feeling much more comfortable. She decided to text Venetia. 'Do you know anything about his divorce?'

A little later the reply came back. 'Think his wife went off with his best friend. Very messy and painful. We think it may have put him off writing. How are you getting on with him?'

Daisy couldn't really tell, so she just put, 'OK, I think. His dog is lovely, though.'

'You like dogs! That's good!'

Daisy didn't reply. She just stirred the dog's dinner.

Rory didn't have any white wine (Daisy guessed his wife had drunk it) but he did have some red and he opened a bottle for them to have with their supper.

'This is really very good!' he said, sounding surprised. 'What is it?'

'Pretty much the same as Griselda's, only with garlic and onions, carrots et cetera. You've got so much good stuff in the freezer.' Someone had obviously stocked up against the storm.

He shrugged. 'Did you manage to find bed linen and things?'

She nodded. 'All folded and ironed in the cupboard.'

'That'll be Mari. She looks after me well. Though I doubt if she'll make it tomorrow, through this snow. Griselda loves her.'

Griselda, who was at their feet under the kitchen

table where they were eating, wagged her tail when she heard her name.

'So, is there pudding?'

'Of course. Bramble crumble. I'll go and get it. Would you like custard or ice cream with it?'

'You made custard?'

'Well, with custard powder. I didn't make it properly. I didn't like to use too many eggs in case we needed them for something else.'

'I love custard made with custard powder,' he said.

Daisy felt it would have been remiss of her not to provide pudding. Venetia would expect it of her. And if she'd failed on the book plate front, she could at least make it up with bramble crumble. She wasn't exactly sure what brambles were until she got them in a pan and discovered they were blackberries, but she was fairly sure Rory liked them, or why would they be in there? She suspected Mari, faithful retainer, of lovingly filling his freezer with his favourite foods. She'd have been very upset about the divorce, thought Daisy, who had a vivid imagination. Mari would always have known that his wife was a 'a flighty piece'. Mari would have a fit if she ever met Daisy, she was sure.

Rory ate his crumble and custard thoughtfully. He regarded Daisy as if she were an interesting specimen. She couldn't tell if his gaze was approving or not.

'I have some work to do. Will you be able to entertain yourself for the rest of the evening?'

A part of Daisy had been hoping he'd suggest coffee and whisky by the fire in the sitting room, but the thought was far from his mind, it seemed.

'Oh, I'll be fine!' she said, eager to please. 'I'll just put this lot in the dishwasher . . .'

'You could leave it. Mari might be able to get here in the morning.'

Daisy smiled. She couldn't possibly do that. 'Would you like some coffee? I could bring it to you?'

Again he seemed faintly startled by this suggestion. 'That would be good, thanks.'

After asking him how he liked it, Daisy delivered it a little later. His room was sparsely furnished with a makeshift desk in one corner. 'Scottish simplicity' certainly reigned here. Rory closed the lid of his laptop as she appeared so she couldn't tell if he was writing another book or playing solitaire.

'Er, we don't get much in the way of television

reception up here – especially when it's snowing,' he said, 'but there are some books in the bedroom next to yours. They were my wife's. You might find something to entertain you.' He smiled. 'Or you might not. Or there are some DVDs.'

'I love reading,' she said and left him to whatever he was doing on his laptop. She realised too late that she was probably stating the obvious. She worked for a publishing house. Of course she loved reading.

Although she found a little single bedroom, lined with bookshelves, some of which contained the sort of fiction she loved, she didn't really want to settle to a book. Looking out of the window to see what the weather was doing, she realised it had stopped snowing, the wind had dropped and the moon was up. She gasped at the beauty and magical quality of the scene before her. The snow-covered mountains reflected the moonlight and created a silver path that led across the loch, which was as still as glass. The trees at the base of the mountains were white. It could have been an image on a Christmas card, and yet Daisy doubted such serenity could really be captured, however skilled the artist.

She stared for a long time and then she realised she had to go out in it, she had to experience the whole scene more intimately. She ran downstairs and opened the big cupboard in the hall, hoping to find wellington boots and a big coat to wear.

It was all there. The boots, too big for Daisy but definitely female, a very new down jacket, a cashmere scarf, were all in the cupboard next to far more scruffy male coats and fleeces. Rory's wife had apparently been fond of clothes but why had she left them all behind?

Wrapped up, Daisy wondered if she should call out to Rory and tell him she was going. She had decided it was better not to disturb him and just go when Griselda stirred herself and came up to say hello. She stretched elegantly and put her head on Daisy's chest and seemed to be asking to go out.

Aware of how he felt about her, Daisy felt she couldn't just take Griselda for a walk in her condition, not without telling Rory although she was still loath to break into his working time. She paused at the foot of the stairs, the dog impatient, she as yet undecided. What would Venetia do? she asked herself. Venetia would tell Rory. She slipped off the boots and padded upstairs.

'Rory? Is it all right if I take Griselda for a little walk? It's lovely out there now and she seems to want to go.'

Rory came to the door. He looked as if he'd like her to fill out a risk assessment form before taking his precious dog out of his orbit. 'Well, take a torch in case the moon goes in. Maybe a stick? And keep her on the lead, she probably won't come back to you, she doesn't know you. And if she took off after a deer or something, it could be fatal.'

'I'll keep her on the lead and be very careful. I'll take a torch. Do I really have to take a stick? I wouldn't have a spare hand for it.'

He considered, as if possibly counting her hands. 'OK. I'll let you off the stick.'

Relieved, she said, 'Would it be all right if I walked down to the loch, do you think?'

'If the snow isn't too deep that should be fine.'

'I won't be long.'

'Let me know when you come back. I'll be listening out for you.'

'I don't have to take Griselda if you'd rather I didn't.'

'No, she does usually have an outing about now. It's probably why she assumed you were taking her.'

'I'll keep her safe, I promise,' said Daisy.

He nodded. As Daisy padded back down the stairs again, she wondered what Venetia would do to her if she did anything to harm Rory's beloved, pregnant dog. Daisy would be lucky to come out alive from that particular carpeting. Except of course that Rory would have killed her first.

Griselda was perfectly happy to stay close, Daisy discovered. There was a loop of lead as she picked her way alongside Daisy. Together they went out of the back door and surveyed the scene for a few moments. It was spectacularly beautiful and icy cold, but the jacket didn't let her down. It was so light she hardly felt she was wearing it and yet she was snuggly warm.

'So, which way, Grizzie?' said Daisy, aware that she had never been in such deep snow before and anxious not to fall over in it. Beautiful as it was, Daisy felt her preference for scenery on screen was justified.

The dog pointed her nose to the left and then Daisy spotted a gate in the wall. There was probably a path leading from it down to the loch.

The snow nearly came to the top of her boots and Daisy took careful steps. Griselda, a little impatient with her handler, looked back, wanting to go faster.

Daisy didn't hurry though, aware she didn't know what was under her feet beneath the snow and wary of twisting her ankle.

She stopped when she got to the loch and just drank in the beauty of it all. Griselda gave her a rather strange look but then squatted to relieve herself. Daisy sensed she'd rather have been off the lead to do this and turned her head away to give the dog some privacy. Her wee could have filled a small swimming pool, Daisy noted.

The snow was far lighter on the shores of the loch and Daisy and Griselda walked along it together in the moonlight. There was no tugging on the lead, just the occasional reproachful look. If circumstances had been different, Daisy would have let her off, certain that she'd have stayed by her side, a stately companion. But she wasn't going to do that, not now.

Griselda stopped and so Daisy stopped too, suddenly aware that they'd gone quite far. 'Come on, Grizzie,' she said, 'we'd better go back or Rory will worry.' She turned and looked up at the little house on the hill and realised it was quite far away. There was a light on upstairs where, she imagined, Rory was writing. Oh please let it be a book, she thought, and not just angry emails.

Although she had Griselda by her side, Daisy felt suddenly lonely in a way she hadn't before. She'd felt a bit homesick and fed up with herself for getting into this ridiculous situation but she hadn't been so aware that she wasn't part of a couple. While she had a loving family and lots of friends, there was no one in her life who cared more about her than anyone else. Rory, who'd had that in his life, must miss the lack of it even more keenly. Daisy herself had had lots of boyfriends, some more serious than others, but she was only in her early twenties. It was far too soon to think about settling down. What was it about the light in the window that made her feel so alone?

She paused in her journey to gaze at the moonlit scene. It was all so vast. There was so much history, so much geography, so much – everything. It made her feel very small and very insignificant. From nowhere tears started to form in her eyes. She'd felt tearful before when she realised how wrong everything had gone but now she was getting on with it and it was sort of OK, she was losing it. It didn't make sense.

Better cry now when she was on her own, she decided. She didn't want to be heard sobbing in her bed by Rory. How embarrassing would that be? She kept her gaze on the silver loch and let the tears trickle down her cheeks, hot for a few seconds and then icy cold.

'Hey! Daisy! What are you doing out here?'

It was Rory, who had somehow arrived beside her without making a noise. Daisy jumped, not because she thought he was a monster or someone likely to hurt her but because she'd been in another world in her head, where there were no other people.

'Grizzie will get cold, standing round like this. Come on,' he went on gruffly. He took the lead out of her hand and unclipped it, letting the dog make her own way.

She knew it was just because he'd been worried about his beloved dog. It wasn't her he'd been concerned about. He wouldn't mind how long she stayed staring in the moonlight. But she couldn't help imagining what it would be like if he cared about her and not just his pregnant dog.

Because she wasn't concentrating, her foot slipped and she nearly fell over. Before she'd fully taken in that she was floundering in the snow, Rory had caught her and hooked his arm through hers. 'Careful!' he said and they set off again.

Daisy found her breath was a little short as they proceded up the hill through the snow together. It wasn't because she wasn't fit – she was. And yet she didn't want to admit there might be another reason for it.

Rory was undeniably an attractive man. Girls in the office had definitely had him on their 'to do' lists although he was far too rugged to be handsome. He wouldn't be a keeper either, they all agreed, he was far too difficult and grumpy, but most of them agreed they wouldn't kick him out of bed.

Daisy felt she knew him a bit better now. Not a lot better, but some. He was difficult and grumpy but he had a kinder side too, and that hadn't made him any less attractive.

These thoughts kept her mind fully occupied until they reached the house.

'Cocoa,' he stated after he'd rubbed down Griselda and given her some biscuits.

Daisy was sitting on the floor, struggling with her boots. 'Do you want me to make it?'

'No. It's my speciality. I can't have you being the only one who can do anything in the kitchen.' He came over to where she was sitting on the floor, took hold of her heel and tugged off first one boot and then the other. Then he put out his hand and hauled her to her feet.

'I could have got up on my own,' she said to his departing back. Then she followed him into the kitchen. To herself she said, 'And I'm quite good at making cocoa too.'

However, she realised he did have a different technique for making hot chocolate. He had opened a tin of condensed milk and was spooning it into a mug. He tipped in quite a lot of cocoa powder and stirred thoroughly. Then he added boiling water from the kettle, stirred some more and sipped. 'Is that OK for you?' He handed her the mug.

She tasted it. It was very sweet but delicious. 'Not quite hot enough,' she said.

'No. I make it in the mugs and then tip it into a saucepan. There are some biscuits in that cupboard. If you want them.'

'No thank you,' she said, watching him tip the delicious-smelling liquid back into the pan.

'Let's take it through to what's left of the fire.'

Later, in bed, wearing some cashmere bed socks and very sleepy, she thought of all the author launches she'd been to, and there was no doubt about it, cocoa-staring into the embers of the fire in Rory McAllan's sitting room was by far the most fun.

As soon as she awoke, she went to the window to see the state of the weather. It had started snowing again and the sky was the same yellowy white it had been yesterday. The silver-gilded sky of the night before was buried deep in grubby marshmallow.

Daisy had a quick shower and put on some clothes. She'd need to wash underwear today – somehow she didn't fancy the ex-wife's knickers, even if they were brand new. Wrapped up in several layers, she went downstairs to see if Rory had been up and the dog let out.

There was a woman in the kitchen. 'Oh! Hello!'

'Hello!' said the woman cheerfully. She was putting a new liner in the bin and Daisy realised this was the cleaner, Mari.

Daisy had imagined her to be a fairly elderly family retainer type, in a wrap-over pinny; instead there was a woman not much older than she was, wearing jeans and a striped apron. 'I'm Daisy,' she said.

'And I'm Mari. Himself has gone out with the dog.'

'Oh good. No puppies then?'

'Not yet. I'm not sure when they're due.' Mari stopped fiddling with the bin. 'So you're from his publishers?'

'That's right. I came up to get some bookplates signed and got snowed in. Or rather, he said the flights would be cancelled.'

'Oh yes. They close the airport before it gets too bad so the planes aren't stranded. No one can use the roads, either. I walked here. I live just a little way along. I saw you arrive,' she added.

'You probably thought I was completely mad,' said Daisy. 'And of course, I was, but I didn't know it at the time.'

Mari, who had been looking a little stern, allowed herself to smile. 'Well, southerners aren't so aware of things like weather.' She paused. 'Rory said you can cook!'

Still keen to get this woman on side, Daisy shrugged. 'Well—'

'You made bread and everything. That's more than Eleanor would have dreamt of doing.'

'His ex-wife? But why were all the things to make bread here? Dried yeast, and a whole sack of flour.'

'She thought she was going to do all those domestic things—'

133

'Rory said "all the gear and no idea".'

'That does about cover it.'

'So what happened to her?' Daisy asked quickly, desperate for information before Rory got back with Griselda, hoping Mari wouldn't clam up and refuse to gossip.

Mari moved the simmering kettle to the hot-plate. 'You must need some breakfast. I'll make something and we can have a little chat. He'll be a little while. He's gone down to the loch to see if it's frozen. He'll be wanting to take the boat out later to fetch some logs.'

Daisy filed this information away for later. 'So? Please tell me about his wife. I'm terrified of putting my foot in it.' She smiled. 'My boss would absolutely kill me if I did anything to upset Rory.'

'So you're not here because you fancy him then?'

Daisy's eyes widened as if in horror. Of course she fancied him, everyone did. He was rugged and moody and very sexy, but she'd never admit it, although she respected Mari's bluntness. It made her own questions about his ex-wife seem less impertinent. 'No! I just messed up big time and as I want to keep my job – the first job I've ever felt like that about – I tried to put it right. Couldn't have done a worse job really, could I?'

Reassured that Rory wasn't in danger of being seduced, Mari put two steaming mugs on the table. Then she put bread in the toaster. 'She ran off with his best friend!'

Venetia had said more or less the same but Daisy felt it was best if Mari thought she was first with the news. 'Oh no! Like that joke? My wife's gone off with my best friend, oh how I miss him?'

Mari looked doubtful. 'Well, maybe. But what he'll really miss is the land.'

'She took the land? How could she do that?' This seemed a bit of a feat, even for the most grasping of ex-wives.

'His best friend owns the estate Rory was going to buy, for conservation reasons. Now he won't be able to afford to because he's got to pay Eleanor off. So Fergus, his ex-best friend, gets the girl and the property. He's not so keen on conservation as Rory thought and is thinking of selling it on.'

'But Rory is one of the best selling authors on the planet! He earns shedloads! What has he done with it all?'

'He's been buying up bits of land – preferably bits of ancient forest – for years. He's got acres and acres of it, but he might not be able to afford the bit he wants most, which is here. It does include the loch and quite a lot of the other side.'

'Blimey, that would be expensive.'

Mari nodded, satisfied that she'd got her point across so accurately.

Daisy buttered the toast Mari had put in front of her thoughtfully. She felt a text to Venetia coming on.

Mari taught Daisy how to make Scotch pancakes, dropping the mixture directly onto the hotplate of the Aga. This kept her happily entertained while she waited for Rory to come back with the logs.

When he appeared, having seen to Griselda's needs, he shovelled three of them into his mouth in quick succession. 'No one makes these like you, Mari,' he said.

'Actually, Daisy made those,' said Mari. 'She's a quick learner.' She undid her apron. 'What's it like out there, Rory?'

'You're off now, then?'

She nodded. 'It's not a day to hang around.'

'You're right there. And I reckon there's more snow up there. You'd better be getting off. Would you like me to come with you?'

'Or I could come with you,' suggested Daisy, who was suffering from cabin fever and desperate to get out into the snow. Secretly, she wanted to go sledging.

'Don't be daft!' said Rory. 'How would you get back here on your own?'

'On my two feet?' suggested Daisy, forgetting for a moment that she shouldn't argue with her firm's most precious author.

'Och,' said Mari, possibly sensing an argument. 'Don't be daft. I got here just fine and I'll get back the same way.'

It was only after Mari had left that Daisy realised she'd only really come to check her, Daisy, out. Daisy completely understood. If a strange young woman from London had called on her boss without warning, she'd want to check her out, too.

'I'm longing for some exercise!' said Daisy later. 'Do let's go out!'

Rory glowered at her. 'You can help me get a load of logs if you like. From across the other side of the loch.'

'That would be fun. When do you want to go?'

'Now. It gets dark so early. We need to do it before lunch.'

'If it's not a stupid question, why do you keep

your logs on the other side of the loch? Wouldn't it be handier to keep them this side? In a basket by the fire, or something?'

Rory couldn't quite bring himself to laugh but his expression indicated mild amusement. 'I do have a log store but it's not full and some trees were felled on the other side and have been cut up for logs. I want as many of them here as possible, in case the loch freezes and we can't restock. I'm just thinking ahead.'

Daisy nodded, sagely, she hoped.

She slipped almost the first moment she got outside. Ice had formed on the path to the loch and for a nanosecond her feet flailed in the air like a cartoon character's. She landed on her back.

'Don't laugh,' she said breathlessly, when Rory showed absolutely no signs of doing so. 'OK, you can laugh, but you mustn't take a video and put it on YouTube.'

This did make Rory smile. He reached for her hand and dragged her up. 'Are you OK?'

Daisy nodded. 'Winded. And I'll have some massive bruises tomorrow.'

Rory's expression was inscrutable. 'Let me know if you want me to rub arnica on them.'

'In your dreams, pal,' said Daisy, secretly delighted

that Rory might have actually indulged in a little flirt.

'That coat looks good on you,' he said, taking her arm, presumably so she didn't fall over again.

She blushed. 'I found it in the cupboard—'

'No, it's fine. Eleanor never got round to wearing it. She didn't take it with her. Probably because it was a present from me.'

'Mari told me about your wife,' said Daisy. 'I'm so sorry.'

'What I mind most was not seeing what must have been under my nose. Her going off with Fergus.'

'It must have been very tough.' Daisy didn't add that she thought Eleanor must have been mad to leave Rory. Although to be fair, she hadn't seen Fergus.

'No one likes to be made a fool of.'

'To be brutally frank, I expect everyone thought it was Eleanor who was the fool.' For a few seconds Daisy experienced the unusual sensation of being able to set her own feelings aside. She knew she was developing a little crush on Rory – who wouldn't in the circumstances? And yet now, she'd rather that he never noticed her as a woman than for him to be unhappy.

'Nope. I should think people understood her wanting a man who was around to pay her some attention and who had a private jet.' He sounded regretful, as if he was taking some blame for Eleanor's defection.

'Oh, he has a private jet?' said Daisy. 'Say no more! All is now clear!'

He squeezed her arm. 'Daisy, I'm sure you know that the PR girl must never take the piss out of the bestselling author.'

'I'm allowed to take the piss out of you,' Daisy explained. 'But I mustn't piss you off.'

He laughed properly. 'And how do you know that the former hasn't caused the latter?'

Daisy didn't waste time trying to work out exactly what he meant – she got the drift. 'Don't tell anyone I said this, but as long as Venetia never finds out, I don't really care!'

'Maybe I'll tell her!'

'But she knows you're really grumpy so I'll just her tell you were in a bad mood.' She paused. 'And she will believe me because to be fair, you are in a bad mood most of the time.'

'Honestly! I don't know what to say about you!'

'If you were a slightly less literary writer you'd know that you say, "What are you like?"'

'That's the thing,' he said seriously. 'I really do not know what you're like.'

Pleased with this conclusion, Daisy didn't say anything else until she was in the stern of the rowing boat being pushed off while Rory clambered in after her.

'Will Griselda be all right while we're doing this?' she asked.

'Mari's husband is coming up in a minute.'

'That's good of him.'

'Yes it is. He loves Grizzie and will make sure there's space for the new logs in the shed. They are both very loyal. I'm lucky to have them.'

Daisy thought it was probably more than just luck that made them such good friends but didn't comment.

Rory was a restful companion, Daisy decided. He didn't need to be chatted to, and while Daisy liked chatting – was good at it – sometimes it was nice not to bother. Instead she drank in the beauty of her surroundings. The white mountains touching the grey, snow-filled sky, leading down to the loch, like dark glass, still, deep and very cold. It was scenery, all right, and yet somehow, Daisy liked it.

They had crossed the loch, filled the boat with logs and rowed back, twice, when Daisy got cold. Before they got back in the boat for a third and final trip, she said, 'Could I have a go with the oars this time? It's getting chilly watching you do it all the time.'

'Can you row?' Rory's eyebrow reached his dark thatch of hair.

'Shall we see? I can give it a go, at least.' She smiled briefly.

'OK. I'll prepare myself to be amused.'

'You know what?' said Daisy seriously, having got aboard and settling herself in the middle of the boat. 'You should practise that. Being amused is a good skill to have.'

'And you know what? You're really helping.'

Daisy smiled, feeling smug. 'I'll tell Venetia. She'll like that.'

They'd travelled halfway across the loch before he said, 'You actually can row, can't you?'

'Yup. One of those things my father thought I ought to learn.'

'So why do you go round looking as if you're a complete ditz? You do have skills and yet you're just a PR girl.'

Daisy frowned at him over her oars. 'You of all

people should know better than that. PR girls work incredibly hard and do a really difficult and important job. And I love it.' She had only recently discovered this.

'And you do it badly.'

'I'm not brilliant at it, I admit, but that's because it's difficult.'

'But you can cook, row, basically do useful things. It's crazy you doing a job you're bad at.'

'If you can think of jobs in London, that pay, that include cooking and rowing, I'll apply right away. Although to be honest, I would need a whole wardrobe change.'

He frowned and shook his head, not convinced she was making sense.

'There are other places to live apart from London,' he said.

'You say that, but I wouldn't want to risk it. I wouldn't want to live anywhere I couldn't pick up a black cab at any time.' She shuddered at the thought. Then wondered if actually, she might learn to cope without them.

While Rory stacked logs, Daisy made some soup using her private, super-quick recipe that relied on Rory's well-stocked freezer and a tin of tomatoes.

She added some dried chilli, hoping its presence in the spice rack meant Rory liked it.

After lunch, Daisy made a cake while Rory sawed and chopped and stacked. She quite liked this sort of job herself but thought he would feel obliged to think up a job for her that involved cooking, rowing and log-chopping. She didn't think he should waste his brainpower. While she creamed and folded, her own brain was focused on how she could suggest to him that he not only offer Athene another book, but instead, four books. That way he would get enough money to buy his beloved loch and the woodland beyond. She'd had another text from Venetia, wanting to know how she was getting on. She'd added a Happy New Year for tomorrow to the text, otherwise Daisy would never have noticed the date.

By four o'clock it was dark. Daisy made tea and cut a slice of cake. She took a mug and the cake up to Rory and then took her own into the sitting room. She stoked the wood burner (no girl whose parents had a place in the country was fazed by a wood burner), put more logs on the fire and snuggled up on the sofa with a book. Then, still feeling chilly, she lit the fire and pulled the throw that was on the back of the sofa over herself. It had presumably been left behind by Eleanor. She might have had a lot of things wrong with her, Daisy thought, but she had good taste and shared Daisy's passion for cashmere. It was hard to remember it was New Year's Eve – Hogmanay up here. Back home she'd be climbing into something uncomfortable but sexy and ringing round her friends for lifts to and from the venue. She didn't seem to mind missing out on all the fun at all. How weird was that?

She was awoken from her comfortable doze in front of the fire by a high, strangled cry. Her first thought was of a fox but then she remembered Grizzie. She struggled upright and went into Grizzie's bedroom. She was there, looking frightened, possibly wondering what on earth was happening to her.

Daisy ran up the stairs, calling as she went. 'Rory? I think Grizzie's in labour!'

He appeared at his office door, looking dishevelled and worried. 'Are you sure? How do you know? She's not due for a few more days!'

'Come and see for yourself.'

She went back quickly, certain he would mow her down in his eagerness to get to his beloved dog.

145

Griselda was very pleased to see her master.

Her master, on the other hand, was not pleased to see Griselda obviously suffering – from confusion if not from real pain. 'I'll ring Hamish,' he said.

Daisy made sure Griselda had water and food available and that there were plenty of newspapers around. Then she trawled the house for things she might need.

There was a generous stock of hand towels in the airing cupboard. Eleanor obviously had a small White Company addiction for which Daisy was now grateful. She took several of them, sure Griselda would appreciate her puppies being born into such fluffy luxury. She found a couple of single sheets and added them to her pile. Then she went to the kitchen and found scissors. She put them in a pan and boiled them for a few minutes and then tipped them out onto a towel. She didn't know if all this hygiene was necessary but she was sure Rory would appreciate it.

She put her birthing kit into a box lined with a bath towel and took it all into what she thought of as Griselda's birthing suite. Then she plumped up Griselda's duvet and went to get her book. She settled on the sofa. She knew it could take a long time for anything to happen.

Rory came back into the room. 'Hamish is on his way,' he said. 'I'll boil some water.'

'I'll make tea for him when he gets here,' said Daisy, making it clear that boiling water probably wasn't necessary.

But Rory had already left the room.

Daisy followed him into the kitchen. 'It could take ages, no need to do anything now. Unless you want tea yourself?'

He looked at her, his expression wild. 'I want whisky but I won't, not until we know it's all over.'

'Very sensible. Although it is New Year's Eve.' She looked at him. 'Why don't you go and sit with Grizzie? She'd like you to be there with her.'

'How do you know so much about it? Oh, don't tell me – your parents sent you on a course.'

Daisy giggled. 'Of course they didn't. If they'd thought I could be a vet they'd have made me go to uni. But my mum has Cavaliers and they've had a couple of litters.'

'Cavaliers? Aren't they really small? It won't be the same at all.'

Daisy shrugged, not sure if it would be the same or not. 'Never mind. Hamish will be here. How long will it take him?'

'Normally about forty minutes but in this, I'm not sure.' He looked out of the window and Daisy followed his gaze. It had started to snow again.

'I'm sure he has plenty of time to get here,' said Daisy. 'Tell you what, we'll have tea and something to eat while we're waiting. It'll help to pass the time.'

'Not for me. Well, tea maybe, but I couldn't face food.'

Daisy shook her head. 'Ooh, we've got a right one 'ere.'

He glared at her. 'Are you teasing me?'

'Just a little bit,' said Daisy, not quite as brave as she sounded.

She left him alone with Griselda for a short time. She put more logs on the fire and got in another load from the woodshed, selecting the most seasoned. She realised she wasn't hating this whole situation nearly as much as she would have thought. She was actually good at country skills and now she was surrounded by it, found she quite liked scenery, even when it was mostly white. She wondered briefly if it was Rory's presence that made it all so appealing but pushed the thought firmly away. A PR girl having a thing with a top author would be such a cliché.

'How's she doing?' she said a few minutes later.

Rory was sitting on the sofa, looking distraught, his hair obviously mangled by anxious fingers. 'I don't know. Look, would you stay with her? I'm going to give Hamish another ring. I just hope he hasn't gone out to a party.'

'Bit early isn't it?'

He glanced at his watch, shook his head as if confused, and left the room.

Daisy settled on the sofa with her book and the cashmere throw.

Rory came back a few minutes later. 'He doesn't think he can get here.' He looked as if he could hardly believe this terrible news. 'What are we going to do?'

'Well,' said Daisy. 'You could ask Grizzie if she could put off having her pups until the snow's gone—'

'Don't be so bloody ridiculous.'

'Or we can just see how it goes. Do our best to help her.' She frowned slightly. 'The hard part will be keeping us amused while we wait. We could probably hear her from the sitting room and watch a film but I—'

'We're not leaving her alone!'

'No.' She paused. 'Have you got any cards, Rory?'

He looked bemused. 'What, business cards?'

'No! Playing cards. You know, with numbers and pictures on!'

His expression cleared. 'Oh yes. Good idea. I'll find them.'

Daisy found a small table they could play on. Her training as a PR girl – always looking ahead to see if anything was required to make things go more smoothly – hadn't been entirely wasted.

Rory brought a large jar full of small change as well as the cards.

'We don't need money for snap do we?' asked Daisy.

'We're not playing snap – we're playing poker.'

'Oh.'

'Don't tell me you don't know how to play poker, Daisy-the-PR-Girl!'

'Well—' Her parents had suggested it was a good idea to learn at least the rudiments of bridge but poker wasn't on their list of things a young woman should know.

'Share out the money. Any you win, you can keep,' he said.

'Thank you,' she said and began counting coins.

He'd taught her the basics and Daisy had won a few hands and was enjoying it more and more.

'This is the best fun I've had with my clothes on!' she said delightedly. And the best New Year's Eve she'd had for years, but she didn't say this out loud.

'There is a version you can play—'

She scowled at him, knowing perfectly well what he was referring to. 'No,' she said sternly.

He shrugged. 'Maybe it is a bit cold for strip poker.'

'And imagine if Hamish arrived and we were both half naked. Not a good impression.'

Rory laughed. 'I didn't think you were prudish.'

'Oh I'm not – at least I don't think I am – no one ever thinks they're prudish, do they? No, I was talking from a PR point of view.'

He shook his head, tutting. 'PR my elbow. Your deal.'

Daisy was about to put down a very good hand and claim a huge pile of money when Griselda decided it was time to stop the fun. She gave that strange, high-pitched cry that made both Daisy and Rory throw down their cards. A black, shiny parcel was appearing from Griselda's back end.

'Oh my God, I'm going to faint,' said Rory. 'I'll ring Hamish.'

'Stop being such a wuss! Hand me that towel,' said Daisy. 'I'll catch it. It's quite a long way down.'

Daisy took hold of the bundle emerging from Griselda, overcoming her own anxiety and squeamishness, and passed it to the new mother.

'Oh my God, she's eating it,' said Rory.

'No. She just breaking it out of its sac. And yes, she is eating the afterbirth but that's supposed to happen.'

'You are amazing, you know that?' said Rory.

'Griselda is amazing, that's what. I'm going to change her sheet round a bit so she's not lying in the wet.'

'I didn't know we had all this stuff for her. It's fantastic!' said Rory.

'Not sure your ex-wife had Griselda's puppies in mind when she bought it, but I'm sure she'd be happy to know she had them on thousand thread-count sheets.'

'What the hell are you on about?' Rory was calmer now, watching Griselda wash her pup with a thoroughness that was almost rough.

'The sheets are very high quality,' said Daisy. 'Oh, it's amazing, isn't it? I feel quite tearful.'

Rory put his arm round her and gave her a squeeze. 'So do I.'

When they'd made Griselda and the puppy comfortable and it had made its bumbling way to a teat, Daisy said, 'So, tea? Or more poker?'

'Poker. I was about to take you to the cleaners.'

'You were so not! Look!' Daisy proudly laid down her cards.

Rory poked them with his finger. 'Sorry, Daze, that's a nine, not a ten. My four aces beats you.'

While Daisy laughed and teased and attended to Griselda, who seemed to appreciate having her chest rubbed while she waited for her next pup, she was aware of how much she liked sitting next to Rory, feeling his large, warm presence beside her as they played. While he was outfoxing her at poker, he seemed to forget his worries about his dog and to lose his gloomy persona. Daisy wondered how much of that gloom had been due to his unhappy marriage and now, the loss of both his wife and his friend.

'I'm hungry,' he said, having swept up a pile of pennies and added them to his hoard.

Daisy looked at her watch. 'Ten o'clock! And we didn't have supper. Shall I make us something?'

'No, I will. I can make sandwiches if I have to, but if a puppy comes, I won't know what to do.'

'Good timing,' said Daisy, when he came back some minutes later. 'Look!' Griselda was giving her second puppy a jolly good wash. 'It's a little girl, and she arrived while you were out of the way.'

'Men have no place in a delivery room,' he stated firmly. 'It was one of the few things my ex-wife and I agreed on. Not that we had any children, of course.'

'Oh,' said Daisy as they ate their sandwiches. 'I think I'd need someone in there with me, who I knew. But I haven't got any children either. Not likely to for years and years.'

'But you want them eventually?'

'Oh yes! I should think so.'

'How old are you, Daisy?'

'Twenty-five.'

'That is young. Very young.'

'True,' said Daisy, 'but you know the weird thing?'

'What?'

'You were twenty-five once.'

He laughed. 'You know what, young Daisy – I think I can call you that now with confidence – I've had more fun with you and a couple of packs of cards than I've had for ages and ages.'

'I'll tell Venetia. She'll think I'm doing my job properly for once and be pleased.' She was ecstatic herself but didn't want him to know that.

'It's not all about your job, Daisy. None of what you've been doing lately has been on your job description, now has it?'

She relented. 'Well, not everything I've been doing, admittedly. But Venetia expects all her team to provide any service required by our authors.'

'And that includes being a midwife to their dogs?'

'From now on, it'll be added to the list.'

He chuckled, and put his arm round her. This time, instead of just giving her a squeeze, he kissed the top of her head. Daisy supressed a little sigh. He was so gorgeous (she now let herself admit it) but he would think she was far too young for him. He was treating her like a baby sister, which was not what she wanted at all.

It was eleven thirty, and Griselda was the proud mother of five puppies when one got stuck. She pushed and cried and caused Rory to breathe quickly. 'You could go and ring Hamish,' suggested Daisy, who was frightened herself.

'No point. I had a text while I was making sandwiches. He's got no chance.'

'Just us then,' said Daisy. She swallowed and looked at the lump protruding from Griselda. The dog was in pain and the puppy could easily die. What worried Daisy more was what would happen to Griselda if all the afterbirth didn't come away, if there were more pups stuck in the queue. Then they'd really need Hamish. 'Could you hand me a towel?'

As gently as she could, trying to set aside her fears, she took hold of the puppy and pulled and turned it a little. To her enormous relief if came out and she was able to lift it away. It was very still though and trapped in its bag. 'Scissors,' she said softly. Rory handed them to her and even more careful now, she cut until its face was no longer covered. It hadn't moved. Griselda was panting her way through another contraction so Daisy did what she'd seen her mother do, and rubbed the little creature briskly, roughly almost. At last it squeaked. Daisy sighed deeply and handed it to the dog who had looked up anxiously when she heard her pup make a noise.

When Daisy had dealt with the afterbirth she felt suddenly very tired and emotional. She knew it was mostly relief that all seemed to be well, but it made her feel rather wobbly. She looked at Rory and realised he was wobbly too. It seemed natural to take him into her arms and give him a hug. He hugged her back, and they stood there, both holding on tightly.

At last Daisy felt she should break out of where she really wanted to stay for ever. She looked up, about to say something about a cup of tea. Rory was looking down at her, his mind obviously on something quite different. Daisy took a breath. What was about to happen was not professional, but it was what she wanted more than anything. His mouth came down on hers.

Hardly had his lips met hers than there was a frantic banging on the back door. For a second they stared at each other. Daisy felt horribly caught out as if somehow work had discovered she was about to kiss their top author. Rory was confused for a moment and then he grinned.

'It must be after midnight. That's the sound of a first-footer if ever I heard one!'

They went to the door together. Mari and two men Daisy didn't recognise were there. The one nearest the door had hair the colour of soot. But it wasn't his hair colour that had Rory so delighted.

'Hamish! You made it!'

'I got as far as these guy's—' He indicated Mari and a man Daisy took to be her husband. 'They said they'd come with me.' Without wasting time on either ancient rituals or formalities, Rory led Hamish to where Griselda and the pups were.

Mari was in a little less of a hurry to see the new arrivals, although only slightly. 'We knew the puppies would be here or nearly here, so we said we'd come first-footing and get an early look. Oh, Daisy, this is Ian, my man, and this is Daisy.'

Ian smiled down kindly at Daisy, his red hair making him look far more Scottish than the dark-haired Hamish. 'I've heard a lot about you, Daisy.'

Daisy shuddered. 'I'm not even going to try and find out what.'

Rather than overcrowd the new mother, Daisy went to the kitchen and put the kettle on. Then she found glasses and got out the cake.

Mari joined her shortly afterwards. 'They're not what you'd call cute, but adorable for all that. And seven of them! That's a good number.'

Daisy nodded. 'I feel as if they're my puppies too! Now what will people want? Whisky or tea?'

'Whisky. And traditionally we'd eat Black Bun with it.'

Daisy frowned. 'What on earth is Black Bun?'

Mari laughed. 'It's a cake. You've got a cake there. I've brought shortbread with me. Oh, and some coal – don't ask—'

'Even I know that coal is to do with the first-footing thing you go in for up here.'

Mari laughed again. 'We have to buy some specially. We all use wood burners up here. Ah, here they come. I'll get pouring.'

The kitchen was suddenly full of men laughing and banging each other on the back. Daisy and Mari handed out tumblers of whisky, cake and shortbread. Suddenly there was a silence. Rory raised his glass. 'A toast! To Daisy! She may be a rubbish PR girl but she's a brilliant midwife when it comes to puppies!'

Daisy realised no one but she and Rory had a clue what a PR girl was and accepted the toasts, the kisses and the appreciation that came her way.

'I must say,' said Hamish, 'speaking as a vet, you did all the right things with Grizzie. Rory was very lucky you were there.'

Daisy realised she was blushing. 'I've seen puppies being born before.'

'You were still brilliant,' said Rory.

Daisy found herself looking up into his eyes and

blushed some more. There was respect, appreciation and something she really hoped was lust in them. She wished she could magic away the other people and see if he would really kiss her then.

'Let's go by the fire and sit down,' he said a second later. 'I'm exhausted. And you guys must be too. Walking all that way in the snow.'

Then the cosy sitting room was full of people, easily taking up the two armchairs and the sofa. The room looked lovely, Daisy thought, having lit the candles while Rory made up the fire. Hamish went round topping up glasses and Mari muttered about making crumbs with the shortbread. It was a delightful party.

Daisy found herself with nowhere to sit and somehow ended up on the rug in front of the fire, leaning against the armchair Rory was sitting on. He offered her the chair but she declined. 'I like being able to really see the flames,' she explained and he didn't argue.

Daisy didn't really know any of these people and yet as she listened to their chat she realised she felt quite at home among them, which was ridiculous. She had as much a place in their lives as one of those orchids that last forever did among the heather, or the wild mountain thyme.

She was just starting to feel more than a little sentimental when everyone was on their feet and going.

There was a lot of hugging and seasonal greetings and then suddenly everyone was gone. It was just Rory and Daisy, confronting each other. No one spoke for long seconds. Daisy caved in first. 'We'd better check on Grizzie,' she said.

Rory nodded solemnly. 'Yes. She was only checked by one of the best vets in the Highlands a few minutes ago.'

'Well, I haven't seen her for a while!' said Daisy and tiptoed into her room.

Griselda lay, almost as long as a man, on the special bedding Hamish had brought with him, her pups all latched on, sucking away. She raised her head when Daisy entered and lifted her tail, half proud and half bemused by what had happened to her.

It took Daisy a long time to convey to Grizzie just what a clever girl she was and how beautiful her (slightly rat-like) puppies were. Rory came in just as she was finishing. He took Daisy's hand and raised her to her feet.

'I'm going to sleep in here with Grizzie. Hamish says these big dogs can be a bit clumsy.'

'Well, let me know if you'd like me to take a turn. I wouldn't mind at all.'

'I know you wouldn't. You're very loyal.'

'Well, to Grizzie, I am!' said Daisy.

'To us both, you are.'

Daisy was suddenly desperate to get away. She'd longed for him to take her into his arms, to his bed, but now she didn't seem able to handle the situation.

'You go to bed now, Daisy,' he said gently. 'You must be exhausted.'

She was awoken the following morning by the smell of bacon frying. For a while she lay there, wondering what was going on, and then she remembered the puppies. She got out of bed and grabbed Eleanor's abandoned dressing gown (also cashmere). She was still doing it up as she ran down the stairs to see how Griselda was getting on.

She was lying on her side, seven rat-sized puppies kneading her side as they had their breakfast. The previous evening they'd been tube-shaped. Today, they were little balloons. They'd obviously been feeding all night. Rory came in while she was still kneeling, telling Griselda what a good and clever dog she was.

'It's amazing, isn't it?' she said, looking up at him.

'It is. And there's breakfast. Come and have some. Grizzie will still be here afterwards.'

Daisy got to her feet and tightened her dressing-gown belt. 'I'll pop up and get dressed.'

'Don't, come as you are. You look enchanting. I like you without make-up and your hair in a bird's nest.'

'It took me hours to get it like this,' she said solemnly.

'Yes, about eight hours,' he said, grinning. 'Come and have bacon and eggs.'

There was definitely a feeling of celebration as they ate the enormous breakfast cooked by Rory.

'I don't usually have much first thing,' said Daisy, on her second slice of toast having eaten a very 'full Scottish'.

'Well, it isn't first thing, being ten o'clock,' said Rory. 'Are you sure you won't try the fried haggis? It's very tasty.'

'I'm sure it is but I've eaten enough bacon and eggs for six PR girls already. I couldn't manage another thing.'

He leaned forward and scooped a tiny blob of marmalade from the corner of her mouth.

'I'm going to get showered now,' said Daisy, suddenly feeling very underdressed.

She came down a little later, showered, dressed and with a bit of make-up. It was all very well for Rory to say she looked good without it but she knew better. She'd replied to a long text from Venetia who was pleased about the pups but wanted to know if she'd managed to ask Rory to sign up for the four books Athene so wanted from him. Daisy had replied she was waiting for the right moment when in fact, she'd forgotten all about that. She just wanted to think about Rory, Griselda and the puppies, not book deals.

She went into the kitchen, prepared to tidy up after last night's party and today's breakfast. To her surprise, the kitchen was in pretty good shape. She did some wiping down and putting away but really Rory had done a very good job. She had put the kettle on for more tea when the back door opened and Mari came in.

'I had to come and peek at the bairns,' she said, apparently a little embarrassed. 'I'm not here officially.'

'Well, it's lovely to see you whether you're official or not,' said Daisy. 'Cup of something?'

'Tea please. I'll just go and see Grizzie.'

Daisy went to join Mari and Rory in their puppy adoration and then Mari said, 'Come on, you two need to get out. I'll watch the babies.'

Daisy suddenly yearned to leave the house and go out in the snow. She didn't know how much longer it might last. When the snow went, or even partly went, she would have to go too.

'Are you up for it, Daisy?' asked Rory, as if she might not be.

'Oh yes. We need to walk that breakfast off.'

Well wrapped up, they walked in silence for a bit, finding the effort of walking through the snow enough without speaking as well. Eventually they stopped. They were on a ridge overlooking the loch and the mountains beyond.

'I'm going to miss this,' said Daisy. 'I never thought I'd say that, but I really am.'

'So am I,' said Rory.

Daisy looked at him. 'What do you mean?' A tiny part of her hoped he was going to say he would miss her. Most of her knew he wouldn't.

'I might have to sell it. I have an expensive wife to pay off and a one-time friend who isn't as interested in the environment as I thought he was. As he thought he was, to be fair. Don't tell me,

Mari didn't tell you all about it. She's not a gossip but she likes people to be informed, which is how she defines it herself.'

Daisy didn't speak immediately, then she plucked up her courage and said, 'There is a way you could get money. Lots of it.'

'I'm not selling that bit of land those foreigners are after,' he said swiftly. 'I don't care how much they're willing to pay. It's possible there are wild cats on that site and I won't have it built on!'

'Oh! Mari didn't tell me about that. Perhaps she thought I didn't "need to know".'

He relaxed. 'Sorry. All my friends – the few I've got I trust – have said I should just sell that little corner and all my troubles will be over, but I can't. I worked damn hard to buy it and I'm keeping it.'

'My idea was different.'

'Tell me.'

'You may not like this idea either.' She knew, because Venetia had told her yet again in her previous text that he had always completely rejected the idea of a contract for more than one book. But Athene wanted more than one book, four books for preference, for all sorts of reasons Venetia didn't think she needed to share with Daisy.

'What? It's getting worse in my imagination all the time.'

'Turn off your imagination! It's agreeing to sign for four books and not just one. Athene would pay you shedloads.' She didn't know exactly how enormous the sheds were, but Venetia assured her they were massive.

'Oh.' He sounded as if this was an entirely new idea. 'I've always insisted on only signing for one book at a time. I don't like to be tied down by long contracts. I might want to give up writing.'

'Well, it's up to you of course. It's a solution though, that doesn't mean you have to lose any of this.'

She made a sweeping gesture at the stunning scene before them.

He didn't speak for a long time. Daisy spent the time drinking in the beauty of the mountains, the snow, the silver light on the loch, the dark of the distant tree trunks contrasting with the snow weighing down the branches.

He cleared his throat. 'How much do you think I'd get?'

'I don't know. But I suggest you ask your agent for how much you want and then leave it with him.'

He gave a long sigh and then said, 'I've always loved this place, but just recently I've come to love it more. Losing it would be incredibly painful.'

'Then don't lose it, keep it,' said Daisy.

He took an agonisingly long time to think about it. 'All right. I'll tell David that's what I want to do. See what he says.'

Daisy didn't comment. Rory's agent was notorious for getting fantastically large deals. She only hoped she wouldn't be held responsible if the deal completely bankrupted Athene.

'It's getting dark,' said Daisy a little later. 'And it's only lunch time.'

'We should go back,' said Rory. 'Mari will be wanting to go home.'

Two days later the thaw came. They heard on the news that the roads were beginning to clear and that normal service was resuming. Reluctantly, Daisy made plans to leave. Rory didn't suggest she stayed any longer and besides, Daisy needed to get back, back to real life and the hustle and bustle of London and her job.

Rory insisted on her keeping the cashmere dressing gown and Daisy felt that if it meant she had to check in her luggage and not just have carry-on, it was worth it. It was a fabulous garment! But in her heart she knew it wasn't just because it was beautiful and warm and suited her that she wanted it, but because it would always remind her of her time with Rory. He also said she should wear the coat and scarf and boots, too. The boots she had arrived in were ruined so she didn't argue too much. But again, it was the memories, not the clothes themselves, that made her want them.

She had said long and fond farewells to the puppies, who all now had names, and a longer one to Grizzie, who now felt like a sister, they had shared so much.

She was very businesslike with Rory. 'Thank you so much for not kicking me out into the snow,' she said, jumping up slightly so she could kiss his cheek.

'Thank you for delivering Grizzie's puppies. I was hopeless.'

'You'd have managed just fine,' she said briskly, looking about for her case.

'Daisy—'

She looked up. He put his hand on her cheek and held it, looking into her face, his expression unreadable. 'You're very young.'

Daisy understood. She was too young for him; that was why he hadn't kissed her again, or never shown if he had feelings for her. There had been a moment when she felt she'd spotted something in his expression that indicated there might have been a hint of desire. But now he was being practical, and she must be the same. 'I know,' she said. 'I think it's a good thing!'

'Generally, it's good,' said Rory, slightly rueful. 'This time...'

Just then the hooting of the taxi horn stopped him saying more. Daisy wondered if they were destined always to be interrupted just as Rory might be about to say or do something lovely.

'I'd better go.'

'Yes. You'd better.'

She had just set off down the track towards the waiting taxi (it was the same grumpy driver – she recognised his car) when she turned round and came hurrying up the hill again.

'What? Have you changed your mind about going?' said Rory. His voice sounded as if he might be smiling.

Daisy didn't allow herself to look at him, to see if he would like it if she had changed her mind. She just flung her case on the floor and opened it.

170

'The bloody bookplates! I never got you to sign them!'

A month later, Daisy was at her desk. Her trip to Scotland, such a mistake in many ways, had led to her being promoted. This, Venetia had told her, was not just because she'd managed to get Rory McAllan to do what no one else had ever managed and sign a four-book deal, but because her time in the far north had made her much more sensible. Daisy had not argued. She'd learnt a lot up there in the mountains and she knew her time there had been very special for lots of reasons, some of them perfectly sensible, but the dominant one just a dream.

She was planning a small tour of the west of England for one of her authors (she had her own now, and didn't just assist other publicists with theirs) when she heard a bit of a commotion. She looked up and saw Rory.

For a moment he looked so out of place she didn't properly recognise him, which was ridiculous. She hadn't known he was coming and she felt caught out. Her breathing was severely affected by this and, as he strode over towards her desk, she worried that she wouldn't be able to speak. She just had time to take a sip of water before he arrived.

'Hello, Daisy,' he said.

'Hello,' she whispered. Her brain flashed back to the time in Scotland when she had teased him and they had played poker while Grizzie had her puppies. She could speak OK then.

'Will you come out for lunch with me? Now?'

She looked at her desk full of half-completed tasks and then at her phone, which told her it was half past eleven. 'Um—'

From nowhere Venetia appeared. 'Off you go, Daisy. This will all wait.' She found Daisy's coat from the back of the door and wrangled her into it. 'You can take as long as you like. You've worked very hard lately.'

Daisy looked at her boss, still incredulous. This generosity over lunch hours was unheard of.

'Off you go, Daisy,' Venetia insisted. 'I'll cover for you.'

They didn't speak in the elevator. Daisy was overcome with shyness. He was in her space, it was all wrong. It only worked between them in Scotland, where he felt at home.

'Venetia sorted out a table for me,' he said as they walked along the pavement. He stopped and ushered her into a very lovely restaurant only very special authors got taken to. Daisy wasn't often invited to those lunches.

An agonising lifetime passed while they were seated, presented with menus and ordered drinks. Rory ordered Famous Grouse, Daisy a spritzer.

'How's Grizzie?' said Daisy when Rory didn't say anything for an ominously long time.

'She's fine. Sends love.'

Daisy relaxed a little and smiled. 'Send mine back. And to the little ones.'

'Not very little now. It's amazing how quickly they grow. It's like one of those speeded-up films.'

'Have you got homes for them?'

He shook his head. 'The interview process takes ages. It's easier to adopt a baby than to buy one of Griselda's puppies.'

'So, how many are you going to keep?'

He laughed properly. 'Actually, I didn't come all this way to talk about Griselda.'

'No?' She felt more relaxed now. He was behaving like the Rory she had got to know, not the London Rory, who scared the hell out of everyone. Even Venetia.

'I've got something to ask you. A proposition.'
'Oh?

'Daisy, my agent says I should consider having a permanent person looking after my PR. He says if I don't it's possible my profile will get smaller. I could drop off the radar. I need someone on the case day and night.' He glanced quickly up at her. 'Will you consider the position? I'm afraid it does mean you'd have to live in Scotland.'

Daisy considered. Then she put her head on one side. 'Your agent said that? Your agent said your profile could get smaller when your latest telly adaptation just got enormous ratings and the TV tie-in of your latest book has been at number one for weeks? I think you'd be better off employing me as a kennel maid. There you might actually need my help.'

He sighed. 'OK, no. My agent didn't say that. But I had to have some excuse to come and see you. I miss you so badly. I had to think of a good reason.'

'It's a pathetic reason. And you don't need to make excuses! You're Rory McAllan, you can do and have exactly what you want!'

'But I want you, Daisy. Can I have you?'

She allowed her heart to beat a few times before she answered. 'I'm very young. You mentioned that several times.'

'I know, but I don't think it's as important as I once did. And I promise I won't bury you in the wilds of Scotland. I won't be such a recluse—'

'Rory.' She put her hand on his to stop him talking. Probably a first, she realised.

'You don't have to change anything for me.'

He lifted her chin and looked into her eyes. This time she had no difficulty in reading love, longing and, reassuringly, lust in his expression. 'I love you, Daisy. I missed you so much. Mari, Hamish, they all said I had been mad to let you go back.'

'It's only because I can cook and am good with dogs.'

He shook his head. 'How quickly can we eat this lunch? And when can I carry you off?'

When the waiter came to take their order they were kissing. And when they left without ordering anything, he just smiled and shook his head.

They were very late getting back to the office. Daisy had been hoping to sneak in, unnoticed. Not that she minded being late, she just didn't want to have to explain why.

They had no chance to sneak anywhere. Venetia appeared the moment they got out of the lift.

'Well, I hope you two are engaged!' said Venetia. 'I've got fizz and a cake!'

'Good about the cake,' said Rory to Venetia. 'We missed lunch . . .'

Cheeseboard

Staying Away at Christmas

'If you could just stop moaning for a minute and keep a look out for the turn,' said Miranda to her eldest daughter, 'I don't want to miss it.' She was creeping down the Devon lanes looking for the holiday home they'd had such fun in that summer. It was only four o'clock in the afternoon but it was already dark. And these winding country roads were bad enough to navigate in the light. 'I know you don't want to be here, you've told me, but could we at least get there before we have the whole argument again?'

Isa, who was sixteen, sighed. 'I just think if we couldn't go to Granny's it would have been better if we'd stayed at home for Christmas. Then at least we'd be able to see our friends.'

'I know, darling, but we're here now. Is Lulu still asleep?'

Isa looked over her shoulder at her sister. 'Yup. Shall I wake her?'

'Let's get there first.' Miranda glanced at Isa, feeling guilty for what could have been the wrong decision. 'We'll make it fun, really we will.'

Isa grunted. 'Well, it wasn't all that great at Dad's last year.'

'You got lovely presents, though,' said Miranda, secretly relieved that the gifts showered on her daughters by their father and his new wife didn't make it a great Christmas.

Isa sighed. 'Yeah.'

'Are we nearly there yet?' came a voice from the back seat. Lulu had obviously woken up.

Isa giggled. 'Silly! And yes we are, if we don't go wrong.'

Miranda relaxed a little. Now Lulu was awake, Isa would be less teenagerish, although at sixteen, she was entitled to be.

'I think it's here.' She slowed to a stop by a narrow turning, barely visible from the road. 'Do we agree? This is the last turn?'

'Yes!' yelled Lulu, filled with ten-year-old confidence. 'There's the white stone in the hedge!'

'Well spotted, Lu,' said Isa, and Miranda turned into the lane.

After what felt like at least a mile of uneven driveway, they pulled up in front of a converted barn, framed by two little bushes with fairy lights on them. The light above the door was on, and there was a wreath on the door.

'Oh wow!' exclaimed Miranda as she struggled with the key. 'Sheila's really made it Christmassy.' As the door opened she said, 'Come on girls, it's lovely and warm inside.'

Together they went into the hall and from there into the huge room, which was a kitchen first, a sitting room in the middle and a dining room at the end. The kitchen was separated by a half wall so you could cook and still chat to people in the sitting room but you didn't have to look at the dirty dishes while you ate. In the summer they'd kept the French doors at the end open and watched the swallows in the evenings. It had been a brilliant holiday.

'It looks amazing!' said Lulu, running into the place that, ever since the summer, had somehow felt like it was theirs. 'I wasn't expecting a Christmas tree!'

Miranda wasn't either, although Sheila, the woman they'd hired the house from, had said she'd do her best to make it Christmassy. There was not only a tree but other decorations as well, and with the several sets of fairy lights that Miranda had packed, they'd soon make the house festive.

It was hard being a single parent at Christmas when everything on television and in every magazine assumed everyone was part of a family with two parents. It was all right – sort of – when they could go home to Miranda's parents because they recreated something similar to the Christmases Miranda and her sister had shared as a child. But that year her parents had been invited to spend Christmas with old friends and when Miranda discovered this, and that her mother was planning to refuse, when really, she yearned to have a Christmas off, Miranda said she was taking the girls away and it would be a great adventure.

The girls had not been enthusiastic but eventually Miranda's best friend had said, 'You know what? You go through a lot of Christmasses in your life – some are better than others. Get over it.'

Now, Isa volunteered to light the wood burner while Miranda and Lulu chose bedrooms and got the cases upstairs. They were still doing this when Isa called urgently up the stairs.

'Mum! There's a car in the drive!'

As the drive was only for their house, Miranda

came downstairs. There would be a knock on the door, someone would be lost and she'd have to try and remember the way back to the main road.

There was no knock. The door opened and a teenage boy, a shock of dark hair that was at once modern and romantic, and made him look like he should be famous, came in.

'Oh!' he said. 'What are you doing here?'

Isa, who was wearing long woollen tights and a very short skirt, hooked one leg round the other in a gesture she'd had from childhood. 'We're, like, staying?'

'What's the problem, Dan?' said a deep male voice from behind.

'It's like, occupied.'

Miranda placed an arm around Isa's shoulders, not so much to protect her daughter from a dangerous stranger but to support her in the presence of a boy when she hadn't had at least three hours' notice.

'Hello!' she said, knowing she was embarrassing her daughter but unable to stand there in silence. 'Can I help?' She looked beyond the beautiful boy to the man, who was tall, dark and clearly tired. He was obviously related to the boy but the beauty had been eroded by time and care.

'We've rented this house for Christmas,' he said, his jaw firmly set. 'And you're in it.'

'We've rented this house too. I mean, you've probably got the wrong house.'

'No!' He glared at her. 'I've got very clear directions. This is definitely the right house.' That he had made a mistake was not a possibility.

'Why don't you come in and we can sort this out?' said Miranda, fairly sure she and her daughters were in no danger from more than irritation.

The man grunted. 'Hang on, I've left my youngest in the car. She's asleep. I'd better check she hasn't woken up.' He went back into the darkness.

'Come in,' said Miranda to the boy, unrepentantly hospitable. 'I'll put the kettle on.'

The boy followed her into the kitchen. 'It looks really Christmassy. I wasn't expecting that.' He scowled. 'Dad bought a fake tree – we probably won't need it.'

'Dad' appeared a few moments later with a girl of about seven.

'Well, come in, do,' said Miranda. 'Then I'll ring Sheila. She'll know where you're booked in. I know she has several houses she rents out.'

She felt confident that all would be well and was pleased that the fire was going and that the house looked so welcoming. It wasn't her house of course, but she had a strong sense of ownership. It was why she'd wanted to come here for Christmas. It was like home, having spent their summer holiday here, but without the depressing absence of her husband, which her real home still held, even after two years.

She smiled and held out her hand. 'I'm Miranda, this is my daughter Isa, and here's Lulu.'

The man frowned. He didn't seem happy to be put in a social situation with strangers when he was expecting to move into his holiday home. 'I'm Anthony Berkley, this is my son Dan. And this is Amy. But we won't take up your time having tea. I think maybe you should be getting your things together. I assure you, this house is ours for the Christmas period.'

Miranda didn't react but carried on making tea. It would keep her going until the moment this man and his beautiful family had gone and she could open the wine. 'I'll ring Sheila—' she said.

'I'll do it,' said Anthony, pulling out his phone and clicking on a number.

As Miranda would have taken a while to find the number, she felt obliged to forgive him for his high-handedness.

He moved out of earshot which Miranda found rather rude. It was a shared problem, after all. She decided to abandon the tea. She found the bottle of wine, which was part of the welcome package, and the corkscrew. Possession was nine-tenths of the law and having a glass of wine in her hand would definitely declare her ownership.

Dan stood still, watching what was going on but not speaking. Isa, who was probably dying inside, Miranda felt, was fiddling with some of the decorations. Although Miranda felt a strong antipathy to Anthony, once everything was sorted out and he and his family were in the right rental property, which would probably be nearby, it might be nice for Isa and Lulu if they arranged to meet up in a couple of days' time. It would be some sort of a social life and it would stop them missing their friends so much.

Anthony stalked back into the kitchen looking furious. 'She's coming over,' he said, 'to sort things out.' He looked enviously at Miranda's wine.

Miranda considered offering him a glass but his referring to Sheila, who worked so hard to make everything nice for her tenants, as 'she' had annoyed her.

'Don't think,' he said, 'the fact that you have a

glass of wine and I haven't will make it so I have to move and not you.'

Miranda took a sip. She might as well take advantage.

Lulu had sloped off to the living end of the room and put the television on and to Miranda's relief Isa went to join her. Amy soon followed and then Dan. A discussion about what to watch went on briefly and then a familiar theme tune was heard followed by general sounds of approval.

Had the situation been remotely normal, Miranda would have said something along the lines of 'It's good they seem to be getting on', but the situation wasn't at all normal and Anthony's prickly attitude wasn't helping.

Shortly afterwards, the back door opened and Sheila appeared, looking harassed, notwithstanding a trail of tinsel in her hair, which didn't seem to have been put there on purpose.

'I'm so sorry! And I would have been here sooner only we've got a family party going on.'

'So sorry to have troubled you,' said Miranda, who felt awful dragging her out here on Christmas Eve.

'Can you sort it out, please?' said Anthony, just

the right side of rude. 'This muddle? How two families seem to have been double-booked into the same property?'

Sheila produced a book and put it on the kitchen table, then ruffled through the pages. 'I'm terribly sorry,' she said to Anthony. 'I thought you'd changed your mind and cancelled.'

'Why did you think that?' he demanded.

'You didn't pay your balance. I asked you for it but you never sent it,' said Sheila.

Anthony peered over her shoulder. 'Oh God, I really thought I had.'

The hot air leaked out of him slowly but inevitably. Possibly sensing this, Sheila took the upper hand. 'I'm afraid if I don't get the balance, the booking isn't confirmed. I sent you at least three emails telling you this.'

'God, what a mess,' he breathed. 'I'm afraid my secretary left and I got a new computer at the same time. A lot of things fell through the cracks.'

'Well,' said Sheila, 'I could offer you a little two-bed but I haven't been in it since October and it hasn't got a wood burner or a fireplace or anything.'

'That doesn't sound very festive,' said Anthony and for the first time smiled somewhat ruefully.

Miranda felt a moment of relief – and triumph – that she had been in the right. And then the spirit of Christmas kicked in and she made a decision. Before she could change her mind she said, 'You could stay here.'

Anthony looked at her, frowning slightly. 'What do you mean?'

'I mean, there are four double bedrooms, you could stay here. We could both have the house for Christmas.'

'We couldn't possibly impose—' Anthony began.

'Otherwise it's the two-bed with no wood burner,' said Miranda.

'That I haven't been in since October,' finished Sheila. 'You only need pay half each this way,' she added, glancing at Miranda, possibly guessing that this was a consideration for her.

Anthony looked at Miranda as if for the first time. He'd done nothing but huff and puff since he'd arrived and now all the huff and puff had gone out of him. 'We should ask the children,' he said.

'Yes,' agreed Sheila, 'but can I suggest you ask them all privately?'

'Good idea,' said Miranda. 'I'll ask Isa first, she's my toughest.'

She went to where sofas were arranged round

191

the wood burner. Isa was sitting cross-legged on the floor, her back against the sofa. It was how she always sat. Dan was on the sofa and looked pretty relaxed. Lulu was on the other sofa, playing a board game with Amy, her long fair hair hanging down over it. Amy was giggling.

'Isa? Can I have a word?' said Miranda. 'It's important.'

Isa frowned but didn't argue and got up. Miranda drew her into the ground floor bedroom she had been looking forward to sleeping in – it had such a sumptuous en-suite bathroom. 'Isa, there's been a mix up. There's nowhere else for that other family to go. They won't find a hotel now and I don't know how far they'd have to drive if they went back. Would you mind if they stayed here?'

'What? And we'd have Christmas with them?'

Miranda nodded. 'I'm not sure how we'll work things out but there's room for us all, in theory.' She hesitated. 'I know you think I'm mad but I really wouldn't feel happy about turning them out into the snow – figurative snow—' she added quickly, seeing her daughter's eager glance towards the window. 'But on the other hand, if it would ruin your Christmas to have them—'

'No, it's cool,' said Isa with a flick of her hair.

'Christmas has been pretty much ruined anyway since you and Dad split up. It'll be different.'

'Can you ask Lulu to come and see me?' said Miranda, shocked that her daughter felt like that about Christmas, but relieved she had accepted the plan so easily.

Lulu came skipping in a moment later, a lock of hair now disguised as a Christmas decoration. 'Yeah?'

'Darling, those people have nowhere else to go. Would you mind very much if they stayed here and we all had Christmas together?'

'No, that would be fine. It would be a bit "no room at the inn" if we threw them out now. And Amy is sweet and Isa fancies Dan.'

'Lulu! How do you know? And don't say that to anyone else. Isa would die.' Miranda couldn't help feeling sorry for Isa, having such a perceptive sister.

'She wouldn't actually die you know, Mum.' Lulu skipped off again.

Miranda went back to the kitchen. Sheila was there with Anthony. She assumed he'd spoken to his two.

'Well?' asked Sheila, 'are your girls happy to share their Christmas?'

193

'With strangers?' added Anthony.

'What do your two feel about it?' said Miranda. She didn't want to say her girls were fine about it if his children had said they'd die rather than share Christmas with them.

'They're fine,' said Anthony, tightly.

'Excellent,' said Sheila. 'Now, have you got enough bedding? Do you need another put-you-up?'

'We'll be fine,' said Miranda, 'you go back to your party.'

'But we might need a put-you-up,' said Anthony. 'I mean—'

'There are four double bedrooms,' Miranda reminded him, 'and a put-you-up in a cupboard.'

'How do you know?' Anthony asked, apparently not pleased about her greater knowledge. 'I mean about the cupboard?'

'We stayed here in the summer.'

Anthony nodded. 'Oh, OK.'

'Are you sure you'll be all right?' said Sheila, addressing them both but looking at Miranda.

'We will. We'll be fine,' said Miranda sounding more confident than she felt.

'I'm only up the hill if you need me,' said Sheila.

'We will be fine,' said Anthony, much more convincingly.

After a little more protest, Sheila left, clearly eager to be off now the crisis had been averted.

'Right, well, we'd better sort out bedrooms,' said Anthony.

Dan wandered into the kitchen. 'We've done it,' he said. 'Miranda will have the downstairs bedroom. Dad'll have the room at the end, I'll have the other double and, and the girls are all going in together.'

Both adults looked at him in surprise. 'I don't think you should have a room on your own,' said Anthony. 'What about – Isa?'

'She and Lulu always share at Christmas,' explained Miranda.

'Yeah, and they asked Amy if she wanted to go in with them. Isa said it was quite a big room.'

'Right,' said Anthony with a frown. He was obviously accustomed to doing the organising and now it had been done behind his back.

'Why don't you go and see where you're sleeping?' Miranda suggested to him. 'I'll unpack our car. I haven't brought the groceries in yet.'

'We're getting hungry,' said Dan.

'Then help Miranda with her stuff,' said Anthony. 'You don't mind if he calls you Miranda?'

'Of course not.'

195

*

Miranda was a little embarrassed by the amount of food she'd brought, given that the shops would be open the day after Boxing Day and when she'd gone shopping, she'd only been shopping for three. But filling the house with food – be it her own home or this temporary one – made her feel more Christmassy. She didn't need to do it when they went to her parents' because her mother was of the same ilk and also bought far too much.

She hoped that Dan, being a boy, and about the same age as Isa, wouldn't realise how much she had over-catered.

Her hope faded the moment she lifted the door to the boot of her car.

'Wow, were you going to have a party?' asked Dan, hefting a large cardboard box.

Briefly, she considered making up a lie about her plans but abandoned them.

'Nope. I just got a lot of stuff.' She hefted a box of her own and followed Dan into the house.

She couldn't criticise his helpfulness. He carried on unloading her car while she stowed things, grateful that the capacious cupboards got it out of sight quite quickly. She could hear giggling from upstairs and it made her smile.

Assuming Dan would go back to doing whatever other young men of his age would be doing in the circumstances, Miranda was surprised that he stayed in the kitchen, picking up bottles and cans at random. Then he opened the fridge and shut it again. 'No turkey,' he said. It wasn't a question.

Miranda shook her head. 'There are only three of us. I didn't want to be eating it till the end of the holiday.'

'No worries, we've got a turkey,' he said.

At that moment, Isa and Lulu came into the kitchen. 'We're hungry,' said Lulu, 'and so is Amy.'

Miranda put the oven on. 'I brought a lasagne. It'll probably be enough. I've got garlic bread and I'll make a salad.'

'You make it yourself?' asked Dan.

'Don't be rude,' said Anthony, appearing from upstairs, presumably having been wrestling with the put-you-up.

'No, it's a fair question,' said Miranda, not at all offended. 'Yes, I did. It's all home-made.'

Dan nodded approvingly. Miranda felt relieved.

'Dan? Would you mind getting our stuff in?' asked Anthony. It was more of a command than a request.

Dan sighed but went.

'I've got wine – and some champagne. Would you like a glass? Or are you happy with the red?' Anthony was making an effort but Miranda could tell he wasn't yet resigned to the situation.

'I'm fine. And there should be enough to have with the lasagne.'

'We won't run out, I have a case of it. Red, I mean. And white, and—'

'Why?' Miranda was suddenly worried that she was about to spend Christmas with an alcoholic.

'I ordered a mixed case but didn't have time to choose my favourites, so I just put the lot in the car.' He raised his eyebrows, possibly reading her anxious thought. 'I wasn't intending to drink it all, and Dan always has a glass at Christmas.'

Miranda, who had the lasagne and the garlic bread in the oven, warming, was starting on a salad. 'So, if you don't mind me asking, why did you come away for Christmas?'

He hesitated before answering. 'We usually go to my sister's but this year she was also inviting her old friend, newly single, and on the lookout for a husband. I'm not in the market for a mother for my children just now.'

Miranda felt herself blush and opened a cupboard door at random, to hide her embarrassment. How awful if he thought she was on the lookout for a husband. And what had happened to his wife? There was no polite way of asking.

'So, what about you?' he said.

Miranda went back to grating carrot. The salad, if it was to feed six instead of three, would have to be substantial. 'Oh, we usually go to my parents' but they wanted to spend Christmas with friends this year.' Without thinking, she went on, 'If we'd just stayed at home it would have felt lonely without – my ex-husband.'

'So he's still alive then?'

'We're divorced. Two years ago. I don't miss him at all but I do miss being a proper family.'

'I do miss my wife but she died a long time ago, when Amy was a baby.' His expression became set, reminding Miranda of how he had been when he had arrived. 'Please don't feel obliged to express your deep compassion – we're fine as a unit, we don't need to "complete it" by adding a stranger.'

'Right,' said Miranda, and looked in the fridge to find the celery she knew she'd packed. She was offended although she knew she shouldn't be. It hadn't occurred to her to make a move on him because he was a widower. She didn't want a new relationship herself – life was tough enough holding it all together for the children without adding a random man who could cause all kinds of trouble.

'I'm sorry,' he said a couple of moments later. 'I've been under a lot of stress lately.'

She looked at him, impressed by his quick, sincere apology that came with an endearingly shy smile. 'It's OK. And don't worry. I'm not looking for a relationship either. I have enough on my plate.'

The smile broadened. 'Now we've got that out of the way, I'd better go and wrap some presents.'

Alone in the kitchen Miranda thought, yes, it was Christmas Eve and you're a man. You will have presents to wrap at the last minute. Her ex-husband had been spectacularly bad at present buying and Isa had always done his wrapping.

Miranda had finished making the salad and taken her glass of wine into the sitting room. She was enjoying the guilty pleasure of watching a celebratory special when Anthony appeared.

'Sorry to disturb you, but have you seen Amy?' It was not a casual enquiry. He looked worried.

'She's probably with my girls. Have you asked them?'

'Of course,' he said shortly and stalked away.

She was off the sofa and after him in seconds. 'There's a big cupboard on the landing. Have you looked in there?'

'Yes,' he snapped. Dan appeared in the hallway. 'You should have kept an eye on her!' said Anthony.

'Excuse me, but you're the dad here, Dad!' said Dan.

'I can't be everywhere!'

'Well nor can I! And it's not fair to blame me because Amy's gone missing. Again!'

'She has a habit of wandering off on her own,' said Anthony. 'She's always very surprised to find that we've been worried sick. I'll ring her friends' parents and see if she's been in touch and said anything.'

He got out his phone and began scrolling through his address book. Dan scowled at his father, obviously just as concerned.

Isa and Lulu appeared at the top of the stairs looking anxious. Miranda hurried upstairs to join them.

'Have you found her?' Isa asked.

'I didn't mean to.' Lulu's voice caught on a sob.

'What's the matter, darling?' said Miranda quietly. 'If you know anything, tell us. No one's going to be cross.'

'I'm sure it's nothing to do with you, Lu,' said Isa, trying to be comforting.

'I shouldn't have told her—'

'Excuse me!' Anthony called up the stairs. 'If we're discussing Amy, could you please involve me?'

Miranda threw him a look and then returned her attention to the girls. He was desperately worried and it made him angry. She wanted to protect her girls from it if she could. 'Have you any idea where Amy might be?' she asked.

Isa shook her head. 'Not really.'

'We were telling Amy about how wonderful it is here. I mentioned the look-out point,' Lulu said, fighting tears. 'Amy got up . . . we thought she'd gone off to find Dan. You don't think she's gone there do you, Mum?'

'OK, we'll go and tell Anthony about this.'

Anthony listened while Isa explained what had happened. It was to his credit, Miranda thought, that he didn't shout. 'OK, can you tell me how to get there?'

'It would make more sense for me to go,' said Miranda. 'I know where it is.'

'Amy is my child! I'm responsible for her!'

Anthony obviously didn't think it was so

necessary to keep his temper when he was talking to Miranda.

'But I know where she might be.'

'Then we'll both go,' said Anthony.

'Shall I come, Dad?' said Dan.

Anthony considered. 'No, you stay here and take any calls from her friends' parents. I've left so many messages—'

'I could do that, if you like,' suggested Isa.

Anthony shook his head. 'No. If she came home, it would be nice if Dan were here.'

The plan agreed on, Miranda hurried into her boots and coat, whilst Lulu and Isa hovered beside her.

'Try not to worry, girls. We'll find her, I'm sure. Now keep the fire going, Isa, we'll need it when Amy comes back. Oh, and make sure the lasagne doesn't burn.'

'I'll take care of that,' said Dan.

After everyone had promised to call the moment there was news, Miranda and Anthony headed off into the night, torches in their hands. Anthony agreed to go in the direction of the village and then if he didn't find her, he was going to drive round the lanes. Miranda was headed for the point.

*

Miranda didn't much like the dark. It wasn't a real phobia but at home she always made a point of putting a light on in her bedroom before she went to bed so she wouldn't be going into a dark room on her own. She had a time switch on lamps in the sitting room too, so no matter how early the evenings were drawing in there would always be a light on when she got home from work. But now she set off up the path as fast as she safely could. She felt sick and her mouth was dry. She didn't know Amy, she'd exchanged very few words with her, but she was a child and was lost – and because her own daughter might be inadvertently to blame for her disappearance, Miranda felt responsible. She must do everything she could to help.

Miranda knew where she was going. The girls had told her about this little ruined building up on the cliffs that had a wonderful view of the village and the harbour beyond. Then they'd taken her there with a picnic. Isa had pretended to be blasé about it but Lulu had loved it. She had taken a rug up there one day and spent hours looking out at the world and reading. If Lulu had told Amy about it and Amy was prone to running off, it might easily be where she had headed.

As she walked, her eyes grew accustomed to the

light level, and it didn't seem nearly so dark. There was a moon somewhere behind the clouds and a few stars pricked through.

Miranda turned off the torch and put it in her pocket. She wanted both hands free in case she stumbled and needed to stop herself falling.

She wished she'd brought a walking stick – there was a collection of them in the utility room along with the torches. Just for a second she allowed herself to think about how she would feel if she had to come back alone. She was sick with worry now but how much worse to be sick with despair.

She reached the brow of the hill at last and had to walk the same distance again to get to the building. She could see its outline now and thought she glimpsed a light in it. Then she realised it was probably just her imagination. She was hoping to see a light, that was all.

When she was on the flat she started to run. She had to know as soon as possible if Amy was in the look-out building. If she wasn't then she, Miranda, should be somewhere else, not wasting her time on random notions.

As she got closer she realised there was indeed a light but it was intermittent and even when it was on it was very faint. She tried to go faster but she wasn't a runner and already sweat was running down her spine. She was hampered by her heavy coat too.

At last she got there. She dug for her torch in her pocket and switched it on. 'Amy?' she called, as she wriggled through the narrow doorway.

Miranda could see the little girl crouching there, her eyes wide and frightened. She was clutching one of those key-ring torches you had to hold on. 'Hello,' she said huskily.

'Are you all right?' asked Miranda.

'Not really,' said Amy after a few seconds and Miranda could tell she'd been crying. 'I came here because it sounded so lovely and then I remembered I didn't know the way back.'

'Well, you did the right thing, staying put,' said Miranda, rummaging in her pocket for a sweet. 'Here,' she said, handing her one.

Amy took it. 'Is everyone very angry with me? I know I shouldn't have done it but sometimes I feel I have to be on my own.'

'You could have been on your own without scaring us all,' said Miranda, trying to sound calm.

'I know, but it's better if I can just go.'

'Not for your dad,' said Miranda.

Amy put her head in her hands and began to cry.

Miranda longed to take her in her arms and hug her, tell her how no one was angry and would just be pleased she was found. But she didn't know Amy and didn't know how Anthony would react. Some parents did want to beat their children about the head with relief when they reappeared after an absence. She wasn't like that herself but it was a common reaction.

'Let's tell him you're found, shall we?' Then she realised, in spite of all their plans and precautions, she'd forgotten to put his number in her phone. She sent Isa a text instead asking her to tell Dan, who could tell his father.

'Shall we go back now?' Amy nodded.

The two of them walked along the path that Miranda had run down just a short time before. How different this journey back was! She just hoped that Anthony had got the news that Amy was safe by now.

'Dad does get angry,' Amy said quietly, a little later.

Miranda chose her words. 'When someone you love very much goes missing you do get angry because you're so worried about them.'

'I hate it when they shout.'

'Who?'

'Dad and Dan. I hate it when there's a row.'

'Was that why you went? Because they were rowing?' She hadn't heard anything herself, but she'd been engrossed in *Celebrity Come Dine With Me Christmas Special*.

'They were going to. I could hear Dan getting rude and Dad hates that.'

Miranda didn't have sons but felt that like daughters with their mothers, there was bound to be challenging behaviour. Which meant rows. 'I think if you came home safely they'd be so thrilled, they wouldn't think of rowing.'

'Dad will shout at me.'

'I won't let him,' said Miranda rashly, wondering what on earth her chances were of preventing a man she didn't know reacting in a way that was normal for him.

'Could you stop him?' Amy sounded doubtful too.

'I might not be able to stop him entirely but I promise you I'll get him to stop really quickly. Once I explain how you feel and it being Christmas, he won't want to shout.'

The little girl shivered and Miranda put her arm round her. 'Let's hurry!'

'If you promise it'll be all right?'

'I promise,' said Miranda but her fingers were crossed in her pocket. She wasn't in a position to promise really but she wanted to get Amy back to her family as soon as possible.

Amy held the torch as they increased their pace. Miranda felt her phone vibrate and saw there was a text from Isa. She paused just long enough to read it. 'Dan's dad knows she's safe. See you soon.'

Suddenly there was a gust of wind, blowing away the clouds and revealing a bright full moon. Stars appeared too and one, fairly low, seemed to settle across the bay, shining over the hills.

'Look, Amy!' said Miranda. 'Look at that star!'

'It's like the Star of Bethlehem!' Amy said in awe. 'It's magic!'

They stopped to look at it, Miranda with her arm round Amy's shoulders and just then, the sound of singing came wafting up the valley. It took a few moments but then Miranda recognised it.

'It's "Once in Royal",' she said.

'Yes! I wish it was "O Little Town of Bethlehem",' said Amy.

'They might sing that in a minute. I think they've just come out of the pub. Let's walk along to their rhythm – it'll get us home quicker.'

The sound grew nearer and they heard rich male

voices singing familiar melodies. Amy took hold of Miranda's hand and although she couldn't be certain, she felt the little girl was happy again, her anxiety swept away by the moonlight, the twinkling stars and the sound of carols. As the party of carollers grew nearer they could see pinpricks of light. They were obviously carrying lanterns. It was, Miranda thought, the perfect way to celebrate Christmas Eve.

They were on the way down the drive, nearly back, when Miranda felt Amy freeze beside her.

'You promise I won't get into trouble?' she said desperately, clinging to Miranda's hand, her voice tense with anxiety.

'Sweetheart,' said Miranda. 'I can't absolutely promise there won't be – say – one or two shouts, but then it will be over. Your father will be thrilled to see you. That I absolutely guarantee.'

Still the little girl wouldn't move.

'Come on, honey, you stand behind me.' Without giving Amy more time to get anxious Miranda dragged her forward and opened the door. Then she thrust her behind her. 'Amy's back!' she called. 'I found her at the look-out point.'

Anthony appeared, mobile in hand. 'She's here!' he said loudly into it and threw it on the stairs.

'Now really,' said Miranda, who could feel Amy pulling away behind her, 'you mustn't shout at her!' She was looking intently at Anthony and for a moment caught a glimpse of the desperate father, worried sick about his daughter, drawing breath to relieve his tension by letting her know, loudly, exactly how worried he'd been. She held his gaze, willing him to take a few seconds before speaking.

'Amy, sweetheart, we were worried,' he said calmly, and Amy threw herself into his arms.

Miranda had gone into the kitchen to give father and daughter time alone when she suddenly remembered the lasagne and garlic bread she'd put into the oven who knew how long before. It was unlikely Dan had remembered to do anything about it. She pulled open the oven door thinking that burnt offerings were the last thing people needed when she saw that the lasagne was golden brown and perfect. She pulled out the garlic bread and unwrapped the end. That wasn't burnt either.

Dan, who had been greeting his sister in the hall, came in. 'I kept an eye on it for you. It should be OK.'

'Bless you! It would have been so awful if it

had all been burnt.' Anthony came in just then. 'Dan has saved the day,' she said. 'Or rather the dinner.'

Anthony put his hand on his son's shoulder and gave it a squeeze. Whatever their differences had been they were over for the time being.

Miranda waited for a couple of moments. 'Where's Amy?'

'She's upstairs with the girls. Isa is giving her a bath.' Anthony sighed. 'I'll have to have a talk with her later. She's done this before and it's so terrifying. I'll never be able to thank you enough for finding her.'

'It was just lucky I had an idea where she might have gone. Really, it was nothing.'

'Rarely, if ever, has that word been used so inappropriately,' he said and then smiled.

Miranda felt as if the sun had come out just for her. Her stomach flipped over and it was only with a huge effort of will was she able to remind herself that all this warmth was gratitude for finding his daughter. It wasn't personal.

'I think we should eat as soon as the girls appear,' she said, hoping she didn't sound as flustered as she felt.

'Give the girls a shout,' said Anthony as Dan left

the room. 'You can relax now and have another drink. You deserve it. I see you have lemons – I'll make you one of my famous hot toddies.'

Shortly afterwards he put a glass into her hand. 'Now, go and sit down and rest. We'll do dinner from here.'

She was nursing the drink which was so fantastically strong and lemony she could practically feel it killing germs as it went down her throat, when Isa appeared.

'Well done, Mum, for finding Amy.'

'Thank you, darling, but it was Lulu who gave me the tip. Is Amy OK now?'

'Yeah, she'll be fine. She and Lulu are playing happily – you know, little girls' stuff.' She smiled at her mother, then said, 'Shall I set the table?'

This was almost unheard of. Setting the table was Isa's least favourite job and she usually had to be blackmailed or bribed into doing it. 'That would be lovely. I've got some Christmas napkins in one of the bags.'

'Will there be enough for tomorrow if we use them now?' Then Isa raised her eyes to heaven. 'Don't tell me – you've got two sorts.'

Miranda laughed. 'Really, my little napkin obsession is quite harmless.'

Her daughter laughed too. 'I suppose it is.'

Ten minutes later they were all seated round the large, dining-room table. 'Well, this is very nice,' said Anthony, sounding, to Miranda's annoyance, slightly surprised.

Amy was in her dressing gown and everyone was eating the lasagne with enthusiasm, which gave Miranda a pleasant glow of achievement.

'What would you have done if we hadn't been here?' asked Dan.

'Sorry?' Miranda didn't think he was being rude but couldn't be sure. She had very little experience of boys. He'd been so helpful up till now.

'I mean, there'd have been a lot left over if we hadn't been here to eat it,' he said.

'There'd have been a lot left over full stop,' said Isa. 'Mum always cooks too much. She can't help it.'

'Thank you, Isa,' Miranda said good-humouredly.

'I'm glad you made too much,' said Amy.

'So am I,' said Anthony.

'Me too,' said Dan, with a surprisingly charming smile.

'I think we should discuss our Christmas Day

routines,' said Miranda, wanting to move on from the lasagne.

'Stockings, walk, then presents, then lunch,' said Lulu.

'We don't have stockings,' said Dan.

There was a gasp of shock from Isa and Lulu but Miranda was relieved they didn't actually say anything.

'Too much for Dad,' said Amy. 'He says he can't be doing with such a commercialised myth.'

Anthony nodded. 'I'm afraid that's true.'

It had sounded like a direct quote. Miranda's girls looked at each other with a mixture of absolute horror and compassion.

'OK, so what do you do?' asked Miranda.

'Dad makes breakfast and then we go to my aunt's,' said Dan. 'We open our presents and then have lunch.'

'Before that there's a row about the turkey,' said Amy, with a shudder.

'Aunt Flo puts it in the Aga at midnight on Christmas Eve – before sometimes I reckon – and so by lunchtime it's turned to sawdust,' Dan explained, disapproval evident in every syllable.

'Right,' said Miranda.

'Dad cooks a great breakfast though,' conceded Dan.

'I know Flo isn't a great cook but it's very kind of her to have us every year,' said Anthony.

Dan sighed. This was obviously not a new argument.

'What do you do after lunch?' asked Miranda.

'Wash up. It takes for ever,' said Dan.

'Then we watch telly while the adults sleep,' said Amy.

'Sounds, like, really good,' said Isa, catching Dan's eye. He flicked his eyebrow in reply.

'We'll have to think up something that suits us all,' said Miranda, shocked about the stockings herself. Her girls seemed to like them the best of all the Christmas rituals.

'Yeah,' said Dan with surprising firmness.

'Have we all finished?' said Anthony a few moments later. 'Get the plates together, guys.'

'Would anyone like pudding?' said Miranda, having handed her plate to Amy.

'I've got ice cream. I expect I could make some sort of sauce . . .'

'I have some very nice cheese,' said Anthony.

'Oh, much better,' said Miranda. 'Will you lot be OK with cheese?'

'I'll have ice cream but I can get it myself,' said Lulu. 'Amy, would you like some? Shall we go and get it? We can put drinking chocolate on it.'

'It's nice for Amy to have some female company,' said Anthony when he'd brought in the cheese and biscuits and the younger girls were still making ice-cream concoctions in the kitchen.

'She does go to an all girls' school,' said Dan.

'I meant out of school,' said Anthony. 'I've just remembered! There's a bottle of port in that case of wine. I'll get it.'

Aunt Flo may not have been much of a cook but her washing-up training must have been first class. The kitchen was clear in no time and Miranda was able to get her presents in from the car and retire to her bedroom. It was late, but she had a lot to do before she could go to bed. She'd have done it earlier in the evening if she hadn't had to help look for Amy.

There was the briefest knock on her door and her daughters came in. 'We're going to do stockings for them,' said Isa.

'Though we can't do one for Anthony,' said Lulu. 'Too hard.'

'And he doesn't believe in them anyway,' said

Isa. 'But Amy must have one. Poor little thing. She must have been terrified on her own, before you found her.'

'And we can't leave Dan out,' said Lulu.

Having had a think, Miranda said, 'OK. I've wrapped up what I've got for your stockings but I can't remember what the things are. Except they will all be girly.'

'We'll just have to unwrap everything to see what we've got. We'll do Dan first as he's the hard one. Amy is easy,' said Isa, taking control.

Miranda watched as her girls opened the packages, tossing anything remotely male into a pile. They seemed to be enjoying this as much – or possibly more – as having the things for themselves.

'It would be better if we didn't try and fill the usual stockings,' said Miranda. 'I've got a couple of pairs of new socks. They won't take so much filling.'

'Good plan, Mum,' said Lulu.

'Can you get them?' said Isa. 'When we've done Dan's we can easily do the others.'

Miranda found herself sacrificing her new toothbrush (after she'd found her old one was still in her washbag) and Isa came up with a face flannel. A lot of what Miranda put in her children's stockings was edible and useful but Isa declared she would not put facial scrub into Dan's stocking.

'It's unisex,' said Lulu. 'Boys get spots too.'

'Of course they do!' said Isa angrily. 'But we don't want to draw attention to it! They've got, like, feelings!'

'I know!' said Miranda after they'd sat in silence for a few minutes. 'There was a little bottle of truffle oil I meant to give to Grandpa but forgot. I'm fairly sure it's still in with the groceries I haven't unpacked yet.'

'Perfecto!' said Isa. 'Go and get it.'

'Please!' said Lulu.

Isa gave Miranda the lopsided smile that so often got her out of trouble.

Miranda went into the kitchen. The Berkleys were all watching television and didn't notice her rummaging in her box. She found the little bottle and went back to her bedroom.

'OK,' said Isa, after the girls had wrapped and filled Dan's stocking. 'Do you mind going out for a bit, Mum? We've got things to do.'

'But this is my bedroom!'

'I know, but currently it's Christmas Central,' said Lulu. 'Out!'

Obediently, she left the room.

*

Much later, Miranda hung four fat, red socks on the mantelpiece and admired the effect. The room was all so Christmassy, partly thanks to Sheila's tree and decorations, but also because someone had lit a Christmas candle and the smell lingered. The fairy lights had been left on and it almost did look like a magazine Christmas. She smiled. It was all going to be very different but it was going to be fun. Having turned off the fairy lights, she went back to bed.

Miranda was awoken the next day by Lulu and the smell of cooking. She looked at her watch. It was half-past nine. It was unheard of for her to sleep this late, but she had been really tired.

Lulu was holding a cup of tea. 'Get up, Mum! There's breakfast and we're all waiting for you.'

Miranda sat up and took the tea. She could smell cooking but couldn't identify it. 'So what are we having?'

'Scrambled eggs and smoked salmon. I don't think I like smoked salmon do I?'

'You might like it now.'

'I'll try it. Now hurry up.'

'Should I get dressed? Is everyone dressed?'

Lulu thought about it. 'Yes, but you don't have to be. You'll be ages and we can't start anything until you get there. Just wear your dressing gown.'

Miranda's dressing gown was new, a Christmas present from her mother, she had chosen it herself. 'Oh, OK.'

She took the time to fluff up her hair and put on enough make-up to feel human, and went into the kitchen. She couldn't remember a Christmas that had started with a cup of tea and breakfast cooked by someone else. Her ex could hardly make toast.

Anthony was by the cooker. 'Happy Christmas,' he said, apron on and smiling. A million miles away from the man she'd first encountered yesterday afternoon.

'Happy Christmas back,' she said, aware that she was happy. It was all so different from the usual disappointments that Christmas sometimes brought with it. She didn't need a husband today.

'I have a very limited repertoire,' said Anthony, indicating the saucepan he was stirring eggs in, 'but what I can do, I do well.'

Dan was buttering toast. The table had been set and someone had lit the wood burner. Miranda checked to see the stockings wouldn't be scorched

221

when she noticed there were now five. A silver spangled sock sat fatly beside its scarlet companions. She smiled.

'More tea or coffee?' asked Dan.

'Tea. Milk, no sugar. I don't much like coffee.'

'Coming up.'

'He works in a restaurant sometimes,' explained Amy, bringing in a plate full of toast. 'I couldn't find a toast rack.'

'That's OK.' Miranda could have told her where to find the toast rack but something about Amy suggested she was expecting criticism and she didn't want to imply that toast on a plate wasn't fine.

Dan then swooped in with three plates of scrambled eggs, one of them balanced on his arm. Anthony came in with two more and Lulu brought the last one. 'This is mine,' she explained, 'with no smoked salmon.'

Miranda realised that Anthony must have cooked hers separately and appreciated the gesture.

'OK everybody, eat it before it gets cold,' he said. Having just sat down he got up again. 'Talking of cold, I have some fizz. Glass of fizz, Miranda?'

'Oh yes please,' she said. This was getting better and better.

'With or without orange juice?'

'Without.'

'Kids, you have to have it with. Lulu? Do you like Buck's Fizz?'

'Never had it,' said Lulu, obviously impressed.

'But you like orange juice?'

'Oh yes,' she said enthusiastically.

Anthony was very skilful with the champagne and orange juice, Miranda realised. He adjusted the amount of each to suit each person. Amy, the youngest, had orange juice with just a splash of fizz, enough to be festive but not enough to make her drunk. Isa, she decided, had probably had a touch too much fizz when she clapped her hands. 'Stockings!'

'We don't do stockings,' said Anthony.

'We do,' said Isa, 'but I'm afraid you haven't got one.'

'They are only for the children,' Miranda hurriedly explained, and then found herself presented with the sparkly sock. 'Oh.'

'This year we did one for you,' explained Lulu. 'And for Amy and Dan.'

'Cool,' said Dan, looking at his, slightly perplexed.

'Can we open them now?' asked Amy.

''Course,' said Lulu.

'We should all open them together,' said Isa. 'Otherwise it's embarrassing.'

There was a short silence broken by the sound of rustling and paper ripping.

'Thank you so much for this, girls,' said Miranda, undoing a little packet. It had a box of false eyelashes. 'Oh goodness. I have no idea how to put them on.'

'Wait until after brekkie, Mum, I'll show you,' said Isa, undoing some heart-shaped Post-it notes.

'These are lovely!' said Amy, holding up a pair of earrings Miranda had bought for Lulu.

'I have a toothbrush and some soap,' said Dan, although he didn't seem to mind.

'Don't forget to eat,' said Anthony.

'We usually open stockings in Mum's bed,' said Lulu.

'It might have been a bit much, us all piling in,' said Dan. 'We haven't known each other twenty-four hours, yet.'

Maybe it was the champagne, or the unexpectedness about everything, but breakfast was extremely jolly. When she'd initiated clearing up afterwards, Miranda said, 'Presents?'

'Actually,' said Dan, 'if you don't mind, I'd really like to crack on with lunch?'

This was a bit a shock. 'Aren't I doing lunch?' said Miranda.

Dan shook his head. 'Na-uh. You didn't even buy a turkey. We've brought one from home that's been in brine. I've had enough sawdust turkeys.'

'Dan is very foodie,' said Amy, apologetically.

'I even brought my own knives.' Seeing Miranda's bemusement he went on, 'I read that in Elizabeth David – always take your own knife on holiday.' He grinned.

Miranda stared at him for a few seconds thinking he was very strange but rather wonderful. 'Oh, no, that's fine!' she said. 'I don't mind not cooking it, I'm just falling into my default position. But I'm very happy to be galley slave and do the potatoes and things.'

She looked at Anthony for guidance.

He shook his head. 'I think the kids want to do it.'

'It is quite boring hanging round waiting for dinner,' said Isa.

'Oh,' said Miranda, not sure if she was offended or not. 'But you've got your presents to play with?'

'Mum!' said Isa, as if her mother was just the stupidest person on earth and shouldn't even attempt to make a joke.

'I'm going to be sous chef,' said Amy.

'I'll be in charge of sticking plasters,' said Lulu.

'And what shall I do?' asked Miranda.

'We'll go for a walk, in the direction of a pub, and leave this lot to it,' said Anthony. 'It's OK, Dan's a very good cook and a tyrant in the kitchen. And Amy has promised faithfully not to leave home without telling us again. We'll come back in a couple of hours.'

While Miranda was getting dressed, including finding her thick socks and scarf, she lured Isa into her bedroom. 'Are you sure you're OK with this? Cooking your own Christmas dinner?'

'Mum! I'm not a child. I can help Dan cook.'

Miranda opened her mouth and then closed it. It wouldn't do to ask Isa if she fancied Dan. She was fairly sure she did or she wouldn't be so obliging and helpful. 'OK, just checking.'

It took Miranda some emotional effort to leave a house full of children cooking Christmas lunch. She couldn't decide if it was a wrench or a liberation. It kept her silent for the first part of the walk, which, as it was uphill, was probably a good thing. Although it was lovely to be outside. It was frosty and cold but the sun was shining, giving the day a proper Christmas sparkle.

'Which way?' asked Anthony. 'You know the area.'

'Over the fields and down to the shoreline. It means another walk uphill home but if we're going to eat a huge meal it's probably a good thing.'

'I hope you don't mind Dan taking over. He's really interested in food and cooking and my sister is very territorial about her kitchen. Men are only allowed in to wash up.'

Miranda didn't answer immediately. 'I don't think I mind at all. After all, even if it's a disaster – and I'm sure it won't be – it's not like in the olden days when it was one of the few good meals to be had.'

'It won't be a disaster – he's a very good cook – but you're right. My sister thinks the sky will fall in if the gravy isn't perfect.'

Miranda nodded. 'Actually I'm a bit fixated on gravy myself. It took me so long to learn how to make it, now I have, I get grumpy if I don't think it's perfect.' She paused. 'But only if I've made it. I'm very tolerant of other people's cooking.'

'I think something very bad would happen to my sister if Dan was allowed to cook the Christmas meal,' said Anthony. He paused. 'Miranda, I haven't thanked you properly for finding Amy. I was beside myself. As you've gathered she's run away before. I never know if I should be furious or just desperately relieved when I find her.'

'So which are you?'

'Both! The first time I'd sent her off to school with some other children and their mum and she just came home and hid in the garage. The cleaning lady found her. She did it again a bit later and last time we had a very long talk about how worrying it was and I thought I'd convinced her not to do it any more.'

'She said it was because she hates rows. You and Dan—'

There was a short silence. 'Ah. It's tough to be a parent of a teenager without rows.'

Miranda sighed. 'Tell me about it!'

'I do try and accommodate Dan as much as I can – which was another reason why I didn't want to go to my sister's this year. It wasn't fair on him. But he can be really stubborn sometimes.'

As Miranda remembered the main reason he hadn't gone to his sister's was because his sister had laid on an eligible female, she found herself laughing. 'It was a bit "out of the frying pan" though, wasn't it?'

'What do you mean?'

'I mean, you didn't go because your sister's friend was also invited and so you arranged to go away. And then you were forced to share a house with exactly the sort of person you'd travelled miles to avoid. Not that I'm all that eligible, too old and with baggage, but you must see the irony.'

Anthony chuckled, a little reluctantly. 'I'm not against meeting people in the ordinary way – by accident almost – but I hate being set up. Do you get set up by your friends who assume you must want another partner?'

Still giggling Miranda said, 'No chance. There are very few single men about you know. It's a quirk of nature, when men get divorced they find women ten years younger than themselves. A woman my age would only be able to aspire to a man in his late fifties or sixties. Nothing wrong with them, I'm sure, but frankly I'd rather not bother.'

'Is that true?' This seemed a revelation to Anthony.

'Yup. My ex-husband's wife is ten years younger than me.'

'And how old is she?'

'Anthony! That is the same as asking me how old I am, which is very rude.'

'I'd have put you at thirty-seven.'

This gave Miranda a jolt. Was he flattering her? If so, why? It surely couldn't be because he genuinely thought she looked eight years younger than her true age. 'I'm forty-five,' she said. 'There, you tricked me into telling you.'

'I'm fifty,' said Anthony.

'And your sister's friend? Thirty-six?'

He nodded. 'Probably. But not my type at all.'

'Do you have a type?' she asked.

'I don't know. It's hard to say. You're either attracted to someone or you're not.'

Miranda laughed again. 'I think I feel sorry for your sister. Trying to find you a nice woman, mother for your children, and you refuse to co-operate.' She allowed him a second to take this in and then said, 'If we follow this path down here, we can walk along the shore and end up at the pub. It might not be open, of course.'

He took her arm and laughed. 'But it might.'

It was and it was heaving with people. Decorated with paper chains and paper balls, with a huge Christmas tree in one corner, there were fairy lights along every beam. The noise of people talking and laughing almost drowned out Noddy Holder and his pals. There was a tempting smell of wine and spices. Miranda was very glad they'd come.

Anthony fought his way to the bar and came back with two drinks to where she was standing, rammed between two families who had a year's catching up to do. 'I forgot to ask you what you wanted. I got you a mulled wine. It smelt so delicious.'

'Thank you. It's perfect.' She took the glass.

'Cheers and Happy Christmas!' he said. They clinked glasses.

Two drinks later they thought they ought to be getting back. The tide was further out and the wading birds made the most of the newly revealed food source. They wandered slowly along, having decided lunch wouldn't be ready for some time and not wanting to put stress on the cooks by too early a reappearance.

Miranda slipped on some mud and Anthony caught her. When she was steady on her feet again they set off, with his arm still firmly round her.

Maybe I shouldn't have had that second drink, Miranda thought, as they wandered along, but we seem to have come out of the pub more of a couple than when we went in.

'Do you know, by coming to Devon I've missed

231

three Christmas parties,' she said happily. 'Three opportunities to feel patronised by married couples.' She paused. 'I've got one I can't avoid though.'

'Oh? New Year's Eve?'

'I don't mind the friends we go to for New Year at all. I mean, she's my best friend and it's always lovely. No, it's the work do I'm dreading.'

'After Christmas? Unusual!'

'I know! But there wasn't a date suitable before and it's a dinner dance. Can you imagine anything worse? But it's terribly frowned on if you don't go.'

'And you have to bring a plus one?'

'That's it. It's always terribly awkward, everyone being in couples.'

'I'll go with you, if you like.'

Miranda stopped abruptly. 'Don't be silly, you don't want to do that. Besides, I live in Bath. You probably live in North Yorkshire or somewhere equally miles away.'

He shook his head. 'Bristol. It's why we chose Devon – it's not too far.'

'That's why we chose it too!'

'So I'll come to your works do with you.'

'No, Anthony! You'd hate it!'

'We can hate it together.'

'It's too much.'

'Miranda, you seem to have forgotten that you found my daughter. A slightly boring evening – which might well have its compensations – is the least I can suffer if it would make it easier for you.'

Miranda thought of the stir she would create, turning up with a very presentable man. None of the women would pity her for being single and the men wouldn't hit on her because they thought she was desperate. 'That would be really kind. It would be lovely of you.'

'Then you and I shall both go to the ball!'

By the time they got back to the house they were both rosy cheeked and out of breath. 'That last bit was a bit of a killer but at least we can eat every-thing and not feel guilty.'

Anthony looked down at her and nodded. 'There was just one thing wrong with that otherwise excel-lent pub.'

'Oh, what? I thought it was lovely.'

'No mistletoe.'

'Oh there was! A great big bunch of it. Didn't you see?'

'There was none where we were standing. Never mind, if there's one thing I've learned this Christmas, is how to improvise.' Then he picked a spring of rosemary from the bush growing by the back door, held it over her head, and kissed her on the mouth. It was firm and for a moment she interpreted it as a declaration of intent. Her stomach did the turning over thing it had done before and for a moment she wished it didn't have to end so quickly.

'That's good improvisation,' said Miranda, when she'd got over the shock.

'I'm not always a stuck-up old so-and-so who makes mistakes and blames other people,' he said. 'I need you to know that.'

'Oh, I'd stopped thinking you were that ages ago,' said Miranda, slightly pink. 'So it was a wasted kiss.'

'I don't think so,' he said. Then he took her into his arms and kissed her again.

She'd hardly got her breath back before he'd opened the door and ushered her into the house.

'Hi Mum,' said Lulu excitedly. 'We need you to make the gravy! We said you did the best gravy ever.'

Miranda, who didn't want to offend Dan for all sorts of reasons, hesitated. She was still a little flustered from Anthony's kisses. 'I'm sure Dan's got it covered.'

Dan actually looked a bit harassed. He was scraping at the bottom of the turkey roasting pan, presumably trying to get some colour into a sauce that was the unappealing pink of uncooked sausages. 'I give up!' he said, throwing the wooden spoon into the pan.

'Why don't you check the table's set?' said Miranda to the others, not wanting Dan's difficulties to be too public. 'Now,' she said to him when they were alone, 'would you like me to sort it?'

'Yeah. I've never managed proper gravy. If it was beef, I'd just do a jus, but turkey juices aren't the same.'

'I'll just fetch something from my room,' said Miranda, and she hurried off, glad her room was on the ground floor. She came back moments later.

'What's that?' asked Dan, sounding horrified.

'Mother's Little Helpers. Watch and learn.'

'So what are they?'

'Gravy granules and soy sauce,' said Miranda, not sure if she was proud or ashamed.

Five minutes later there was a saucepan full of gravy that Dan pronounced, 'OK.'

Miranda nodded, pleased with his praise. 'Have you got the stuffing sorted?'

He nodded. 'Loads of fresh herbs in the garden. It was easy.'

'Are we good to go?'

He nodded. 'Yup!'

'I think that was the best Christmas meal I have ever eaten,' Miranda said, half an hour later. 'Certainly the best turkey. It was so moist!'

Dan accepted this praise with a nod.

'It was really good, Dan,' said Anthony.

'I think this whole Christmas has been great,' said Isa.

'Yes,' agreed Lulu, 'and we haven't even opened our presents yet.'

'I'd like us to have Christmas like this every year,' said Amy with a sigh.

'What? You'd like us to come to Devon for Christmas every year?' asked her father, frowning slightly.

'No! I don't care where we are,' Amy explained. 'I just want to have it with Lulu and Isa and—' She looked up shyly. 'Miranda.'

Anthony cast an anxious glance at his family. 'Sweetheart, we could do stockings, if you like. I'm sure I'd manage.'

'Oh Dad!' Amy became distressed. 'You don't

236

understand! I just want us all to be together.'

'Like a family?' suggested Lulu, taking Amy's hand.

'Yes!'

'Well, unless you guys live in the north of Scotland,' said Isa, 'I'm sure we could arrange something.'

'Bristol,' said Dan.

'Bath,' said Isa.

Miranda caught them exchange glances.

'Well, I'm with Amy,' said Miranda. 'I think I'd like it a lot if we could spend Christmas together again, too. And not just because I didn't have to cook and Dan is so good at it.' And she meant it. It was the least stressful Christmas she'd spent as an adult.

'But does it just have to be at Christmas?' asked Anthony. 'Maybe we could meet up at other times?'

'Sunday lunch,' said Isa. 'Mum does a great roast.'

'Which you will sample tomorrow, probably,' said Miranda, 'unless you want to go on eating turkey. We were going to have roast beef and Yorkshire pudding.'

'Cool,' said Dan. 'I make great Yorkshires. You could come to ours, too.'

*

It had been a very different Christmas. As they hadn't cooked, Miranda and Anthony cleared up together, chatting randomly, their inhibitions weakened by Anthony's very good wine – and perhaps by their shared kisses. She couldn't help smiling to herself at the memory.

And afterwards, instead of watching television they had got out the many different games the house provided and, as Dan insisted, played them all. Eventually, at about six o'clock, they felt able to face the mince pies that Dan had made (rough puff pastry, just perfect) and they opened their presents. But as they'd agreed only to open presents from people who were there, that didn't take long.

Then Anthony produced the port and a bottle of Madeira and they went back to Monopoly.

Boxing Day had been largely similar – walks, games, food and jollity.

Miranda was thrilled to see Isa having a nice time with Dan. She couldn't quite work out if they were just friends or if Dan fancied Isa – there seemed to be a fair amount of teasing. But whatever it was, Isa was laughing a lot. And Lulu seemed to get on really well with Amy, who, in spite of being younger, was mature for her age and treated Lulu like a loved older sister.

'OK, Isa. Remind me if it's left or right at the top?' Miranda said, as they set off for home, leaving the final look-round and rubbish disposal to Anthony, at his insistence. 'I know both ways will get us to the main road eventually, but which one is best?'

'Honestly, Mum! What are you like? It's right!'

As she had suspected, the helpful, supportive Isa had been left at the house. The old, combative, challenging Isa had returned. She couldn't help smiling.

A little later, Lulu said, 'Dan says his dad definitely fancies you.'

Miranda was a bit surprised. 'What on earth makes him think that?' It wasn't that they hadn't got on – they had, and he had kissed her – twice – but that was because she was there and it was Christmas, and he'd had a couple of drinks. Miranda knew better than to make anything of it.

'Because he wants to meet up and actually got your contact details,' said Isa.

'That's only because he very kindly offered to come to my works do with me. And our families got on,' said Miranda. 'It won't be anything to do with me personally.'

'No,' Lulu went on. 'Amy says there are loads of women who drool over her and Dan just to impress him and their dad never does anything about it. She said there are always women offering to cook meals and he won't have anything to do with them.'

'Dan said he's interested, and he should know his dad,' put in Isa.

'Oh,' said Miranda.

'And we're going to theirs for Sunday lunch next week,' said Isa. 'That's quite soon. If you're just saying, "Oh yes, we'll do lunch" you don't make a definite date, do you?'

'I really can't remember!' said Miranda, beginning to laugh.

'Mum! You're blushing!' said Isa.

'I expect I'm just having my first hot flush,' said Miranda, trying not to show her excitement. But she was feeling the glow on the inside as well. Christmas had really worked out perfectly. And who knew what the New Year might bring?

Dessert

A Christmas Feast

Imogen put down the bubble wrap she'd just taken from round a mirror and listened. It was the day before Christmas Eve and she was unpacking the few bits and pieces she'd brought with her in her brother's van to her newly rented cottage. Yes, it was definitely carol singers. She realised that any normal person would ignore them but she was at the door almost before they'd knocked. She couldn't help herself; she was a music teacher and they needed help.

Before her was a trio of mothers with fairly young children. The mothers were probably a little older than she was; early thirties rather than late twenties. They were holding lanterns and song sheets, with brightly coloured scarves and hats keeping them warm. They could have been put straight onto a Christmas card, thought Imogen, if there had been snow and their singing hadn't been so dreadful. 'You're not very good are you!' she said, but smiling broadly, so as not to seem bad tempered. She didn't think she'd look intimidating in her scruffy pony tail, faded jeans and hut slippers but she didn't want to take the chance.

There was laughter of the kind caused by nerves, and a bit of shuffling of feet.

'I'm sorry!' said one of the mothers, sounding tired but relieved to see a friendly face, and looking fairly 'yummy' in her sheepskin hat and hairy boots. 'All our best singers are away for Christmas this year, so it's just us.'

'So, if none of you can sing in tune – or hardly know the tune,' said Imogen, 'why are you carol singing?'

'Tradition,' said another yummy mummy. She wore a trapper hat with flaps that came down over her ears and a scarlet scarf. 'The village always sing carols to Miss Wentworth. She's your nearest neighbour.'

'Why?' asked Imogen. It seemed a charming thing to do.

'She taught music here for centuries and now can't get to church any more to hear them. Some kind person—' she sounded as if she wanted to say 'idiotic' — 'thought up the idea of bringing the music to her. It's been going on for years.'

'Then why are you singing to me?'

'Practice,' said the least glamorous mother, in a fleece and beany hat. She was clutching a toddler to her. The toddler was wearing very similar clothes and looked heavy.

'Well, I do think it's lovely that you go and sing carols to an old lady.' Although this was true, Imogen suspected there was more to it.

The women looked at each other. 'She's not a sweet old lady we bring seasonal cheer to,' said one. 'She's a witch and we're all scared of her. But we have to go. Village tradition.'

This was interesting. 'I think you'd better come in,' said Imogen, holding her door open wide. 'It's freezing outside and you need help. There's plenty of room. I haven't got much furniture.'

The little group made their way into Imogen's new home, moved into only hours before. Outside the air sparkled with frost and while no one expected snow, it was still very Christmassy and pretty. Imogen was grateful the heating system in her new home seemed very efficient.

'I thought a family lived here,' commented the woman in the sheepskin hat, looking around. 'The

Smiths. I knew they were moving, but not just before Christmas, surely?'

'They actually moved about a month ago,' said Imogen.

'Oh,' said the woman, looking guilty. 'I thought I hadn't seen the mother at school but you don't see everyone every day.'

'It's nice, isn't it?' said the one in the trapper hat, also looking about her. 'Lots of period features, it could be really sweet. And a really pretty fireplace that looks like it functions.'

'I must say, I was thrilled when I saw it,' said Imogen. 'When you're renting, you're not too fussy, but this is perfect, really. I'll light a fire later, when I'm a bit straighter. They promised me it did work.' She'd made sure there were a few logs and some kindling in among the bits and pieces she'd brought with her.

'So how do you think you can help us?' asked the woman in the fleece, who had put down her toddler and pulled off her hat.

'With this,' said Imogen. She went over to her flute case and opened it. She took out her flute and, after a little tweaking and adjustment of the head, put it to her lips. A couple of test blows and she was ready. 'Now, what were you singing?

"Ding Dong Merrily"? I think I know that one by heart.'

Seconds later the room was filled with the golden, tuneful sound of the familiar carol. Even the children who'd begun to chatter stopped to hear it.

'That was amazing,' said the mother in the sheepskin hat. 'I'm Fenella, by the way. Could you play it again a few times so we really get the tune?'

'I'll do better than that,' said Imogen. 'I'll rehearse you for a bit and then I'll come with you to Miss Wentworth's. I ought to meet my neighbour anyway. I'm Imogen. And I'm a music teacher.'

'This is like a game. I'm Samantha, and I'm a full-time mum to these two, Teddy and Annabelle,' said the one in the trapper hat.

The woman in the fleece ensemble said, 'I'm Susie, and this is Rodney. I know, I know! It's a family name. We call him Rodders.'

'All right,' said Imogen. 'I'll just find some biscuits for the kids, if you don't mind, so we can do a bit of work.' She retreated into the kitchen and came back with some chocolate-covered reindeer. 'Are they OK with chocolate?'

'It's Christmas,' said Fenella. 'Annabel Karmel has gone out of the window.'

While the children unwrapped the reindeer intended for Imogen's nieces and nephews, she got businesslike with the mums. 'Sorry to be bossy,' she said, 'but presumably we haven't got much time. Which carols do you know best?'

Fortunately, Imogen's first job had meant she quite often had to rehearse groups of children in corridors and other random places and the women, being mothers of small children, were equally adaptable. After half an hour Imogen put down her flute. 'Actually, you've all got really nice voices, you just need a few lessons. You could be good.'

'Oh! Thank you. I never sing at home because my husband complains,' said Fenella. 'But you're really giving us confidence.'

'If you think we're OK now, shall we go and sing to Miss W?' said Susie. 'I need to get back. My To-Do list is so long I'm thinking of papering the downstairs loo with it.'

'Oh yes,' said Samantha. 'I just can't serve an un-iced Christmas cake to Martin's family again. They already think I'm useless because I won't make my own Christmas puddings. And I expect Imogen's got things to do.'

Imogen nodded. 'Let's get going. Then you can all go home and I can open a bottle of wine.'

'What are you doing for Christmas?' asked Fenella. 'Got family coming? Going to family?'

'Going to family, but not until after Christmas. And please don't be sorry for me. The thought of a few days to move in, spend time on my own without children – although I do adore them – is quite blissful.'

Fenella looked dubious. 'Are you sure?'

'Really, really sure. I have turned down more offers to come for Christmas than you three combined have cooked turkeys, I swear. Now shall we go?'

'Better get the chocolate off these guys first,' said Samantha. 'Miss W is bound to comment otherwise.'

'So she isn't an apple-faced sweet old lady with twinkly eyes?' asked Imogen, producing a packet of Santa tissues from her bag.

'No,' Samantha replied. 'Think more sharp-eyed, terrifying old lady, with pointy fingers who smells strongly of peppermints.'

'There are worse things to smell of,' said Fenella. 'Darling!' she addressed one of her children. 'If you don't let me get this chocolate off, you will look very like cake and Miss Wentworth might be inclined to take a bite out of you.'

This dire threat had the desired effect and after a bit of shoving the group set off, Imogen pulling her coat and woolly hat on as they left.

Imogen felt a little bit nervous. Although her most-recently-formed-choir was much improved since she first met them, they still weren't great and also, the prospect of spending Christmas next door to the local witch was not cheery. But she was intrigued to meet this formidable-sounding woman who had started a whole village tradition. She always liked a challenge and this little outing certainly qualified as one.

They assembled themselves into a semicircle in the space outside Miss Wentworth's house. It was large and Victorian, painted white, with Gothic overtones, and to Imogen's slightly overactive imagination, it seemed a little spooky. It was surrounded by an overgrown laurel hedge which, in spite of the white paint, made it all seem gloomy.

Not surprisingly, their cheery ring wasn't answered for a long time. The choir had got through the whole of 'Ding Dong', 'Oh Little Town' and 'Silent Night' (in badly pronounced German, as Miss Wentworth preferred it in German) before at last the door opened and Imogen saw her new neighbour.

Hmm, she thought, interesting. She could understand the witch description. She was thin and had been tall but now was quite bent over. She had a lot of white hair in a bun, held in place by combs. She wore a cardigan over a high-necked blouse and over that, a shawl. Her skirt went to the ground. Imogen could see why the locals were nervous of her – she did seem to come out of a different century. Imogen was glad her new life as music teacher with the local comprehensive and, eventually, some private pupils would not give her much time for elderly neighbours.

Fenella cleared her throat. 'Happy Christmas, Miss Wentworth!' she said, obviously hoping that some Christmas cheer would conceal her nervousness.

'We've come to sing to you,' said Susie, hugging her toddler to her like a riot shield.

'Come in then, don't dawdle!' said Miss Wentworth, whose voice was crisp and imperious as they shuffled into her hall, which was large but cheerless. There was a table with a vase of dried flowers on it and numerous small pictures and yet it had a museum-like quality that seemed to add to everyone's nerves.

At last the singers were placed to Miss Wentworth's

satisfaction with Imogen facing them, flute in hand. She was hoping she could conduct with facial expression alone. But as they weren't used to having a conductor it might not make any difference anyway.

They got rapidly through their programme and then looked hopeful. Imogen realised they weren't hoping for mulled wine and mince pies or even a contribution to a local charity, they were waiting to be dismissed.

'There aren't so many of you this year,' said Miss Wentworth.

'I know,' Fenella began to explain apologetically. 'Our best singers are all away for Christmas. So it's just us.'

'And who are you?'

She addressed Imogen, who had explained who she was earlier but was prepared to repeat herself. 'I'm your next-door neighbour—'

'Yes, I know that, but you play the flute. Why have you moved here?'

'I've got a job teaching at the secondary school. Music. I hope to get some private pupils too. I teach flute and piano.' Imogen was aware of a child saying, 'Can we go now?' who was then hushed by his mother.

'Ah! Now I understand. And are you going away for Christmas?'

'No, not until a few days afterwards. As I've just moved in, I'll have plenty to do. I'm just staying here.'

'I, on the other hand, have not just moved in,' Miss Wentworth said. 'I too am just staying here.'

Imogen sensed a wave of collective guilt go through the mothers. They were already exhausted by Christmas but they wanted to be with their families and not have Miss Wentworth sitting by the fire casting a pall of gloom and criticism over the party. They had their own relations to do that. She decided to take one for the team – the team of women-kind at Christmas.

'Well,' said Imogen, 'I would be delighted to invite you round for a glass of sherry or something.' There was bound to be somewhere she could buy a bottle of sherry between now and Christmas Day.

'I would very much prefer it if you came to me. For lunch.'

'Oh Miss Wentworth!' said Imogen, horrified by the suggestion. 'I couldn't possibly put you to the trouble of cooking Christmas lunch for me.'

'Oh no, dear,' said Miss Wentworth. 'I would expect you to do the cooking.'

Imogen gulped and heard the others gasp. She'd helped her mother cook Christmas dinner for years but she'd never actually taken responsibility for a turkey herself. 'Er – have you got everything for it?'

'No. We shall make do with what we have. As you can imagine I am a little disappointed that none of my many nieces and nephews – two generations of them – have seen fit to invite me to share the festivities with members of my own family but so be it. That's the younger generation for you.'

As Miss Wentworth was surrounded by members of the younger generation – two generations in fact – who had all put themselves out to come and sing carols to her, Imogen thought this extremely unfair but she didn't say anything. Still, she hated the thought of Miss Wentworth being on her own at Christmas. It was different for her; she had delightful plans for a couple of days later. Miss Wentworth probably hadn't.

'I'll come round at twelve,' she said firmly. 'I'll bring anything I have that's suitable. And some wine.'

'Thank you.' Miss Wentworth inclined her head. 'Now, before you go, I'd like to hear "Little One Sweet".'

'We don't know that one,' said Fenella bravely, freedom in sight.

'Really?' said Miss Wentworth, aggrieved. 'You sang it to me last year.'

'We had our best singers last year,' said Fenella. 'We're the second division, I'm afraid.'

'I'll play it for you,' said Imogen, adjusting her flute again. As she played she resolved to teach her new choir the carol for next year. It was so lovely.

'Very nice, dear,' said Miss Wentworth when she'd finished. 'Now, bowl in the corner, something for the little ones and off you go!'

The children moved swiftly towards the bowl and each took a bag of chocolate coins. At last Imogen understood how they had all managed to be so good during what for them must have been torture.

The party made their goodbyes and soon afterwards, their escape. As one of the children said they needed to wee now, Imogen invited them back to her house.

'Oh God! I am so sorry, Imogen,' said Fenella, once they were gathered in the warmth and safety of Imogen's little cottage and Samantha was unwrapping her small child in the downstairs loo.

'Yes,' agreed Susie. 'If you hadn't come along to

help us you wouldn't have got roped in to cooking Christmas dinner for her.'

Samantha, when she came back, was almost speechless with guilt. 'We should invite her to ours,' she wailed. 'But Bill just wouldn't stand for it. He can't bear my relations anyway without adding Miss Wentworth.'

'It's fine,' said Imogen. 'Really, I don't mind. I was only going to unpack and sort things out. I'm having my Christmas later. It's no sacrifice, honestly.' She didn't want these lovely women having their heavy guilt-burden added to by her. Although she was a bit worried about it.

'You could have curled up in front of the Christmas specials with a box of chocs and a bottle of wine,' said Samantha. 'Which is what I always yearn to do.'

'Not really, you don't,' said Susie. 'You only think you do. But Imogen, I'm going to come and get you sometime when you're free. You must come for a walk, or for a meal, or something. You've been so kind to us, when you don't know us from Adam.' She glanced around. 'OK, Eve, then.'

After a certain amount of teasing and discussion about which of them was most grateful to Imogen, the other women made similar offers of hospitality.

By the time they all left, she'd been invited to a lunch and a fancy dress party. When Imogen finally closed her front door behind them all she felt she already had friends in the area.

Her house did feel rather empty now the women and their children had left but Imogen ignored a sudden pang of loneliness. She hadn't moved far away from family and friends for a bad reason – she had a very good reason – but just now she sort of wished she hadn't. Everyone would be madly wrapping presents, watching *Nativity!* on the telly, and the children would all be rolling around the floor in her brother's house. This was the first year she wasn't there to prevent the tree from being knocked over. She hoped someone would catch it.

When she'd applied for the job as music teacher in this charming, if rather far south for her family, who all lived north of Birmingham, area, it was because it was near an orchestra she longed to be part of. She didn't think she'd ever be a full-time musician – she'd always teach as well, and as she loved teaching this wasn't a hardship – but she did want to be a member of the best orchestra she could be part of. And for that, she had to live a bit nearer.

The Aphrodite Orchestra was over a hundred years old and had a reputation that could be envied by professionals. In fact, Imogen had discovered, a lot of its players were professional musicians happy to play for nothing when they weren't doing paid work so they could be part of such a group. You had to be really good to get in.

Imogen's older brother had bitten his lip and shook his head when he heard her plans to move away from home so she could be near enough to audition. 'I know you're good, Imi,' he had said. 'But supposing you don't get in? You'll be miles away from all of us, lonely, living among a lot of posh Southerners who'll despise you.'

'Then I'll come home,' said Imogen. 'If I'm unhappy and it all goes wrong, I'll give in. I'm not proud. And you've been saying "I told you so" to me ever since I was born; I'm quite used to it.'

She hadn't actually told anyone that she'd already applied and had an email back saying she'd hear more after Christmas – which could mean March. But she felt it was a gesture of her faith in herself to make contact even before she lived in the area.

But she was heading home as soon after Christmas as she could manage, and she was going to bring with her a gingerbread house. That way her nephews and nieces wouldn't feel too bad about her abandoning them just so she could join an orchestra. Making it would be a very good way of passing Christmas.

However, since her offer to cook for Miss Wentworth, it all had to be done in one day. Her plan had been to make the pieces on Christmas Eve and spend Christmas Day assembling it. She wasn't a particularly experienced baker but she wanted to prove something to her older brothers and her family. If she appeared with a proper gingerbread house, still intact after a car journey, they'd be reluctantly impressed. She'd bought tiny battery-operated fairy lights to go inside it. And if it went to plan, she'd make the door large enough so she could put a tea light in there, to satisfy her mother's love of candles. She was going to show her family that she hadn't made a mistake and could cope perfectly well without them living down the road.

As Christmas Eve turned out to be a lovely day, and Imogen was in a new area, she just had to spend at least some of it exploring on foot. She found a lot to be happy about and was already looking forward to having her nieces to stay. The nephews, three and four, would have to be a bit older before they could have a sleepover with her now she lived further away.

There was a little park by a pond that was perfect for sailing boats on, a walk that went along the river and ended up back in the village, and a very attractive church that she would visit sometime over the festive period. She might see if there was a Christingle service as walking back by herself after Midnight Mass might be a bit scary until she knew the area better.

After she got home – she was beginning to think of it as home – she made a sandwich and then braced herself and found the mixing bowl and scales. She hadn't brought much stuff with her; she was determined to find out what she needed before dragging it out of her parents' attic and cluttering up her new home. But she had made sure there would be no obstacles to making her gingerbread house.

At last she was able to pronounce her ginger-bread house finished. At least she'd made all the pieces and that felt like a triumph after she'd had to throw away a few attempts (over-baked, aka, burnt). She looked at the clock. It was gone six! She had missed the Christingle service, and, more importantly, she had nearly missed the shop. It had said on the door that it would close at seven. She pulled on her coat and ran.

She arrived at the counter out of breath and panting. 'Hello,' she said. 'I need to buy Christmas dinner. Can you help?'

As she spoke she realised the shop was really quite small. It wouldn't be able to provide a turkey, sausages, stuffing, potatoes, or at least not all of those things.

The man rested his elbows on the counter. He was late middle-aged and obviously wanted to help. On the other hand, he wasn't a miracle worker. 'You might find something in the freezer but it won't be a whole anything. Might be a duck breast or two.'

'Oh, that would be perfect,' said Imogen, refusing to be cast down. 'What about potatoes?'

'I've a few spuds left and some cabbage.'

'That would go well with duck, I'm sure. Have you a tin of cherries?'

'I've probably got mandarin oranges in a tin but if you want cherries, it's jam.'

Eventually Imogen assembled a collection of items that wouldn't have looked out of place in a competition called 'Make a meal out of this lot if you can'. But she was a positive soul and felt alcohol would fill in the missing pieces. Miss Wentworth was elderly and slight; a couple of glasses of sherry would prevent her noticing any deficiencies.

'And a bottle of sherry. What do you think Miss Wentworth likes? Bristol Cream? Amontillado? Or dry sherry?'

The man she now knew as Bob, as they'd become friends during her search for Christmas dinner, shook his head. 'She doesn't drink sherry. She likes a Whisky Mac.'

'Which is?'

'Whisky and ginger wine. I have those, if you want to buy them. Not cheap, needless to say.'

'It's Christmas. I'll buy them. And if it makes Miss Wentworth happy, it'll be worth it. Oh, and I'll have a packet of icing sugar. I've got two at home, but I might need extra.'

It was nearly midnight before Imogen was happy with her gingerbread house, but she was very happy. There might have been some wonky corners that would have worried a surveyor had it been a real house, but the plethora of icing, sweets like jewels and very convincing trees growing up the side of it (courtesy of a few Curly Wurlys) and the lights shining from inside, made it magical. Her nieces and nephews would love it. Her place as favourite aunt would be unchallenged.

Although she was very tired, as she showered off the icing and then climbed into her fleecy pyjamas, she knew that the young mothers she'd met would be even more so, and probably had to cope with being woken in the very early hours. At least she could sleep in for a while before she had to face Miss Wentworth and her scratch Christmas dinner.

When Imogen heard the doorbell and saw it was only seven o'clock in the morning, she wasn't exactly delighted, but thinking it might be something to do with Miss Wentworth, she ran down the stairs to answer it as quickly as she could.

It was Samantha. 'So sorry to disturb you, but I've managed to tunnel out for a few minutes. I've brought you this.' She held out a cling-film covered paper plate. Imogen couldn't identify the small brown object beneath the film. 'They're just some cookies the children made. I think they're edible. I wanted to help you out in some way. I didn't think you'd want the giblets from our turkey to make gravy, or bath bombs, so I brought these. Oh, and a bottle of sloe gin. It's from last year. My aunt gives us some every year and we never get through it.'

'Thank you very much,' said Imogen, a bit husky. 'How kind.'

'I'd better go. Happy Christmas!'

Inside, having put the kettle on, Imogen inspected the offerings. She sniffed them. They smelt spicy and gingery. They didn't look very appetising but she thought they might be useful for something. She hoped that she'd be back here by teatime, having exhausted her hostess with duck a la confiture de cerise – or whatever the French for cherry jam was – but one never knew. If she didn't make the Whisky Macs strong enough, she might have to listen to the Queen's Speech with Miss Wentworth. And then she might have to provide something to eat that was faintly teatime-ish. She nibbled a bit of cookie thoughtfully. She rather hoped not – their edibility was borderline.

Three times during the morning, in between Imogen answering Happy Christmas calls and texts, getting showered and dressed, and searching on the internet for suitable recipes, there were knocks at the door. Two were other members of her impromptu choir but one was a stranger. They all brought food items. Fairly random food items. She ended up with a jar of pickled pineapple (home-made), some cheese straws (Imogen tasted one and it was delicious), a couple of jars of chutney, and a small Stilton. Everyone had heard how she was spending Christmas Day with the village witch and felt bad about it. They expressed this with food. And Imogen was very grateful but uncertain as to how she could introduce these items into a Christmas meal.

But that wasn't the point. It really was the thought that counted. These people, who lived in the village she'd only moved into days before, were acknowledging her presence and her good deed. It lifted her spirits. When she'd closed the door on what she hoped was the last caller, she picked up her flute and played her favourite carol, to celebrate her positive feelings and to put her in the mood for what might be quite a difficult day. It was 'Tomorrow Will Be My Dancing Day'. It was only after she'd put her flute safely away in its case that she realised there was a certain irony in her choice. Tomorrow she could dance; her Christmas duty would be over.

Feeling very like Little Red Riding Hood, with her basket of provisions, as Imogen knocked firmly on

Miss Wentworth's front door, she realised the difference was Miss Wentworth was already as scary as
a wolf. Seeing the house in daylight, she realised
it was really quite handsome if only someone
would cut back the hedge that seemed to absorb
the light. It had a forgotten-about look, and with
the hedge, Imogen thought Sleeping Beauty would
feel right at home here.

Hoping Miss Wentworth would come to the door
before she became overcome with thoughts of fairy
tales, she took a deep breath and chided herself for
being whimsical. She was supposed to be an adult,
after all.

'Well, you're on time, at least,' said Miss Wentworth.

'Happy Christmas!' said Imogen determinedly.
'How are you? Not too tired after our performance
the other day? Shall I come in? All your heat is
flowing out of the front door.'

Miss Wentworth opened the door a bit wider
and stepped aside. Imogen entered a large hallway
that cried out for a Christmas tree. She had quite
wanted one herself but decided that it would be
all dried up and dead when she got back to it after
staying away so hadn't bothered.

Although there was a table with a bowl of dried
flowers on it, there was nothing seasonal or fresh.

She had only briefly noticed these things when she and the yummy mummies had come carol singing. Now she realised just how alone Miss Wentworth was in her grand house.

'Shall I take the food through to the kitchen?'

Miss Wentworth nodded. She indicated one of the doors that led off the hall.

Imogen went in and put her basket on the scrubbed wooden table. It was an old-fashioned family kitchen and contained enough original features to make an interior designer weep for joy. But even though it was midday it was dark and although there was an old-fashioned range it was unlit. The kitchen was cold. Miss Wentworth followed her in.

Imogen was by no means an alcoholic, but she said, 'Shall we have a Christmas drink? Then I'll get on with the cooking?' The thought of cobbling together a Christmas meal with random ingredients in this sombre and probably poorly equipped kitchen without a sip or two of Dutch Courage was beyond even Imogen's usually optimistic self.

'I never drink alcohol before six o'clock,' said Miss Wentworth.

'I do if it's Christmas,' said Imogen firmly, opening a cupboard in the search for glasses. 'And

I'm dealing with a difficult old lady,' she added silently.

'Not those glasses,' said Miss Wentworth, when Imogen had found a couple of tumblers. 'We'll use the ones in the cabinet. It is Christmas, after all.'

At last! thought Imogen. You noticed.

Miss Wentworth left the room and came back with the glasses she thought suitable (still tumblers, but Waterford Crystal this time) and Imogen set about making the drinks. 'Would you like ice?' she said, having contemplated the two bottles she'd brought with her.

'No thank you.' In this simple sentence Miss Wentworth managed to convey that she considered ice to be vulgar.

It was probably just as well. There was a huge old-fashioned refrigerator, shuddering away, in the corner of the room but it didn't look as if it produced ice. It probably considered it to be vulgar too.

Unwilling to ask any more questions, like 'How do you make a Whisky Mac', Imogen decided she'd prefer to practice mixology without an audience.

'Why don't you go through and sit down? I'll bring the drinks.'

'Very well.'

Working on the principle that the first named ingredient should be in a greater quantity, Imogen poured two large double whiskies into the glasses and then added some ginger wine. She took the two glasses through to the sitting room. The house was very quiet – such a contrast to Christmases at home with her family. The sitting room was stately with French doors and a grand piano. A marble fireplace surrounded an empty hearth, and although the room wasn't cold, Imogen yearned for some living flames. There were quite a lot of small tables dotted about the room and on them a wide selection of photographs in silver frames, small silver and dark wood boxes, china shepherdesses and crino-lined ladies. Miss Wentworth obviously liked the odd knick-knack.

Miss Wentworth was perched on a chair that actually had an antimacassar draped over its back. Imogen had never seen one in use outside a costume drama. But although Miss Wentworth was in more or less modern dress – twentieth century at least – she would have fitted in well in an episode of *Downton*. A twinge of unease went through her as she passed her the glass. 'It might be a bit strong. I've never made a Whisky Mac before.'

Miss Wentworth sipped. 'Delicious, dear, thank you.'

'Oh!' said Imogen, pleased.

They perched and sipped for a few seconds and then Miss Wentworth said, 'The door knocker hasn't stopped all morning.'

'Oh?'

'Yes. People bringing food offerings, as if I was a god or something. I didn't ask for explanations. I just put the things over there.' She gestured to a side table, which Imogen now noticed was covered with the kind of wrapped shapes that she had herself received. 'It seems the village knows I'm on my own for Christmas.'

'Well,' said Imogen, offended by this, given that she wasn't on her own for Christmas. 'You did tell the carol singers the situation. I expect word has got about. Shall we see what we've got?'

Considering that Imogen had been given pickled pineapple and a small Stilton, it was disappointing that most of Miss Wentworth's presents were various forms of chutney, although there was a chilli jam that Imogen thought looked interesting but didn't think it was something Miss Wentworth would like. And maybe it was a good thing that no one had presented Miss

Wentworth with a pheasant. Imogen really wouldn't have known what to do with one in its feathers. 'Well, we'll be all right when we get to the cheese and biscuits stage. But that reminds me. I've got some cheese straws.' She got up. 'I'll fetch them.'

'I rarely eat cheese,' said Miss Wentworth. 'It gives me indigestion.'

'It's a shame none of the neighbours brought round a nice bottle of Gaviscon,' muttered Imogen as she left the room.

She brought in the cheese straws and offered them to Miss Wentworth, who took one.

'I unwrapped one of the presents earlier,' Miss Wentworth said. 'What are they?'

She held out a bowl with three pastel-colour spheres in it.

Samantha had obviously found a home for her surplus bath bombs. 'They fizz when you put them in your bath.'

'I never have baths. Dangerous at my age.'

Imogen took another sip of her drink. It was very strong but warming. 'I'd better get on with the lunch.' It was going to be a very long day.

She had just got up to go back to the kitchen when there was a sharp rap at the door.

'Oh do open that for me,' said Miss Wentworth. 'I'm tired of people bringing me things I don't want.'

Feeling a flash of sympathy, Imogen put her glass on a lace doily and went to the door.

A man holding a cardboard box stood there. He was wearing a long navy coat and a scarf looped round his neck. He was tall and, Imogen thought, fairly good-looking and very slightly familiar. He didn't speak when he saw Imogen so he obviously didn't know her. She helped him out. 'Hello! Shall I take that for you?'

'Is my aunt in?'

Pennies began to drop. 'Is your aunt Miss Wentworth?'

'Yes,' he said.

Imogen was about to let him pass her and then felt maybe she should check his credentials, at least a bit. 'I'll just ask her. You might be anyone, trying to get into her good books, selling something.'

'On Christmas Day?'

Imogen nodded. 'It would be a good day. The old and vulnerable are feeling lonely, they'll let you in, offer you a sherry, have one themselves, and there you are. Double glazing sold, no problem.' She suddenly became aware of the Whisky Mac she'd been drinking. It might have gone to her head.

'I'll check with Miss Wentworth.' When she reached the sitting-room door she realised she'd forgotten to ask for an important bit of information. She turned round. 'Name?'

He shook his head. 'She won't remember. We've hardly met. Say I'm Glenys's boy.'

Miss Wentworth was putting down her glass as Imogen entered. 'It's one of your nephews. Glenys's boy. Shall I let him in?'

She considered. 'Glenys? Did she have a boy? I'd forgotten.'

'He's come a long way.' She didn't know this but allowed herself some artistic licence.

'I thought she only had girls...'

'He's brought a present.'

'Oh very well, bring him in.'

As he entered, bearing his box, he was, Imogen decided, what Miss Wentworth's generation would describe as a fine figure of a man, the sort of nephew any great-aunt would be proud to have. He instantly made the room seem smaller and more full of knick-knacks.

'So you're Glenys's boy,' said Miss Wentworth, frowning at him. 'I could have sworn she only had girls.'

'Three girls, then me. I'm the afterthought,' he said.

'Hmph. So, what are you doing here?'

'I'm just back from Germany. I heard you were going to be on your own for Christmas so I've come to collect you, to take you back to my mother's house.'

'Glenys? Never one of my favourites. Besides, I'm having Christmas with this – remind me of your name, dear?'

'It's Imogen. But, Miss Wentworth, you're likely to have a much nicer lunch – dinner – with – Glenys. We've only got duck breasts and cherry jam. All that I could get from the shop at the last minute,' she added, for the nephew's benefit.

'Oh I doubt it. Glenys was never much of a cook.'

'I'm not much of a cook,' said Imogen.

'I'm sure it will be fine,' said Miss Wentworth. 'Besides I wouldn't like to travel so far on Christmas Day.'

Imogen began to see why Miss Wentworth found herself alone at this time of year. She was just too difficult to please.

'I have a very comfortable car,' Glenys's boy persisted. 'I could have you back here by supper-time, easily.'

'No thank you,' said Miss Wentworth. 'Now, what's this present you've brought me?'

'Why don't you open it and see?' he suggested.

He unbuttoned his coat and Imogen took hold of it and laid it over the back of a chair. Just by handling it she knew it was cashmere and the lining silk. He was a high-status nephew. Probably worked in IT or was a banker. She turned her attention back to Miss Wentworth and the present.

'Imogen, dear, do you think you could give my nephew some sort of refreshment? He's travelled a long way.'

'Open your present first, please,' he said. 'If you don't like it you might not want me to be refreshed.'

It was possible he had a sense of humour, Imogen thought. That was good.

'Oh very well, then.'

It was beautifully wrapped. Imogen, from her own trips abroad, recognised the hand of a European shop assistant, who seemed naturally skilled at handling paper and ribbon.

'I picked it up in Munich,' he said, as if reading her mind. 'I do hope you still like these things, Aunt Dorothy.'

At last Miss Wentworth arrived at the box.

Carefully, she took out its contents. It was a ceramic figure, which, when Imogen moved so she could see it better, turned out to be a violinist.

'It's a musical box. Turn the key on the bottom and it plays. Shall I do it for you?'

The tune 'Silent Night' came tinkling forth. 'Oh, how charmingly sentimental. Thank you, Jamie.'

He smiled. 'I was wondering if you were going to remember my name or if I would have to remind you.'

'I'm not completely poggled you know. I knew it would come to me eventually. Now, Imogen, dear, would you mind very much—'

Imogen jumped up. 'Of course. What would you like? I haven't found my way round the kitchen yet but I'm sure I could do coffee, or tea or something?'

'What are you two drinking?'

'Whisky Macs,' said Imogen, although she had resolved not to drink any more of hers. 'But I don't expect you'd want anything like that, if you're driving.'

He looked around him and took stock. 'No, I'll have a Whisky Mac. I'm staying.'

'What do you mean?' asked Imogen, hoping

there was another interpretation that could be put on this word.

'I'm determined that my great-aunt should spend Christmas with at least one member of my family. And that's me. I'm sure there's a spare bed somewhere. I've got a sleeping bag in the car so as not to put her to any trouble. So I'll have a Whisky Mac, please.' He seemed abashed for a moment. 'I do hope you'll have enough food.'

'I'm sure we'll manage,' said Imogen, feeling only slightly like the waitress. She could feed him pickled pineapple and chilli jam if necessary. It would serve him right for turning up on Christmas Day without due warning. Besides, this nephew – Jamie – turning up meant she could go home. He and his great-aunt would want to talk about family and they'd prefer to do that without a stranger present. They could have jammy-duck-breast – she could make some delicious variation of cheese on toast for her own meal. That's what she hoped, anyway.

She brought through his drink in the kitchen tumbler his great-aunt had shunned.

'Here you go. Now, maybe in a minute, if you came into the kitchen, I could show you what you've got for your Christmas dinner? Not conventional, but it was all the shop had just before closing on Christmas Eve.' She sensed disapproval. It was from the way his dark, thick eyebrows drew together. Imogen felt she should explain. 'I only met your great-aunt the day before Christmas Eve. We agreed to spend Christmas together, but if she's got you and won't be on her own, I'll be fine. So I'll just pop off home now.'

'Oh, please don't do that,' said Jamie, who probably couldn't cook any better than his mother.

'Imogen, dear, please don't leave us.' Miss Wentworth might have had the same misgivings as to the cooking. 'My nephew and I would very much like you to join us for Christmas. You've been so kind—'

She had made a great effort to show gratitude and Imogen appreciated it. 'It's really very kind of you—'

'Please stay,' said Jamie. 'And not just because you can cook. I'll help you all I can with that, of course.'

Imogen's gaze flicked to his eyes. She couldn't interpret his expression clearly. In among the polite concern was command. This was a man who was used to having his orders obeyed. He was obviously a captain of industry – maybe even a General.

Then she looked at Miss Wentworth. She was a proud woman with a sharp tongue but she did seem to genuinely want her to spend Christmas with her.

'If you stay,' said Miss Wentworth. 'We could have some music. I would very much enjoy some music.'

'Would you like me to put a CD on, Aunt Dorothy?'

'No, no! I mean real music. Imogen is quite a passable flautist.'

'Oh,' said Jamie, sounding surprised.

'So if you could be persuaded to stay, maybe we could have a little concert later.' She paused. 'Young Jamie plays a little.'

Imogen met 'Young Jamie's' eye and suppressed a smile.

'So, Imogen,' said Jamie. 'Will you stay? Please?'

'Well, if you're sure you wouldn't prefer to keep it as a family occasion—'

'We're sure,' said Jamie quickly.

'Then I'd be delighted.'

A little while later, Imogen and Jamie surveyed their ingredients. 'My aunt has potatoes and frozen peas.'

281

'There seem to be plenty of eggs. I could make Yorkshire pudding,' said Imogen. 'It's my signature dish.'

'I'm not sure it's a whole dish,' said Jamie. 'More of an extra.'

'As far as I'm concerned, it's a dish and it's nice. But if you're a great cook yourself, you can think of something to do with two duck breasts and some jam. Bearing in mind there are three of us now.'

He sighed. 'I'm not a great cook but I like to eat. Shall we see what we can do?'

Imogen had long abandoned her resolution not to drink any more alcohol and also her slight shyness with Jamie. He wasn't the sort of man she normally mixed with, who were usually teachers, less well-groomed, and more relaxed, but he had a kind heart, something that was revealed further as they prepared vegetables together. He was chopping onions with a blunt knife and she was doing her best with an ancient potato peeler with string round the handle. Aunt Dorothy was in the sitting room 'resting her eyes' with a Bach string quartet on in the background. Jamie had persuaded her to overcome her objections to non-live music. Maybe the musical box had helped.

'So what made you come and visit your aunt on Christmas Day?' she said, poking at a blemish in her potato.

'I got back last night – I've been away for a while – and heard no one from the family was seeing her.' He blinked hard, eyes streaming. 'I was appalled. I know she's difficult but she shouldn't just be forgotten, not at Christmas.'

'I suspect she likes you – once she remembered you existed – that probably makes you think better of her. She is fairly formidable.'

'I know but – well – Christmas. No one wants to be alone then.'

'To be honest, I was perfectly happy about it. None of my family were, and I'm looking forward to seeing them shortly, but I would have been fine.' She would have been fine, she was convinced, but she wouldn't have enjoyed herself in the way that she found she was enjoying herself now.

'Possibly. But you had the prospect of seeing your family. Poor old Aunt Dorothy didn't have that.'

Imogen picked up another potato.'I did realise that, which was why I offered to spend it with her. Have you seen her much lately?'

'No. I've been working away for some years now.'

'Well, I only met her the other day and she is fairly terrifying.'

'Really?'

His disbelief was galling. 'Yes. There was this trio of mums with their babies who felt obliged to go to her house and sing her carols when I don't think they do it for everyone. She was very critical.'

'I don't expect they were very good.'

'Well, no, they weren't brilliant, but they had come out on a cold night to sing to her. Apparently it's a village tradition.'

'Oh?'

'Yup. It's to do with her not being able to get to church to hear them. Apparently the good singers were all away this year. They came to me first and—' She hesitated, aware she would come across as very bossy if she wasn't careful. Quite why she minded how she came across she didn't ask herself.

'What?'

'I sort of took them under my wing. I'm a music teacher. They needed help. I got out my flute and accompanied them.'

'Ah! That's why Aunt Dorothy said you were a passable flautist.'

'She exaggerated my talents.'

He laughed. 'I doubt that very much. Exaggeration is not her way.'

Imogen laughed. 'I think I'd already picked that up. Now, have we enough vegetables?'

'I think so. And the duck is ready to cook when everything else is. The jam is bubbling away nicely. That drop of sloe gin was a touch of genius though I say it myself.'

'A great cook and modest! What a combination.' Imogen was teasing but she was enjoying this slightly bizarre cookery session. Savoury smells scented the air and the kitchen was warming up now all the burners were going. Christmas had finally arrived in Miss Wentworth-land!

'Not that modest actually.'

Imogen laughed again. 'So are you just in England for Christmas? Flying back the day after Boxing Day?'

'No, actually. I've applied for a position in this area. I haven't decided if I'll take it yet, though. I thought if Aunt Dorothy didn't want to come to Mum's with me, I'd stay and check out the area.'

'Oh! A bit like me. Only I have accepted the position. I start next term. I just hope it works out OK.'

'No reason it shouldn't.'

'I know, but I moved away from family and friends to take it. If it doesn't work out—' She stopped. She didn't want to tell this man she'd only just met all her reasons for uprooting herself.

He picked up a wooden spoon and stirred the sauce. 'I'm sure if you can get a group of mothers and babies to perform half decently with no rehearsal, you must be good at your job.'

She laughed. 'I'm quite good at people-wrangling, that's true.'

'Well, then. No need to worry. And very nice for my aunt to have such a kind and caring neighbour.'

Imogen realised if he'd described her as a super-sexy, drop-dead-gorgeous neighbour it would have been embarrassing, but somehow she wished she'd come across as more than just kind and caring. Nothing wrong with those things of course, it's just they were rather – unexciting.

With permission, Imogen decided to make the dining room look festive. She rifled Miss Wentworth's cupboards and found all the best china and glasses. She found a white linen table cloth, place mats, candlesticks and (after a rummage in the cupboard by the electricity meter) some candles. She also found some holly and a few brave early primroses in the garden and made napkin rings with ivy and rosemary.

'Oh wow!' said Jamie, who'd she left slicing the duck breasts so they'd stretch to three servings, as he came in. 'That looks beautiful! My aunt will love it.'

'Why don't you get her in? I'll get everything else on the table.'

'Good idea.'

By the time Jamie had roused Miss Wentworth from 'resting her eyes', the table was loaded. Imogen had put everything they had in little dishes. There was a cut-glass bowl of pickled pineapple, which looked festive at least. The Stilton was on a dish on the sideboard and Imogen's Yorkshire puddings were piled on top of the roast potatoes. Various chutneys and jams were distributed as appropriate.

'Well!' said Miss Wentworth, leaning slightly on Jamie's arm. 'That does look delightful. A real Christmas feast. I knew you were both just making a fuss when you said there wasn't enough food. We'll do splendidly. And it's so nice to see my lovely things in use. But please be careful when you do the washing-up. They are all very precious to me.'

It occurred to Imogen that the large drink followed by a good nap had done wonders for Miss Wentworth's spirits. She was unlikely to try many of the dishes on the table but she had enjoyed the spectacle. The washing-up was a bridge to be crossed later.

Jamie and Imogen shared a bottle of wine he found in Miss Wentworth's larder while Miss Wentworth had another Whisky Mac. Jamie mixed it this time so it was probably not as strong. Dishes were passed, plates were filled and then they began to eat.

As Jamie and his great-aunt reminisced, Imogen discovered things about her neighbour. She had been a very renowned teacher of music in her time and had endowed the village hall with quite a large sum. This was what had started the tradition of singing carols to her when she declared she could no longer get to church to hear them sung there. Imogen had known about the carols but she hadn't known about the endowment. It all made a bit more sense now.

She wondered what Jamie did for a living but she didn't ask because if he said something like 'international finance' she wouldn't really be any the wiser and she might feel a bit differently about him. She felt she'd rather focus on the attractive, kindly, faintly musical man she was getting to like.

At last everyone had stopped eating and Miss Wentworth declared a desire for a cup of tea. Imogen agreed with her and got up to make it. She took as many bowls and plates as she could carry and went through to the kitchen.

She was joined shortly afterwards by Jamie, who'd found a tray and loaded it.

'This was so kind of you,' he said, when he had put it down.

'What? Making space so you could put the tray down?'

'No! Doing all this for my aunt.'

Imogen laughed and began spooning chutney out of its cut glass dish and back into its more plebeian jam jar. 'It was a pleasure. Anyway, you did it too.'

'We did make a good team! But she's my aunt, you didn't have to sacrifice your Christmas Day for her. And if it had been left to me it wouldn't have been nearly so festive, and decorative. She's really loved it. I can tell.'

Imogen was very pleased. 'It was huge fun. And I've given us a huge amount of washing-up.'

'I'll do that later, after my aunt has gone to bed.'

'I couldn't possibly let you do that.'

'You might have to. She wants her tea and she wants some music.'

'And you can play the piano?'

He smiled. 'A bit, yes.'

Imogen studied him for a moment. From his expression she couldn't tell if he could just plonk out 'Away in a Manger' or was concert standard. She decided to wait to find out. 'OK, then. But first I've got a little present for her. Only some home-made biscuits but I wanted to bring something.' She looked at him and felt sad. 'I would have made some for you if I'd known you were coming.'

'And I'd have bought you some chocolates and a cuddly toy and maybe a novelty apron, because I don't know you at all and that's what men do in those circumstances.'

Imogen laughed. 'I've been spared then. Come on, I'll find my present and then pop home for my flute.'

*

Imogen took a tray of tea into the sitting room and found Miss Wentworth kneeling on the floor in front of a chest of drawers. The bottom drawer was open. She was searching through it.

'Oh good, Imogen, you're here. Help me up, do. This is all my music. I want you and Jamie to play me something.' She had a sheet of music in her hand. 'Now, take me back to my chair please. I really shouldn't have got down on my knees like that.'

Imogen settled her back down and then handed her the tea. She'd taken a risk and got out the tea service in a glass-fronted cabinet, hoping she wouldn't be told off for using the best china. But Miss Wentworth didn't comment and so while she was sipping, she found the bag of biscuits in her handbag.

'What's this?' said Miss Wentworth sharply when Imogen put it in her hand.

'It's a little present. Just a token. As it's Christmas.'

Miss Wentworth regarded the cheery red paper suspiciously and then pulled out a cellophane packet. In it were half a dozen ginger Christmas trees with icing decorations. 'Hmm. Quite pretty,' she said. 'Thank you. Now go and get your flute. It's time for music!'

Imogen went and while she was in her own house, she scouted round for a little something for Jamie. Somehow it seemed wrong not to give him anything. She found the suitcase full of presents she had wrapped for her family. She found a large bar of chocolate that was an extra gift for her brother. She took it with her. It was perfect. Not enough to be embarrassing but a gesture. He might even open and share it. That would be a plus.

She found Miss Wentworth's sitting room slightly altered when she returned. The grand piano was pulled round and open. Jamie was leafing through music and Miss Wentworth had her chair placed so she could hear perfectly. Imogen found herself cast back to when she was doing her grade exams, piano only to begin with and then piano and flute. The earlier grades were always taken in someone's house for some reason, which somehow had made it even more nerve-racking. She felt exactly the same now, Miss Wentworth being so formidable. She knew any little mistakes would be picked up on. She had to remind herself now that it was only carols round the piano, nothing she hadn't done with her family every year she could remember.

Partly to cover her sudden attack of nerves and partly so it wouldn't melt in her hand, she went over to Jamie and handed him his present. 'Don't get too excited. It's only something I was going to give to my brother.'

'Oh! That's really kind. You shouldn't have.' He unwrapped it. 'Actually, you won't believe this, but this is my favourite kind of chocolate. Thank you so much.' He bent and kissed her cheek.

Imogen felt herself blush. There was something about the feel of his face brushing hers that affected her in a way she hadn't expected.

She moved away and inspected her flute as an excuse to lower her head. She rationalised it. She hadn't been in a relationship for a little while. That would be it. The sudden whiff of maleness, after-shave, and the feel of skin against skin; they had all combined to create this frisson.

'Maybe this would be the moment for you to have my gift,' said Miss Wentworth. 'Fetch it for me, Jamie.'

This was another shock. 'Really, Miss Wentworth. It's not necessary.'

'I know,' she said crisply.

Jamie put a small parcel into her hand. Miss Wentworth hadn't used the wrapping paper her own Christmas present had come in so Imogen realised she must have thought about this before.

'Open it, then. I want to get on with the music.'

It was a tiny gold charm in the shape of a violin.

'Wrong instrument, of course, but it was the best I could do in the time. One of mine. No longer needed. Not a great gift.'

'But, Miss Wentworth, it's lovely. And far too precious to give to someone you've only just met.'

'Not at all. It's a trinket. I thought it might amuse you and if it has, maybe you can amuse me?'

But before obeying orders, Imogen found the gold chain she was wearing round her neck. Currently it had a cross on it but she undid it and added the violin. Then, although she was very used to doing it, her fingers had become slippery and she found it hard it fasten.

'Here, let me,' said Jamie.

The feeling of his fingers against her neck felt like so much more than the casual, inevitable touches incurred by doing up a gold chain. She actually shook her shoulder a little, to try and get rid of the feeling. She liked it too much and it wouldn't lead to anything, she was sure.

'Very nice,' said Jamie, looking at the little gold violin now nestling on Imogen's chest.

'It's gorgeous,' said Imogen, fingering it, feeling

slightly breathless. 'Thank you so much.' For a moment she was moved to go and kiss Miss Wentworth in gratitude but then realised this would probably not be welcomed.

'Please stop thanking me and get on with the music.'

Jamie was an excellent pianist and accompanist and Imogen soon forgot her nerves and just let herself relax into her playing.

Miss Wentworth barked out requests, some of them really challenging, but in spite of a few stumbles, she and Jamie got through them. Sometimes Miss Wentworth made corrections as if forgetting she wasn't actually teaching. At first Imogen accepted them out of good will but then swiftly realised they were perceptive and useful.

Imogen lowered her flute. She was aware it was dark outside and that her arms were very tired. Jamie removed his hands from the piano. Miss Wentworth appeared to have nodded off.

'I think we should stop. We've gone through almost all the carol books,' she said.

'You're a very good sight reader,' said Jamie. 'I'm impressed.'

Imogen hid her pleasure behind a self-deprecating

smile. 'That's because I've played them every year – more often really – since I was a little girl. We do a lot of singing and playing round the piano in my family.'

'And mine,' he said. 'My grandmother was very fond of what she called "community song books". She'd had them passed down by her mother.'

Imogen was delighted. 'What a strange thing to have in common. Singing round the piano – you don't often meet people who know anything about that.'

'It's nice, isn't it?'

Somehow the word 'nice' meant more when he said it. Imogen sighed – partly from tiredness but partly because she felt a sudden rush of happiness. She wasn't quite sure why.

'You're also a very accomplished flautist,' he went on. 'My aunt wasn't exaggerating your talents at all.'

Imogen swallowed. 'She certainly underestimated yours. You do more than play a little. You obviously play a lot.'

He laughed. 'Not as much as I once did.'

It seemed as if he was going to say more but just then Miss Wentworth opened her eyes. 'Well, thank you, both of you, for that. Can I ask you to play this? Not easy to read, I'm afraid. I wrote it. But give it a go, please.'

Imogen went over and fetched the proffered manuscript paper. Glancing at it she realised the composer was right, it would not be easy to read. She studied it for a few seconds before handing it over to Jamie. It was a very pretty tune. If they could manage to play it, it would be lovely.

Jamie also studied it for a few moments before placing it on the piano. 'You'll have to really lean in if we're both going to be able to see it. Let's have a go.'

While Imogen was adjusting her flute she caught sight of Miss Wentworth. She was sitting bolt upright on the edge of her seat, obviously really eager to hear her piece.

'I do hope we can do this,' she muttered to Jamie.

'We can,' he said definitely. 'Don't worry.'

After a couple of false starts they got the feel of the piece and got through it fairly successfully.

'Not bad,' said Miss Wentworth, back in teacher mode. 'Could we have that again please?'

Imogen forgot her aching arms and the blister forming on her right thumb from supporting the flute. She just wanted to get it right. Jamie obviously felt the same. They went through it until at last Miss Wentworth said. 'That's it! Well done.'

This was praise on the same scale as a croix d'honneur from Miss Wentworth.

'It's a lovely piece, Aunt Dorothy,' said Jamie, 'but it needs words, really. It's a song.'

'I know. Sadly I'm a musician, not a poet.'

Imogen dismantled her flute and put it back in its case. 'It's still lovely.'

Imogen realised how much she had enjoyed herself but she suddenly wanted to go home and sit on the sofa in front of the telly, and not perform any more.

'It's getting late. I think I'm going to leave you both to the rest of your day. Thank you so much for making me part of it.'

She was grateful that they didn't press her to stay. She sensed that Miss Wentworth was very tired. Jamie would look after her, see she had everything she needed and then probably find somewhere to put his sleeping bag. There was no shortage of space, anyway. It was thoughtful of him not to put his great-aunt to the trouble of dealing with his sheets. She did like him.

'Jamie will walk back with you,' said Miss Wentworth, stating a fact.

Imogen didn't bother to argue. She felt drained of energy. She'd been up very late the previous night and although she'd really enjoyed herself it had been a very busy day.

She gathered her empty basket, her flute, and other bits and pieces and then Jamie was ready to walk her the few yards to her house.

They didn't speak on the way but when they reached her back door Imogen stopped. Whether it was from politeness or because she felt she wanted to spend a little longer with him, she said, 'Do you want to come in for a few minutes? Have a quick cuppa or glass of wine before you go back?'

'That would be nice. The antimacassars and ornaments are a bit oppressive. A short break from them would be pleasant.'

Imogen laughed, revived by the short walk in the fresh air. 'I promise I don't own a single shepherdess or antimacassar.'

She let them in through the back door and they went into the sitting room.

'Oh, you've got a fire already laid!' said Jamie.

Imogen nodded. 'I was delighted to find a proper fireplace in my little rented cottage.' Looking at him, she smiled. 'Yes, we could light it. I was going to anyway.'

'That would be wonderful. Christmas Day without live flames isn't right.'

'I feel just the same which is why I laid it ready for when I got home.'

'Would you mind if I lit it? I've been in centrally heated apartments for years, seemingly.'

'Go for it. I'll get some wine.'

They sat on the sofa, not speaking much, sipping inferior wine out of Ikea tumblers, looking at the flames. It was one of the nicest half-hours Imogen had ever spent.

Eventually, Jamie sighed. 'I'll have to get back to Aunt Dorothy now.' They both got up and looked at each other a bit awkwardly. 'But I'd like to keep in touch.'

'Oh—' Her heart leaped like a startled deer.

'In case there are any problems with my aunt.'

'Oh.' Her heart landed rather heavily. 'I've got a card somewhere.' She found her handbag and dug about in it until she came up with her card case. She handed one of the ones she'd had done with her new address on it. 'Here you are. It's nice to be able to give one away. Although they're very cheap you have to have quite a lot of them.'

He took out his wallet and tucked it away. 'And

here's one of mine. Don't hesitate to get in touch – for any reason.'

'Thank you,' she said.

'So I'll be off. I can't thank you enough for all the happiness you've brought my aunt today. It was really kind of you.' He bent and kissed her cheek. Then he let himself out of the back door and disappeared.

Imogen stood there feeling deflated. It had been so lovely, cooking, playing music with him, and particularly lovely sitting in front of the fire with him, sipping cheap wine out of cheap glasses. Suddenly it seemed unlikely she would see him again. But it had been wonderful, she reminded herself. She mustn't mind it not being forever. She took the card and read it. Suddenly she blushed all over. James Smith-Williams – one of the most famous young conductors ever.

Deeply shocked, she staggered to the sitting room and sank onto the sofa. She'd spent Christmas Day with music royalty. She felt weak. Now she realised why he'd looked vaguely familiar when she first met him, but in all his publicity photographs he had a beard. Did he think she was a fool for not recognising him? Or had he shaved off his beard so people like her wouldn't? She would probably never know.

When she'd recovered a little she thought she wouldn't tell her family until she knew if the gingerbread house had survived the journey. If it all fell apart she would have some gossip that would take their attention well away from any small catastrophes like biscuit-collapse. And she really hoped her family wouldn't notice that her feelings were in turmoil.

Less than an hour after she arrived, her brother turned off the dining-room lights. 'Ta dah!' said Imogen and everyone said, 'Ah . . .'

All the family were there. Her parents, both brothers and their wives, two little girls in matching dresses and tights, the little boys in hand-knitted sweaters and red corduroy trousers. It was, she said to her brother, almost nauseatingly Christmassy.

The gingerbread house, lit from within and dusted with icing sugar, added to the gorgeous festivity. It looked spectacular.

'Oh, Auntie Imi! That looks awesome,' said her six-year-old niece, Elly. 'I can't believe you could be so clever.'

'No,' said Imogen, delighted with the reaction. 'And that's not the only clever thing I can do.'

'Oh yes? ' said her brother, Fred. 'You've been looking mysterious ever since you arrived. You've got news, haven't you?'

'I have. But there is a downside to it.'

'Oh,' said her mother, sounding disappointed. 'What?'

'I've got to go back tomorrow – but it's for a great reason.'

She handed her mother a cup of tea and Fred put the lights back on so the rest of the high tea could be seen.

'So, tell us, darling. You do look very excited, I must say.'

'Well,' said Imogen, taking a chair next to her mother. 'Just before I got into the car to come I had an email – from the Aphrodite Orchestra!'

'What, telling you not to bother them any more?' suggested Fred, with his eyebrow raised.

Imogen dug him in the ribs in response. 'Telling me to come to a rehearsal the day after tomorrow. I wasn't expecting to hear from them for ages but I gather they're short of flutes and they have a concert coming up very soon.'

'Darling!' said her mother. 'That's brilliant news.'

'And I might have time to pop back up after the rehearsal, before the concert, or the start of the new term.' Although Imogen had driven to her childhood home on a cloud of elation – she'd got the email just as she was packing her car – she now felt a bit sad that she was going to have to have such a short Christmas break with her family.

'Well,' said her father, from the head of the table, less voluble than the rest of the family. 'You're good at the flute. They'll be glad to have you. You won't let them down.'

'They haven't actually accepted me as part of the orchestra,' Imogen said hurriedly, embarrassed by public praise. 'I'm only going for a try-out.'

'You'll be fine!' said her mother. 'You're brilliant.'

'So, are we going to eat anything?' said Imogen's other niece, Sophie, who took after her grandfather and didn't say much.

'Absolutely,' said Imogen's mother. 'Let's break into the gingerbread house.'

'And when you've demolished all that hard work and dexterity, I'll tell you who I spent Christmas Day with.'

'What?' said her sister-in-law, Sally. 'Not the sweet little old lady who is really a witch?'

'She's lovely when you get to know her,' said

Imogen protectively, 'but yes, with her, and also her nephew who is—'

'Spit it out, sis,' said Fred.

'James Smith-Williams!'

Sally who wasn't as musically imprinted as her husband's family, said, 'Who?'

'He's one of the most famous young conductors in the world,' said her husband. 'Cor, blimey. And you shared turkey and stuffing with him?'

'Duck breasts and cherry jam, actually,' said Imogen. 'But I didn't recognise him!'

'Really?' said Fred, his voice squeaky with incredulity.

'He's shaved off his beard. He looks quite different without it.' Imogen explained.

'So how come you spent Christmas Day with him?' asked Sally.

'He found out his great-aunt was going to be alone at Christmas and drove down to take her back to the family. But she wanted to stay at home, so he stayed.'

'Well, your new life in the "Nesh South", where they have central heating and hot water bottles, has turned out to be exciting,' said her mother, reaching over to the gingerbread house. 'Now, who's for a bit of roof?'

*

Imogen had gone through everything from wild excitement to deepest dread in between getting the email to say she was wanted at the rehearsal and actually getting there. She'd got home late the night before and had slept badly, having vivid dreams in which her flute had turned into a recorder and made no sound. She'd been glad to wake up in her little cottage.

As she reached the door to the church hall where the Aphrodite Orchestra rehearsed she was shaking with nerves. She was fumbling with the door handle when another woman came up.

'Let me help you with that. It's a bit awkward. Are you new? Don't think I've seen you before.'

'I'm here for a try-out,' said Imogen. 'I gather you're short of flutes.'

'We are. I'm currently the only one. I'm Melanie.

'And I'm Imogen.'

'Let's go in.'

By the time they'd got to their places Imogen was feeling a lot happier. Melanie was really welcoming and friendly and the others around them seemed to be too. Her spirits were raised even further when the conductor called them to order. He seemed lovely – probably approaching seventy, with longish hair swept back from his forehead, a fairly scruffy jumper worn over well-worn trousers and a waistcoat.

'He's Adam,' whispered Melanie. 'We adore him. He's brought us from nothing to what we are now. But sadly, he's just about to retire. This might be his last concert.'

'Ladies and gentlemen. Quite please. First of all thank you for coming when the rest of the world is still slumped in front of the telly eating chocolates. We knew this would have to happen when we arranged to do a concert for Epiphany. Now—' He paused and checked everyone was paying attention. They were. 'I have an announcement. You all know I've been trying to retire for a few years now and haven't because we've not been able to find a suitable replacement. Well, we might have. Obviously he's got to hear you and you've got to decide if he's what you want and need.'

There was a murmur – a combination of regret, curiosity and excitement.

'I think you'll be very pleased when I tell you who it is—'

'Someone faintly famous, then,' whispered Melanie.

'He's going to come and introduce himself to you all at half time. Now, let's get going.'

Imogen thought she knew who it must be; otherwise the coincidence was just too great. How many famous conductors could there be in a fairly small geographical area? She tried to work out how she felt about it. Why hadn't he mentioned the Aphrodite? Then she realised that she hadn't either. She still hadn't decided what she thought by the time music had been found for her and they'd started work.

She managed to forget the new conductor as she threw herself into the music. It was hard work but, as Jamie – James – had said, she was a good sight-reader and as it was a concert for Epiphany, a lot of the music was carol-based and so well known to her. She gathered a choir was going to join them so it promised to be a fantastic concert. Melanie, who managed to convey a lot of information in a few meaningful whispers, indicated it was going to be quite full on. Local dignitaries, a huge audience, all performed in the cathedral, several miles away.

'I'm hope I'm up to it,' whispered Imogen, when she heard this. 'I'm only on trial.'

'You're great,' said Melanie. 'I'll demand they have you.'

Imogen laughed. 'Loyalty amongst flute players.'

'Yeah, Flautists of the World Unite!'

Shortly afterwards it was time for a break. There was a certain amount of milling about while people stretched, chatted to colleagues, walked about and adjusted their instruments. The conductor came up to Imogen. 'Well! What a find you are. I keep forgetting you're new. You seem to know most of the repertoire and are blending beautifully with Mel here.'

'It helps that most of the music is Christmassy or carols,' Imogen said. 'Er, do you think you'll want me to play for the performance? I understand completely if you don't want people who've only been to one rehearsal—'

'We're depending on you being there,' he said. 'And we've got another rehearsal, with the choir, before the day anyway. You'll be fine. Won't she, Mel?'

'Absolutely. It's wonderful not being a lone flute any more.'

'And you came highly recommended. Now, I'd better fetch our new conductor. I do think the orchestra will be pleased.'

Imogen gulped. She could only have been recommended by one person. She glanced at Mel, dreading her possibly accusing her of nepotism. But Mel was busy sorting her music into alphabetical order and she obviously hadn't heard what Adam had said.

She saw him walk down the hall and discovered she really hoped her knowing James wouldn't spoil this all for her. She loved this orchestra already and it being him might spoil it. It was easy enough to fall in love with the conductor without it being someone you already felt yourself half in love with. And while she might not call it love, she'd certainly thought about him almost every minute since Christmas Day.

'Oh my God!' said Melanie, 'Look who it is. It's only James Smith-Williams.'

Imogen tried to look pleased. In a way she was pleased. It was lovely to see him again. But she felt very vulnerable and exposed. She shifted position until she felt less visible.

Although she deliberately didn't try to catch his eye she found herself looking up just as he was looking at her. He nodded gravely, acknowledging her presence but not drawing attention to her. He wasn't at all surprised to see her.

When he was introduced there was a round of applause. 'We are so lucky to get him,' whispered

Melanie. 'I do hope he takes us on!'

He accepted the applause but then raised his hands. 'Thank you very much for the welcome but you don't know how well I've done yet. You might decide you don't want me after all.'

There was quite a lot of genuine laughter.

'Just to give you all a bit of background, I've become a bit tired of the overseas travelling involved with being a conductor so I felt very lucky when I was offered the headship of Wyndham's School of Music, which as you know is a specialist music college for children from age seven to about eighteen. Lots of very talented young people – and I'll promise to syphon off the best ones in this direction if I can. If they're not getting paid work, that is.'

More laughter. Everyone warmed to him. Imogen couldn't blame them but she still felt very odd about it.

'I'm going to take the rest of the rehearsal – a sort of audition for me, I suppose, and if it goes well, Adam and I will share conducting the concert. But there's just one thing. There's a piece of music I want to add to the mix. It's not long. It was written by my great-aunt and it now has words. It's a very pretty little song and I think you'll like it. I've had it transcribed into a legible form and photocopied – with the composer's permission of course – and I'm going to ask Imogen, your newest recruit, to play it for you as she's familiar with the work.'

'Nothing like dumping me in it!' said Imogen, indignantly, hugely embarrassed at being singled out.

The orchestra thought this was hugely funny although she'd been deadly serious.

'Come up here and play, Imogen, if you don't mind.'

Wishing she could say no, Imogen did as she was asked. She didn't want to alienate her new friends; it was too soon for her to be a soloist.

He adjusted the music stand for her. 'You'll find it very easy after last time. Look, actual notes, printed and everything.' He smiled. 'Sorry about this. It's just to save time really. And I know you can do it.'

A tiny part of her felt better. Of course it made sense that she should play it when she'd played it several times before and no one else had.

He was right. Reading the music now was so much easier than it had been before and the lovely melody quickly came back to her. It should have a voice part though.

'So, what are the words?' she said.

'It's a poem by Longfellow, *Christmas Bells*. Not all the verses as some of them are a bit grim. But I think it'll work well.'

'I hope the choir can learn it in time,' said Imogen, still feeling a bit embarrassed.

'I'm sure they will. They're very committed. And if they can't, well, we won't do it.'

Imogen went back to her place and the whole orchestra ran through it a few times. They all loved the piece, which pleased Imogen, for her elderly neighbour's sake.

'So, we'll see you next week for our last rehearsal?' said Melanie. 'And you didn't tell me you knew James Smith-Williams.'

'I don't really. I live next door to his ancient aunt. We met that way. But we don't really know each other.'

'Hmm, he seemed to know you well enough to ask you to play that piece on your own.'

'Well, that's what we did with his aunt. Played carols and things. It was Christmas Day.'

'Oh. Sounds quite intimate to me.'

'It wasn't, really. It was just a neighbourly thing.'

'Oh well, whatever you say,' said Melanie, but she gave Imogen a wicked wink.

*

It was early afternoon and as Imogen entered the cathedral doors she became aware of the wonderful smell. It was a combination of old buildings, old incense and flowers. It immediately made her feel calmer. The thought of performing what was nearly a solo, in front of a huge audience, had made her feel sick all morning. But shortly, the rehearsal would start, the performance would start coming together and the music would take over.

There was so much riding on it. She didn't want to let anyone down: Miss Wentworth, the orchestra, Jamie – herself. At least a problem with her grandmother meant her parents couldn't come. But now she was here she breathed deeply and took in the scene.

Even before all the candles were lit, the cathedral looked magical. The flowers, the decorations, tasteful and old-fashioned. As always when she stepped into a really old building like this Imogen couldn't help thinking about all the other people who'd come here, bringing their sorrows, their joys, their celebrations and their despair. All the emotion seemed trapped in the stones, the pillars, the worn flagstone floors, the tombstones. But there was peace as well and now Imogen felt happy to be here.

Although her normal level of performance anxiety was far higher than usual. Her role as accompanist to the soloist for Miss Wentworth's carol was key. But it should be all right. The words fitted beautifully and at the previous rehearsal there'd been few dry eyes when the wonderful lyric-soprano sang,

> *'Till ringing, singing on its way,*
> *The world revolved from night to day,*
> *A voice, a chime,*
> *A chant sublime*
> *Of peace on earth, good-will to men!'*

There was a run-through – orchestra, choir, soloists and a couple of readings. Then they retired to the room set aside for them to leave their things until they were on. They sipped bottles of water, ate bananas, sandwiches, and, in Imogen's case, read through her music. She nearly knew it by heart now but she wanted to be able to keep a close eye on Jamie as he conducted the piece. It had to go well, for Miss Wentworth's sake. And not just hers.

If Imogen had thought the cathedral was lovely before it was even more so now as the orchestra and choir took their places for the performance. Myriad candles covered everywhere it was safe to have them. There was minimal electric light and if you half closed your eyes you could imagine the audience were in period costume. There were the great and the good, a couple of them wearing decorative chains around their necks. There were ranks of local people, wrapped up in gloves and hats and scarves, who had come to their cathedral to hear sacred music in their special place of worship. And there were the camp followers, friends and relations of the choir and the orchestra. There didn't seem to be a single empty space. And right in the middle, looking regal and very pleased with herself, sat Miss Wentworth.

Her great-nephew, Jamie Smith-Williams, waited behind the scenes, about to make his entrance. Was he nervous? wondered Imogen. Or, accustomed as he was to the concert halls of the world, did he think this was just a little Christmas do? No, Imogen felt she knew him better than that. He would want it all to be perfect, for Miss Wentworth's sake.

Then he entered, and waited until everyone was looking at him. There were some official welcomes and explanations and at last, James raised his baton and they were off.

The applause seemed to go on for ages. Everyone except Miss Wentworth stood. It was a triumph. Then there were short speeches from the retiring conductor who'd conducted half the programme, then from James, from the mayor and a very few words from Miss Wentworth.

'You didn't do badly at all,' she said. 'And that poem went quite well with the music. Thank you.'

But Imogen knew, and thought others did too, that she was utterly delighted. This was the zenith of Miss Wentworth's musical career, even if it took place long after she'd retired.

Imogen drove home feeling very flat. It had been such a magnificent success, everyone had loved everything about it, and now, here she was, in her car, alone (having first given a second violin a lift home) with no one to rejoice with. She knew she would feel better tomorrow. Tomorrow she would remember with joy how wonderful it had been and it would give her courage and inspiration for her first day at her new school. But tonight she felt a bit miserable.

She had no idea when she'd next see Jamie. Of course he hadn't had time to talk to her this evening. She'd last seen him being towed along by a group of dignitaries, just at the moment he'd seen his aunt escorted to a taxi. And the orchestra wasn't convening again for a little while because they hadn't had a break over Christmas. Would she be reduced to watching out for him as he went to visit his aunt – assuming he would visit her. Then what would she do? Rush out and say she was just about to visit Miss Wentworth too? She shuddered at the thought.

She was in the kitchen wondering if she wanted tea or hot chocolate or if she wanted to open a bottle of wine that had been a house-warming present, when there was a quiet knock on the back door. A little startled, she went and opened it.

Standing there, in his long cashmere coat, looking every bit as internationally acclaimed and famous as could be, was James. But as she looked a bit longer she saw that actually, he seemed nervous.

'I'm so sorry I didn't get to speak to you after the performance. I had to meet a hundred different school governors, local business types, teachers, everyone.'

'Right. Well—' She didn't know what to say. Should she ask him in? He would be exhausted, surely. Now he'd said his piece surely he'd want to get off home.

'Can I come in? I'm staying with my aunt and I really wanted to see you.'

Imogen stood back so he could enter. 'Oh, why?'

'To thank you. You were utterly tremendous. And I also wanted to do something I didn't do at Christmas...'

'Buy me a Christmas present?'

'No, kiss you under the mistletoe.'

'But there's no mistletoe!' said Imogen, a little breathless.

'That's a minor detail,' he said and took her into his arms.

Somehow she found herself inside his coat but she didn't mind – she just lost herself in his kiss, which swiftly progressed from an experimental press on her lips to something much more intense.

Her last conscious thought was that he knew about more than just music. They were both breathing a little more heavily when they came apart.

'Goodness me,' said Imogen.

'I've been wanting to do that since Christmas,' said Jamie.

'That's nice,' said Imogen, who was so happy she couldn't think of anything more profound.

'I'm going to be living with my aunt for a

while,' he went on. 'Until I find somewhere more suitable.'

'You'll be able to keep an eye on her.'

'Actually I was hoping to be able to keep an eye on you. Give us a chance to get to know each other apart from at rehearsals.'

Imogen nodded. She was at risk of saying 'how nice' again and it wasn't really adequate for how she was feeling.

'I've brought some champagne to celebrate – the concert, you being so wonderful – everything really. I knew you had an exceptional talent when we played together as well as being one of the kindest, prettiest, sexiest girls I've ever met.'

'Oh.' Her heart was fluttering so hard she could hardly breathe, let alone speak coherently.

'I thought we might light your fire and sit by it? Like we did at Christmas? I loved it so much.'

She got a grip on herself. 'Of course. It's all ready. It just needs a match. I'll get you one.'

He laughed softly as he looked down at her. 'It's very early days of course, but I think I might already have found one.'

Then he took her into his arms again.

Coffee and chocolate truffles

Pink Fizz and Macaroons

'Hello – I wonder whether you can help me,' said Jenny. 'I'm no good at baking, but I need to make a cake.'

In a shop filled with the prettiest, daintiest decorations and cake tins in every shape, Jenny longed to use every tantalising ingredient. But she knew that wouldn't turn her into a baker – any more than buying a set of paints would turn her into an artist.

The woman behind the counter smiled. 'A birthday cake? Special occasion?'

'It's for Mother's Day. Not for my mother, but someone I want to do something nice for. Carrie's my next-door neighbour. She welcomed me when I moved in, making me meals, giving me information. Her family are in Australia, though she Skypes!' She paused to allow the woman behind the counter

325

to admire Jenny's old lady's technical abilities.

'She will keep trying to set me up with people, when I told her I was on a boyfriend-break.' She sighed. 'But she means well, and she told me her grandchildren used to make her cakes on Mother's Day and now they can't. So I want to do it for her instead.'

'Well, traditionally for Mothering Sunday, you'd make a Simnel cake, which is a fruit cake with marzipan. But I'd stick to a sponge if you're new to it.'

'Yes, I'll start with something simple.'

'Or you could buy a cake?' A man's voice from behind her made Jenny turn around. 'From the shop on the corner.'

He was nice-looking – in personality rather than looks – and she didn't want to offend him, but she shook her head emphatically.

'No. I want to make it myself.'

The woman behind the counter agreed. 'It's a fortnight until Mothering Sunday. You've got time to practise.'

Jenny left the shop with a tin, a recipe book and some fail-safes like baking parchment and quick-release oil. 'Do tell me how you get on,' said the woman.

'Yes, do,' said the man. 'You might get into baking. It's satisfying.'

Jenny's first attempts kept the birds amused for days. When she popped in for tea with Carrie, the elderly neighbour who was unknowingly causing her so much stress, she accepted a crumpet soaked in butter.

'You know, I think cakes are overrated,' she said, with her mouth full.

Carrie shook her head. 'A freshly made cake is lovely. Now are you sure about this "boyfriend-break" thing?'

'Yes, I am. Absolutely!'

Carrie tutted. 'My goddaughter's son has just come out of a long-term relationship; he's giving up on women too. How can the world carry on if young people refuse to get together?'

Jenny laughed. 'It's not forever. Don't you think it's good to have some time off between relation-ships?' She hoped this seemed like good sense, not cowardice.

'No, I don't. I believe in getting straight back on the horse!'

They were both laughing. But neither had changed their point of view.

*

'Both cakes have ended up like volcanoes – seen from above.'

The woman, who Jenny now knew as Sylvia, laughed. And the nice man came in while Sylvia was wondering if it was how Jenny greased her tins before putting the parchment in that was making them fail.

Jenny smiled. 'I've been wasting Sylvia's time, trying to find out why my cakes sink. Don't let me hold you up.'

'I can never resist a baking challenge,' he said. 'Are you creaming your butter and sugar together thoroughly?'

'Yes.' Jenny nodded.

'And beating the eggs separately?'

'Yes – of course!'

'Then I think you should try cupcakes. You wouldn't have so much chance of them sinking, and an old lady might prefer individual cakes to keep in the freezer – has she got a freezer?'

Jenny nodded. 'Certainly she has.'

He frowned, considering. 'If you like, I could give you a lesson. At my house, in case your oven's the problem.'

Jenny was pulled up short. She did want to

present Carrie with a cake on Mothering Sunday – and a plate of little ones would be just as good – but…

'It's not a date,' said the man – too firmly, in Jenny's opinion.

'I can vouch for him.' Sylvia smiled. 'He's my daughter's teacher, Mr Edwards. Everyone loves him.'

Mr Edwards blushed. 'Henry, please.'

Henry was a very good teacher. After her lesson in his state-of-the-art kitchen, Jenny was thrilled with her plate of cupcakes. And she adored decorating the spirals of icing (made by Henry) with sparkles and edible glitter.

'Thank you!' She arranged her cakes in a plastic box. 'I am so grateful!'

As she walked home, she wished he'd asked her to stay for a glass of wine. While he wasn't good-looking, really, his kindness, humour and teaching ability had made for a pleasant afternoon. Was she ready to end her boyfriend-break?

The following day, Mothering Sunday, Jenny had invited herself to Carrie's for tea, thrilled that she could present her homemade cakes. She bought a bottle of pink fizz in case Carrie was feeling sad that her family was so far away.

Jenny and Carrie assembled cups and plates. Carrie lit a fire and pulled up a table. Jenny longed to show off her cakes.

Just as Carrie was finally pouring hot water into the warmed pot, the back door opened and Henry walked in. Seeing Jenny, he stopped short. 'Oh! What are you doing here?'

'I thought it'd be nice if we all had tea together,' said Carrie, calm but slightly pink. 'Henry, have you bought a cake?'

'Macaroons. Not that you need them. I happen to know that Jenny's made very good cupcakes.'

Jenny stood up. 'Carrie, I should go...'

Carrie sounded almost cross. 'Henry and I can't eat all this by ourselves.' She frowned. 'I don't approve of this "boyfriend-break" thing. Two nice young people with lots in common refusing to see each other just because you've had a previous relationship. Ridiculous!'

Henry began to laugh. 'You're a terrible old romantic, Aunt Carrie.'

'I'd call you a wicked old matchmaker,' said Jenny, laughing too.

Carrie looked smug. 'I thought there was no

harm in bringing you together. What you do about it is up to you. As long as you both eat some cake.'

Henry and Jenny exchanged glances.

'Honestly, Carrie, going on about missing your grandchildren's cakes when you've had Henry to bake for you.'

'Yes!' Henry protested. 'Making out you'd be alone on Mothering Sunday. It'd serve you right if we left you to it!'

Carrie laughed fondly at him.

'As we're here,' said Jenny, 'we could open the bottle and eat the macaroons. Not sure I can face a cupcake.'

'I'd be happy to give you another lesson,' said Henry. 'If you're still not quite sure about the method.'

'Frankly, I'm not sure I can look a piece of cake in the face for some time. I'd rather go out for a drink.'

'That's possible, too.' Henry took the bottle and eased out the cork.

'Let's have a toast!' said Carrie. 'To the end of the boyfriend-break!'

And everyone raised their glasses, in agreement at last.

The Holiday of a Marriage

When did I realise my marriage had died? Was it when I stopped being excited when I heard my husband's car pull up in the drive? Or when he only ever took me out to dinner because our daughter had phoned him at work to remind him it was my birthday? Hard to tell really, I just knew it had.

It's much easier, in retrospect, to look back and ask yourself when was the last time you sat in bed together, drinking tea and reading your books, or went for a walk on a Sunday afternoon, and held hands, or ambled round Waitrose, discussing what to have for dinner. When you realise it's been months, if not years, since you've done any of them, it's best to be realistic and accept it's over.

Edward and I weren't half-killing each other, but we weren't communicating either. We weren't fighting because we weren't talking beyond the basics. The children had left home and he spent more and more time at work. The bad thing was, I didn't mind that much. I had my own part-time job and was happy to fill the time left over with hobbies. I went to auctions and jumble sales, buying bits and pieces, doing them up, and selling them to local shops and at car-boot sales. I didn't make much money but it satisfied me, and I enjoyed the people it brought me in touch with.

It annoyed me to have to stop messing about with paints, glazes and varnishes to cook him supper, something I'd once loved doing. Now, I was buying all the 'instant and cheating' cookery books and frozen mashed potato in industrial quantities. All that 'fresh and local' thing seemed a waste of time when he just ate, watched the news, read the paper, fell asleep in his chair and then went to bed, without seeming to notice that I stayed up much later than he did.

Currently I was painting a little can, which, when I'd finished with it, would sport an auricular against a pale grey background. I knew just the shop to take it to. The owner's brother sometimes took a turn minding it and he was rather attractive in a laid-back, actorish kind of way. I took the fact that I was even thinking about other men as a sign that things had reached the point of no return. I'd always despised women who played away but now the idea of an affair with a man who really noticed you seemed lovely. I wouldn't do anything about it until I was no longer married though. My marriage vows were still important.

To my credit, I did my best with Edward, but he was so scratchy and irritable. And when the children came round with their partners they noticed he was often quite short. 'What's up with Dad?' my daughter would say. 'He shouldn't speak to you like that. I wouldn't put up with it.'

Somehow I couldn't explain that after being married so long it was hard to talk about your relationship, especially if you hadn't ever made a habit of it, and we hadn't. I didn't think he'd mind us splitting up, really, apart from the upheaval. Emotionally, I thought he'd be fine with it.

But when would I tell him? We'd have to talk about our relationship then. I couldn't just leave a note saying 'It's over.' Edward may have stopped being a good husband but he deserved a proper explanation.

Of course I kept putting it off. I poured all my energy and frustration into restoring things. Had

I had an analyst, they probably would have said I was restoring bric-à-brac because I couldn't restore my marriage. Whatever. But for some reason I didn't want him to have any reason to complain about me. I wanted right on my side. I was also aware that, for an older man, he was quite attractive. He had all his own hair and drove a nice car. I knew someone would snap him up the moment I'd let him go.

Then, just when I was forcing myself to think about Christmas, in late November he told me he'd arranged a holiday for just afterwards.

'We haven't been away for ages,' he said. 'I thought it was time I took you somewhere special.'

Well, I'd been thinking that too, for years, but I hadn't mentioned it. I probably should have mentioned it, because now, it was a bit too late. But when he described what he'd planned, I really wanted to go!

'We'll set off from London City Airport,' he began. 'I know how you hate big air terminals, and fly to Paris. From there we'll go to Guadeloupe, just for a night. And then take the fast ferry to Dominica. Oh, and we'll go business class,' he added.

I absolved him of knowing I was planning to leave him – he just wasn't that sensitive. But if he had known, and had wanted to stop me going, this was the way to do it. I had always longed to go to Dominica, a small, mostly, undeveloped island in the Caribbean that was called the Nature Isle. I loved long walks, following trails and that feeling of history I imagined an island like that would give me. And I had always wanted to travel business class. Edward did a lot, with his work, but on family holidays there were too many of us and we always went the cheapest way possible. We didn't go anywhere very far away, either. So this would be the holiday of a lifetime. Or, the holiday of a marriage.

I justified my rather mercenary decision to go on the holiday by telling myself it wasn't fair to Edward not to. He wouldn't want to go without me and he deserved a holiday. He'd been working incredibly hard. Also, I was bound to be able to find just the right time to tell him. His mobile phone wouldn't ring, a meal wouldn't need cooking and there wouldn't be a property programme I was desperate to watch on television. (I adored property programmes, especially those ones when people went to a whole new location; maybe this was another sign I wanted to move on?)

*

The journey went like clockwork, from the taxi to the airport, via the transfer in Paris that involved a little gentle shopping, to the arrival in the warm exoticism of a Caribbean night. It was perfect. Even the little hotel we stayed in had an unexpected charm. It had only ever been somewhere to sleep before catching the ferry in the morning, but I loved it. In spite of wanting to leave my husband, I was having a good time!

I had decided to wait until we'd recovered from our (rather wonderful) flight, exotic stopover and ferry ride before mentioning being unhappy in our marriage. This meant at least three days of enjoying Dominica, the elegant hotel, the stunning views and the luxurious bedroom before my announcement would spoil it.

Sex had become very infrequent recently – not surprising, really. We were both getting older and Edward worked long hours. The magic had definitely gone out of it for me, and I quite often pretended to be asleep if I thought he might want it. Not that I needed to often, actually.

But that first night, when he moved across the big white bed and took me in his arms, I found something about the scent of ylang-ylang wafting in from the garden, the sounds of the tree frogs and crickets, and, it can't be overlooked, the very good rum punches we'd drunk before dinner, put me in the mood. There's definitely something to be said about a change of scene, good quality sheets and the knowledge that you don't have to get up early in the morning. It was the best sex we'd had for ages. Edward didn't exactly say that, but he did say how wonderful it had been. I had to agree. It made me a bit sad, actually.

Still, one fabulous night wasn't enough to make me change my mind. I was still determined to ask for my freedom, I just had to pick a time.

At the second wonderful hotel, right on the edge of a cliff, where the sunsets were almost too spectacular, we met a delightful honeymoon couple. She was feeling just a bit lonely as you can do on honeymoon, if you don't know your husband well. I was happy to have some female company and the men were both glad to find someone who wanted to go scuba diving. We drank a lot of rum as a foursome, sitting under stars like halogen lamps, breathing in air as soft and warm and perfumed as expensive bath oil, and it was arranged. The boys would leave early and scuba dive, and we women would have breakfast together, lie around the pool and maybe find a craft shop for some gentle shopping later.

We were drinking coffee by the pool, still summoning the energy to put proper clothes on and go shopping, when Julia sighed deeply.

'Are you exhausted? Honeymoons can be tiring.' I thought back to ours – making love several times, night and morning, and it had been lovely, but a bit strenuous.

'No, it's not that. I'm just looking forward to the time when we've been married a bit longer, like you and Edward.'

A flash of guilt stung me. I hadn't told Edward yet, but I hadn't changed my mind. Had Julia been able to guess something? 'What do you mean?'

'Nothing really, it's just you seem so easy with each other. Nick and I still have so much to find out. And Edward adores you!'

'Does he?' This was a bit of a surprise.

'Oh yes. I saw him look at you the other night. It's obvious the sun shines out of you.'

'Oh.' I didn't know what to say, really. I thought Julia must be so loved up herself she was seeing things. But it was rather sweet. Maybe Edward would be more upset than I thought he would be.

'Yes. You'd dropped your hat and were picking it up and he smiled at you with so much love.

You didn't see because of your hat but it made my heart clench.'

Remorse flooded over me. He still loved me! And I had been planning to leave him. How could I have done? Maybe when I'd been feeling neglected he had been loving me all the time. All those little digs he seemed to make probably meant something quite different. How confusing!

I made a big point of being as nice as possible when he and young Nick came back from scuba diving. I got some massage oil from reception and gave him a massage. I was hoping for a bit of 'afternoon delight' but he fell fast asleep. Still, there was always tonight.

As I tiptoed round the bedroom, tidying up, I thought what a lucky escape I'd had. I'd been planning to leave a good and faithful man for reasons that now seemed ridiculous. Thank goodness I hadn't said anything.

A couple of days later, when we'd had a long day following a trail to the most fantastic viewpoint, and had come back to the hotel, he said, 'There's something I need to talk to you about.'

Panic punched me in the solar plexus as I realised what he wanted to say. It seemed so obvious suddenly – he was going to leave me – that was why he'd taken me to this beautiful place, given me such a lovely holiday because he was going to leave me for a younger woman. It all made perfect sense – the late evenings at the office hadn't meant he'd been working, he'd been with Her. His reduced sex drive was because he was getting it elsewhere. I felt such a fool and so sad. Julia must have imagined the smile she'd intercepted. She was young and on her honeymoon; she would think things like that.

I licked my lips. 'Well, what do you want to say?'

'Not here. I want the right spot. We'll both have a shower and change then go to that spot in the garden overlooking the sea where we can watch for the parrots.'

I even thought, as the water poured over my head, that he'd chosen that spot so that if I kicked up a fuss he could shove me over the edge and say I'd slipped. I felt truly ghastly, and wondered if I should leave a note in the bedroom, just in case.

He was definitely edgy as I followed him down the narrow path. This wasn't a pleasant stroll he was taking me on, it was a journey. He had news and I knew what it was.

'Darling,' he began.

That was a little bit encouraging. If he'd called me Anna there'd have been bad news, definitely.

'I don't quite know how to say this . . .'

'I bet you don't,' I said, terrified that I was going to cry. Would that make him push me off the edge and into the sea? It looked quite appealing, actually, very blue and beautiful. But there were a lot of trees to hit on the way down, and rocks at the bottom.

He frowned. 'Sit down.'

I sat, fighting tears. We'd been married for nearly thirty years. Maybe if he was going to leave me I could fling myself down onto those rocks. Then I pulled myself together. That was just silly.

He took my hand. 'Darling – um – you may have noticed that I've been working very long hours lately.'

'Yes,' I snapped, hanging on to my dignity as well as I could.

'It's been for a reason.'

I nodded. The words 'I bet it has' didn't qualify as dignified.

'I've been trying – oh, this is so difficult!'

'Just spit it out,' I said. 'It's going to be hard however you dress it up.' By now I was thinking about the journey home, with us not speaking. I bit my lip.

'OK. I want to take early retirement. I want us to move to the country. I want to be a potter!'

They say shock does funny things to you and they're right. I couldn't take it in. 'What?' It came out as a whisper.

'Oh, I knew you'd find it hard. I'm fed up with working in the oil business. I want to spend more time with you! In the country. Can you bear the idea?'

'You mean, all those extra hours . . .'

'I was doing as many hours, as many deals as I could, so my final salary and my pension will be as good as it can be.'

'Oh.'

'So how do you feel about selling up and starting a new life somewhere else?'

It was hard to put my whirling thoughts into words. He'd never be a perfect husband but I wasn't a perfect wife. What I did know is that I didn't want to stop being one, imperfect or not. Eventually, I managed to say, 'I've always loved those property programmes when they up sticks and move to the country. Now we can do it in real life!'

Then, I'm almost ashamed to relate, he kissed me. And we were late for dinner.

Breakfast with Mr Gillyflower

Hannah's move to the country was working brilliantly. She'd always wanted to move out of the town and live surrounded by fields and woodland, with stunning views. And she saw no reason why she should wait until she was of retirement age to have her dream. The property boom was also a factor. She sold her house in Bristol at the top of the market and bought a tiny, but adorable, cottage – also at the top of the market – in the Cotswolds. She had spare cash with which to do it up from the sale of her Bristol house and she loved her new life. So far, she hadn't had time to be lonely.

She set up a little workspace so she could gaze at hills that gradually became greener as the year edged out of winter into spring. The Severn snaked its silver way to the Bristol Channel and lambs appeared on the hill. Every day she felt joy in her new surroundings, glad that she'd ignored her city friends' negative opinions about turning bucolic so young, and their worries about her having no companions her own age.

'There's a lovely cottage being done up just near me,' she told them. 'A lovely family might move in. The woman and I will start a book group.'

Although she had been joking, the village did have a lot more to offer than many. It wasn't only filled with commuters and retired people. There were many young families and a few newly-weds. She hadn't come across many single people in her age group, but there was a good friendly pub, and a thriving shop with a post office. There was even a hairdresser's which, although more accustomed to traditional wash-and-sets and perms, could do a passable cut-and-blow-dry and keep Hannah in reasonable shape in-between visits to her old hairdresser.

When her work was done or if she needed a break, she climbed the hill so she could see beyond the Severn to Wales. Although she couldn't decide if she was looking at the Brecon Beacons or the Black Mountains, she could pick out the Sugar Loaf and was thrilled to be able to see so far, and to feel ancient ground under her boots.

As winter ended, she worked on her garden. It was pretty and had good soil. There were not too many perennial weeds, apart from couch grass, and even that she found fascinating, as she searched for its pointed root and got it out. The work was satisfying.

The only downside was how steep most of the garden was, and all the sun was at the top, hard to reach without stout boots. The level bit was near the house and in shade a lot of the time. But Hannah was a positive person and she made the best of it. She found a little cast-iron table and chairs in a reclamation yard that she wire-brushed and painted white so when summer finally came she could at least take a glass of wine outside.

However, on her way to the postbox was a garden she coveted. Not directly visible from the road, it was tucked away between two houses, both of which had gardens of their own, so this one wasn't part of their property. She looked at it every time she went to post a letter, but couldn't work out to which house it belonged. Little parcels of land belonging to houses not immediately adjacent to them were a feature of this village, she discovered; relics possibly of property once owned but since sold off.

She longed to get her hands on this garden. It was level, a nice square shape, got the sun all day and had some lovely plants. It was also very over-grown and it was this overgrown-ness that made her want it so much. She didn't want to own it but she desperately wanted to put it in order. No one seemed to be paying it any attention at all and it seemed a terrible waste. She spotted a wooden gate hiding under a lot of a climbing plant that might well prove to be honeysuckle. You had to go along a snicket to reach it, and its inaccessibility made it even more appealing.

She determined to find out who it belonged to and ask if she could tend it for them. She'd do it for nothing, just for the pleasure of seeing those borders cleared, the apple tree pruned and the little vegetable patch productive again. It didn't seem to be attached to a house, but she'd got used to that concept.

Ivy at the shop knew everything. 'Oh, now, that belongs to Mrs Gillyflower. She's in hospital at the moment. She used to spend all her time in that garden. It'll break her heart to see it so overgrown when she comes out. If she comes out,' she added gloomily.

What a wonderful name, thought Hannah,

ignoring the gloom and instantly seeing Mrs Gillyflower as a trim little woman, brown as a nut, her hair in a bun, with eyes bright as a bird's, knowing every plant by name and where it came from. 'Would she mind if I looked after it for her? It breaks my heart to see it like that too.'

Ivy considered, not being one to make snap decisions. 'Well, I don't see the harm in it. You wouldn't be doing one of those makeovers, would you, like they have on television? Putting down slabs? Painting the fence purple?'

'Certainly not!' Hannah hastened to reassure her. 'I'd just tend the beds that are there, get the veg garden clear of weeds and maybe put some potatoes in? Some beans? So Mrs Gillyflower has something nice to look at when she gets back.'

'Well, then, I'm sure that would be fine,' said Ivy, after inspecting Hannah for a while longer.

Hannah walked home and noticed that the house with work going on was developing a rather smart conservatory. She would like a conservatory herself and when she had worked out where one could go, would save up and have one built. But her mind was really on the garden. It was her secret garden.

Then it began to rain. Day after day, water poured down the gullies and gutters, filled the water butts and made the little stream at the end of the lane flood the road. Mrs Gillyflower's garden became more and more overgrown. Hannah could hardly bear to see the hellebores that had flowered so bravely in the late spring covered up with nettles and goosegrass. The celandines, which had looked too optimistic and cheerful, were now taking over.

Every time Hannah went to the shop she asked after Mrs Gillyflower. Apparently she was getting on well and it was hoped she would be home soon. Hannah was beside herself with frustration at not being able to start work on the garden. The moment the rain stopped, Hannah put her garden tools into her wheelbarrow, and ignoring her own garden, wheeled it down the road and started work.

She staggered home some hours later, exhausted. She had cleared half the vegetable patch and created a new compost heap for the weeds. As she watched the water go into her bath, sending up wafts of soothing lavender salts, she hoped she wouldn't have to bag up all those weeds and take them to the tip. The council made compost of them, so it was all right, but the work! And Hannah really wanted to make inroads into the flower beds.

It was a few days later before Hannah was able to go back and she was pleasantly surprised to see how much she'd achieved. She knew she'd worked hard – her muscles were still reminding her – but she didn't remember making a start on that front border or indeed finishing the vegetable patch. But as it had definitely been her plan for that day, she carried on from where she'd left off.

There was a second pile of weeds next to the compost heap she didn't remember leaving there, but it was probably why she'd been thinking about taking some of the garden waste to the tip. She added to the pile and thought how wonderful the garden would be when the roses were out. There was a philadelphus in the corner that would fill the garden with fragrance too.

There were some lovely shrubs in the flower border, but Hannah felt when she'd finished weeding it might look a bit empty, so she made a list of things that were pretty and easy that she would either buy or cadge from neighbours. Old-fashioned aquilegias that Mrs Gillyflower was sure to call 'granny's bonnets', snapdragons, marguerites, pinks and hardy geraniums. She'd put some sweet Williams in the veg patch for planting out next year when they would flower and, of course, some of Mrs Gillyflower's namesake – wallflowers.

Every time Hannah went there seemed to be a

bit more done than she remembered doing. Not a huge amount, but just a bit. After a while she stopped thinking about it.

Then, in May, Hannah was really busy, and it was nearly the end of the month before she was able to go to Mrs Gillyflower's again. She had checked on her progress and Ivy at the shop was able to tell her she'd be out of hospital soon, so things were getting urgent. Then came the morning when Hannah was woken by birdsong and even before the sun was properly up, before she'd had time for more than a cup of coffee, she was down there, overjoyed to be back again.

It was in surprisingly good order. The front border, nearest to the road, which she had more or less cleared, was still weed-free, although the rest of the countryside seemed to be going mad. The vegetable patch was still clear too. She spent a few minutes being surprised then settled down to work, determined to make up for lost time.

She was leaning backwards to relieve the strain on her back when she heard a male voice. 'Hello!'

It didn't come from the road, but from behind her. She turned and saw a man actually in the garden. 'What are you doing here?' she demanded, fright making her abrupt.

'Actually, that's my line.'

He was rather attractive and strangely relaxed considering he'd discovered a trespasser. Hannah took a nervous step back, into the flower bed. 'Is it?'

'Well, my line, my garden, practically the same thing.'

'It's not your garden. It's Mrs Gillyflower's!' Ivy at the shop wouldn't have given her the wrong information.

'I'm her nephew and heir.'

'Well, she's not dead so you can't be her heir, yet!' She paused. 'She's not dead, is she?' Tears sprung to her eyes at the thought, although she'd never met Mrs Gillyflower. Working in her garden made her feel she was an old friend, possibly even a favourite aunt. She didn't want her to die, at least, not until she'd seen her garden again.

'No,' said the man, 'but I'm afraid she won't be able to live on her own again.'

'Oh.'

'She'll have to go into sheltered accommodation. I'm doing up her house so we can rent it out, to help fund her care.'

So the neat little woman with the bird-like eyes and the bun at the back wouldn't walk around the flower beds, admire the veg patch and suggest where the sweet peas should go, happy to see her garden blooming and productive. Hannah sighed. She'd worked terribly hard to that end and now this man was here and had taken her project from her. Him being attractive made it worse not better. 'I'd better go.' She began to gather up her tools, trying not to cry.

'Do you have to? I was really appreciating your help. I've been taken up with the house and haven't been able to do all that much.'

'So you've been gardening here too?'

'Of course! You must have noticed. I thought I'd done quite a lot!' He seemed indignant.

Hannah sighed. 'I suppose I did notice, I just – chose to ignore it, thought…I don't know what I thought.'

'You thought the gardening fairies did it?'

Hannah bit back a sudden smile. It wasn't funny. 'Well, *you* obviously thought they did!' she accused him. 'Otherwise why didn't you stop me? I was trespassing!'

'But in a good way! I was delighted to have help. Between us we're getting on really well! It does seem a shame to stop now.'

'I've worked incredibly hard for nothing!'

'No, you haven't. At least, you were doing it for nothing before.'

'No, I wasn't! I was doing it for Mrs Gillyflower! I imagined her coming back from hospital, dreading to see her garden overgrown and finding it all wonderful!' She paused. 'I feel such a fool!'

'There's no need to feel a fool.'

'I should have noticed the house – which one is it?'

'The one on the corner with the new conservatory. You couldn't possibly have guessed this was its garden. It's going to make it quite difficult to sell if we have to, the garden being so far away.'

'It obviously didn't bother your aunt. It was – is a lovely garden.'

'Yes, and she will see it. She can't come back to live, but she could see the garden and she will appreciate our kindness. As I do. You're a very kind person.'

At that moment Hannah didn't feel kind, she felt stupid and it wasn't pleasant.

'I won't be able to get it all done on my own,' the man went on. 'It would be wonderful if you could help.'

'And what do I get out of it?' asked Hannah, in an effort to sound tough.

He smiled and shrugged. 'The usual? A really good dinner, cooked by me, fine wine, brandy. Are you single, by the way?'

Hannah tossed her head, sure that he knew she was. 'Are you?'

'Yes.'

'You can't bribe me with offers of food, you know.'

'What can I bribe you with, then?'

Hannah had had time to think about this. 'If I help you get this garden in order for your aunt, I want you to help me get my garden in order.'

'You mean you neglected your garden so you could do this one?'

'Not entirely, but it needs terracing.' This idea had only just occurred to her, but it was a good one.

'Well, I could do that, I suppose,' he said thoughtfully. 'But couldn't we do the meal thing too? I've been quite lonely since I've been down here. It's mostly young families and retired people.'

'We could go for a drink. The pub's quite good. It does food, too.'

'But I want to try out the new kitchen.' His eyes crinkled at the corners as he smiled. 'My name's Edward, Edward Gillyflower.'

A most inappropriate thought flickered into Hannah's head as she gave him her name. If she married this man she'd be Mrs Gillyflower and this garden might actually become hers. It was a ridiculous idea and she dismissed it instantly, but she still smiled.

'Well then, Mr Gillyflower, if you promise to terrace my garden, we might well have a deal.'

'It will be my pleasure!' he said. 'Where is your house?'

'Come with me and I'll show you. I didn't have any breakfast. I'll make you a bacon sandwich.'

'If I call you Hannah, will you call me Edward?'

'Maybe.'

At that he hooked his arm through hers and together they walked up the hill to Hannah's house.

A Magazine Christmas

'As it's the first time they've come to us for Christmas, I really do want to get it right.'

Jess knew all this perfectly well. Even if she hadn't endured seven perfect Christmases at her in-laws' Georgian rectory, her husband had been telling her since October. And ever since October, she had been dreading it.

'You did make the puddings when I told you?' her husband went on.

Jess nodded, wondering if she should mention he had a fleck of shaving foam on his neck, or not bother.

'And you ordered the free-range, corn-fed bronze turkey from that farm in Norfolk?'

'What?'

'Through the butcher? You did do that, darling, didn't you? The right bird is crucial.'

'Oh yes. Through the butcher.'

'You should really pick it up today.'

'It's only the twenty-second. Where am I going to keep it?'

'I cleared a space in the shed. It should be fine in there. Oh, and the ham. I hope you ordered a big enough one. I'd better give you some money.'

Dominic, supremely elegant, except for the shaving foam, took out his wallet and produced an alarmingly thick wodge of twenty-pound notes. 'I know old Higgins doesn't take credit cards – lives in the dark ages – so you'll have to pay him in cash. Bloody good butcher, though.'

Jess reflected that 'bloody good' was the right sort of epithet for a butcher.

'Here.' Dominic handed her the money.

'Will it be all that?' Jess looked at it. Living in a mostly cashless society, she had not seen so much of it in one lump for ages, if ever.

'Oh yes, and the rest. Here, you'd better have a bit more.'

'Darling, that's over two hundred pounds! For a turkey and a ham!'

'It's not all for the turkey, Pumpkin, it's for the stuffing. Now don't let Higgins fob you off with ready-made sausage meat, get him to do you some specially. Have you got a list of the other stuffing ingredients?'

'They're in the book, aren't they?'

'Yes, well make sure you don't forget anything, like pine nuts, or pecans. And we need two stuffings, one each end.'

'It's not considered good practice to cook the stuffing actually in the turkey,' said Jess.

'Rubbish! My mother's always cooked the turkey with the stuffing in. Never done anyone any harm.' He pecked her cheek, giving her a good whiff of exquisite aftershave. Sometimes Jess thought his aftershave was what she liked best about her husband, that and his beautiful suits.

When she had loaded the dishwasher with their two coffee cups, two plates, two saucers and two knives, she washed the orange squeezer and the glasses by hand. Dominic didn't like her to put glasses in the dishwasher. As she smoothed on her hand cream afterwards, she wondered about all that money on the kitchen table.

Dominic was a kind husband, at least he thought he was. He didn't expect her to work, while they waited to start a family, and was happy for her to spend a couple of afternoons a week doing watercolours. He didn't even comment on the fact that after three years of trying, she hadn't yet become pregnant – at least, he didn't comment often. He did make reference to his brother's huge and noisy progeny sometimes, implying that if his brother could father so many children, the problem couldn't possibly lie with him. His family, it was acknowledged, was perfect. And, with his family, so was Christmas.

The first Christmas she had spent with them, as a bride, she had been enchanted, if overwhelmed by the ritual, the perfection, the enormous quantity of food, the impression that this was the house on which every magazine Christmas special was based.

The decorations were traditional but perfect. Dominic's mother made her own Christmas wreath out of holly, which obediently produced berries, every year. Swags of greenery decorated both huge fireplaces and even the downstairs loo had a jug of rosemary and box.

The tree, real of course and ten feet high, was decorated with glass baubles from Bavaria, antique angels, real crystal snowflakes and hand-carved cherubs. There was nothing on it that wasn't tasteful, no bells made out of egg boxes and tin foil, Santas made from lavatory rolls and crêpe paper, no cotton-wool snowmen. It didn't even have lights, but proper candles, in holders which had been in the family for aeons.

Jess had never asked Dominic to go to her parents' at Christmas, not after that time when they were first engaged, and he was so stiflingly polite. Her parents were very understanding and never made a thing of it.

This year, because they were having the house re-wired and new central heating put in, Dominic had persuaded his parents to leave their beautiful house in the country, and have Christmas with them, in their terraced house in town.

'We've got to show them that we can do it right,' Dominic had said, so many times that Jess stopped listening. He didn't mean 'we' anyway, he meant 'her'.

It may have been her inability to produce children that made her unsatisfactory to her parents-in-law, but with so many grandchildren, Jess didn't think so. She was unsatisfactory because she wasn't enough of a homemaker, wasn't educated to the required high standard and wasn't connected to any ancient families. She just wasn't posh enough.

So there it was, a big pile of money on the table. She should really have told Dominic that she hadn't made the puddings on Stir-up Sunday, as requested. He'd been away, and she'd gone to see a film with a girlfriend, thinking she'd do it another day. Somehow the day when she felt willing to spend all day cutting special whole candied fruit into cubes, stoning raisins, and getting the grit out of Vostizza currents, and then to fill the kitchen with steam never came.

She also should have mentioned that when she went into Higgins, the 'bloody good butcher', who leered and letched and intimidated Jess, he had gleefully told her that she was too late to order a turkey, and that next year she'd have to be better organised.

So, all that money to spend on a turkey, (and a York ham), and neither turkey nor ham forthcoming. She picked up the money, stuffed it into her wallet, and got ready to go shopping.

She stood at the bus stop, wondering where to buy food of the appropriate quality, and decided on Selfridges. It was a pity that on the way she spotted a little boutique that had a sale on. She hopped off the bus at the next set of lights and went back to it.

She came out feeling light-headed, wearing all her new clothes. She felt so light-headed that she went into a café for coffee and ordered white wine instead.

'What is happening to me?' she wondered, looking at the much depleted amount of money in her purse. 'Why aren't I doing what I was told?'

It was the cash that did it, she realised. She and Dominic shared a credit card, but he went through the bill with a very sharp eye. She couldn't possibly have put the bright, slightly hippy clothes she was wearing on the card. There was a sort of blousy sexiness about the way the top fell off her shoulder slightly, showing far more cleavage than she usually did. Dominic would hate it; he liked her to shop at Aquascutum.

She sipped her wine and considered her plight. She was going to get into an awful lot of trouble. She even wondered if Dominic would instigate a divorce, his grounds being not taking Christmas seriously enough – an especially heinous crime when they were having his parents.

They'd already broken several taboos. They weren't having people in for drinks on Christmas morning, when real people were in their dressing gowns, opening presents, drinking sweet sherry. Dominic's parents, Sebastian and Margot, served Buck's Fizz, hot sausage rolls and mince pies to women who wore court shoes and men who asked Jess every year if she was pregnant yet. When told that she wasn't they told her she was a career girl and that she shouldn't put it off too long. 'The old biological clock is ticking away!' they would say, as if they were the first, and then they would pat her bottom.

Jess had also refused to carve the potatoes into perfect ovals, as suggested by Gary Rhodes. Margot had been doing it for years, long before Gary Rhodes appeared on television and Dominic mentioned them when he was promising to help.

For once, Jess had been adamant. 'If your mother chooses to make sculptures out of her roast potatoes, that's fine, but I'm not doing it. I won't have time.'

'Mother always has time, and she had children to look after.'

'That's low, Dominic, and you know it is!' Using this as an excuse, she had disappeared into the spare room and slept there, glad to be spared his tedious love-making.

She'd also argued against having a starter, but lost that battle. She'd agreed on segmented oranges and grapefruit, in some sort of alcohol. When she'd have a moment to scrape pith off the fruit, which would be walnut-sized by the time she'd finished peeling it with a knife, she didn't yet know. Dominic was going to prepare a timetable for her, which would presumably tell her.

Jess was gloating over the beautiful purple, jewel-encrusted mules she had bought to go with her outfit, when a man asked if he could share her table. Guiltily, Jess thrust the shoe back in its box.

'You're not Cinderella, are you? If so, can I be your Prince Charming?' He was older than Dominic, more solid, with smiling eyes and a very attractive voice.

'I know this is the pantomime season, but no, I'm not Cinderella. I was just admiring the shoes I've just bought, and wondering if they were worth it.'

'Can I get you another glass of wine, then you can show me your shoes.'

Jess may have denied being Cinderella, but he was definitely charming, if not actually a prince. He admired her shoes, he made her laugh, he made her feel attractive, and best of all, he was extremely impressed when she told him what she'd done with the turkey money. 'A woman of spirit, I see. How interesting.'

Dominic had never found her interesting.

*

Jess wore all her new clothes, including the purple mules for Christmas dinner. She had insisted on serving the meal in the evening, or according to the timetable Dominic created on his computer, she would have to get up at 5 a.m. to start cooking the turkey.

Jess felt wonderful; accomplished, beautiful and in control. Aware of the change in her, Dominic gave her a glass of champagne before wrapping himself in blue stripes and heaving the turkey out of the oven to rest. When they all sat down to eat he raised his glass to her admiringly.

'This is splendid darling!'

The turkey was admired by everyone. 'So moist, well done, Jess!' said Sebastian. 'We'll make a cook of you yet.'

'I always do say, buying the right bird is vital,' said Margot.

Jess offered a small prayer of thanks to Bernard Matthews and helped herself to roast potatoes, which, she was pleased to note, were browner and crisper than her mother-in-laws had ever been.

Dominic laughed, sounding terribly like his father. 'I say choosing the right *bird* is what counts.

Eh, darling? You're looking particularly lovely tonight.'

Jess inclined her head. Choosing definitely was important; what to wear, what to spend your money on, and when to tell her husband that she was leaving him – for a man with smiling eyes, who appreciated fabulous shoes and who told her the secret of roast potatoes.

Coming February 2015

A Vintage Wedding

Katie Fforde

Read on for an exclusive sneak peek

Chapter One

Beth Scott glanced at the time, hurriedly disconnected Skype and then her laptop. She was aware that if she didn't get a move on she'd be late for the event at the village hall. Although it didn't sound all that exciting, and she had no idea what it was all in aid of, she had allowed herself to be sold a 'lucky programme' when she was in the village shop. To claim her prize she'd have to be there. Besides, and this felt very pathetic, she might meet someone: a potential friend or, better really, someone who might give her a job. She had lived alone in Chippingford for a week and, so far, had only spoken to people in the shop and her sister Helena, courtesy of Skype. She had been to far-flung friends for Christmas – not having gone home for the first time ever – and so hadn't caught up with her old friends there. She considered herself borderline lonely and on-the-line in need of employment. She wasn't completely broke, but she was having to be very careful with money.

Still, as she went out of her little rented cottage (a holiday let she was grateful to have been lent) and crossed the village green she felt again how lucky she was to have ended up in such a pretty spot. Not quite 'chocolate box', the village was pretty enough, with its trilogy of church, pub and shop all on the green and the school not much further off.

She arrived at the hall, which was behind the church, and realised it didn't quite live up to the charm of the rest of the village. She opened the door feeling shy and flustered. She hadn't even glanced in the mirror, she'd just pulled up the hood of her parka to cover her unfamiliar short hair and run out of the house. But the friendly expression on the face of the woman standing just inside the door made all that unimportant.

'Oh, hello,' said the woman, 'I'm so glad you came! I'm Sarah. We met in the shop?'

'And you sold me a lucky programme,' Beth reminded her. At the time Beth had been reluctant to spend a pound on something she couldn't eat but now she felt it had been worth it. Sarah was attractive, middle-aged and looked as if she might be a little bit scatty. And it was almost as if she had been waiting for Beth.

'This is my daughter, Lindy. She'll look after you. There's another person not yet of pensionable age in the corner. Maybe you'd like to join her?'

'My mum assumes because we're almost the only people here under fifty, we'll become friends,' said Lindy, leading Beth through the crowd. 'She means well and was so pleased when she told me she'd sold programmes to two people she didn't know. She might have discovered oil on the village green, she was so delighted.'

Beth smiled. 'I'm Beth. And I can't believe people would be all that thrilled to have their village green dug up for oil.' She liked the look of Lindy. She too was just wearing jeans and a sweater under her jacket. Her honey-blonde hair was in a tangled knot on her head and she was wearing a Spider-Man badge.

Lindy got Beth's little joke. 'Bad example. But I'm sure you know what I mean.'

'I do.' She thought about her own mother. She grouped people together too. Only her typecasting was based on money, class or status.

Lindy went on shyly, 'Mum thinks I desperately need to meet new people so if she ever sees someone she doesn't know from when I was at primary school, she falls on them and introduces us in the hope they could be what she calls "a bosom buddy".'

Beth laughed. 'And you've probably got loads of friends already.' Lindy was pretty and seemed friendly, and she was local; she was bound to know plenty of people.

Lindy shook her head. 'Not that many, actually. Most of them have moved away and Mum worries. Look, there's Rachel. Mum said she's from London. She lives in that house that's had all the work done. She hasn't been there long.'

'Cool!' said Beth. 'Let's join her.' She felt encouraged. She liked Lindy already and was prepared to like Rachel, too.

Rachel was a bit older than she was, Beth decided. And she looked quite 'London' in a well-groomed, sleek way. Beth suddenly felt slightly grubby.

But in spite of her glossy, straightened red hair and possibly whitened teeth, Rachel smiled as if pleased to be joined by Lindy and Beth. 'Hello, you must be Lindy . . .'

'And I'm Beth.'

'Rachel.'

Looking at her more closely, Beth thought Rachel must be lonely too; why else would she be so pleased to see a couple of women who were probably a bit younger and definitely less well dressed than her? If she hadn't been in her house long, she might not have had time to meet many people.

There was a slightly awkward pause and then Lindy said, 'I love your hair, Beth.'

Beth ran her hand over her head. Her very short haircut was extremely recent and she still hadn't quite got used to it. 'You don't think it looks like I had it cut off for charity?'

Rachel and Lindy laughed. 'No, not at all!' said Lindy.

'*Did* you have it cut off for charity?' said Rachel.

'No! Although I wish I had now, then there'd have been some point to it, rather than it being a spur-of-the-moment thing. I've always had very long hair, you see. My mother didn't ever want me to cut it.'

'It looks brilliant,' said Rachel. 'You've got the face for it. And it makes your eyes look enormous. Sorry, that was a bit personal.'

'Sausage roll, anyone?' asked a cheery-faced

woman of substantial proportions holding a plate of them. 'I made them myself.'

'They are amazing,' said Lindy. 'Mrs Townley's pastry is famous in the village.'

'Thank you, Lindy. Glad to be appreciated,' said Mrs Townley.

Beth remembered she hadn't eaten much that day and helped herself. 'Have a couple!' insisted Mrs Townley.

'It would be rude not to,' said Lindy, encouragingly.

'In which case,' said Beth, and took two.

As she ate, Beth looked around and realised that without the throng of people the village hall would have been pretty dreary. The paintwork was green and maroon and needed redoing. The ceiling was high, with exposed beams and rafters, but it was in desperate need of either a good scrub or total redecoration. 'This could be a lovely building,' she said to no one in particular.

'That's what I thought,' said Rachel. 'But I tend to fall in love with old buildings.'

'Please fall in love with this one,' said Lindy. 'The three groups who use it currently think it's just fine as it is but Mum thinks the roof is about to either collapse or start leaking badly. She says unless people get together and do something about it, it'll fall into total disrepair. She wants to form a "Save the Village Hall" committee.'

'It would be an awful shame to let it just fall down,' said Rachel, staring up into the rafters.

Beth stared up there too and found they didn't look better with closer inspection.

'Here's the wine,' said Lindy after a few moments. 'It may be home-made.'

'I'm sure it's fine,' said Beth. She sensed Lindy was embarrassed about the possibility of home-made wine but to her it felt totally in keeping with what she thought of as life in the country. Beth took a glass being offered by a grey-haired lady wearing a dashing knitted lamé wrap. 'This will be the first glass of wine I've had since I've been here.'

'Are you new here, too?' said Rachel. 'I've only been here ten days. Living here permanently, I mean.'

'Everyone was very excited when you moved in,' said Lindy. 'No one was quite sure who you'd turn out to be. A family? A couple?'

'It's just me,' said Rachel.

Beth couldn't decide if there was a touch of defiance in the way she said this and to cover the slight awkwardness, she said, 'Well, I'm in a rental property.'

'The pretty one with the run-down porch?' asked Lindy.

'That's the one. It's been lent to me by my sister's in-laws-to-be,' said Beth. 'Sorry, that's a bit complicated.'

Rachel frowned. 'Your sister's getting married and her fiancé's parents have lent you a house?'

'Yes! That sounds so much clearer than how I put it. The reason they lent it to me is that I'm organising the wedding.' She paused for dramatic effect. 'Via Skype.'

The other two laughed in surprise. 'That sounds a bit of a challenge,' said Lindy.

'It is – especially on almost no money. But my sister arranged the house for me when I had a major falling-out with my mother and really couldn't go home after uni, so I do owe her. I'm going to try really hard to do a good job,' said Beth.

'Doesn't your mother want to organise your sister's wedding?' asked Lindy.

'Yes!' said Beth. 'She does. But she wants to take over every single detail so Helena asked me to do it. While she's out of the country.'

'I love the thought of a wedding organised via

Skype,' said Rachel.

'You could have the do in the village hall,' said Lindy, 'if we get it restored in time. That would be nice and cheap.'

'That's not a bad idea, actually,' said Beth. 'When is it likely to be restored by? They want the wedding at the end of August.'

Lindy shook her heard. 'Sorry. I didn't mean to get your hopes up. It's not likely to be done this year, not realistically.'

Rachel had been staring at the ceiling again. 'A lick of paint would make a huge difference.'

Beth nodded slowly as the picture formed in her mind. 'It would! With masses of flowers and bunting.'

'Well, I could help with the bunting,' said Lindy. 'I can sew.'

'Is that your job?' asked Beth. 'Sewing?'

Lindy shrugged. 'In a way, but mostly my job is looking after my boys.'

'You've got children?' said Beth. She was surprised. She judged Lindy to be roughly the same age as she was, in her early twenties, and it seemed very young to have children.

Lindy nodded. 'Two of them. Six and three. Little monkeys a lot of the time.'

Beth got the impression she'd added the 'little monkeys' bit for form's sake.

'So, what do you do?' asked Lindy. 'Apart from organising your sister's wedding?'

Beth shrugged. 'Nothing at the moment. I need to find something soon. I've got savings and although Mum doesn't know, Dad hasn't stopped my allowance from when I was at uni, but I'd like to tell him I don't need it any more.'

'Have you just graduated?'

'Last summer. I did what my mother called Facebook and Barmaiding, although there was a bit more to it. I hadn't got the grades I needed for English, which is what she wanted me to do, and picked a course as far away from home as possible. And I'm currently unemployed.' Beth paused, worried that Lindy would think she was a complete flake. 'I did bar work in Brighton up until Christmas but got really fed up.' She made a face. 'My mother said it was my fault for doing such a ridiculous course and did you really need a degree to be a barmaid.' Beth laughed, trying to hide that this had hurt her. 'You don't, really.'

'Do you think university was a waste of time?' asked Lindy.

'Absolutely not. It got me away from home,

I learnt loads about life and how to be independent and had a great time.' Beth paused. 'You didn't go?'

Lindy shook her head. 'No. I got pregnant instead. That taught me a lot too!'

'I bet,' said Beth.

'I love this building!' said Rachel, who hadn't really been listening. 'It's got such rustic charm.'

'You'd love it less if you saw the Ladies,' said Lindy.

'Ah. The Ladies,' said Beth, aware of a need now she thought about it. 'Is it over there?'

Lindy nodded. 'Through the door marked "TO LETS". Someone thought it was funny to take out the "I".'

Beth laughed and set off for the sign. As she left the others she thought she heard Lindy say, 'Good luck.'

The loo was at least clean but it was freezing cold and the seat had a worrying crack in it. Beth felt that even though the building was used by very few, they might have at least replaced that vital piece of equipment.

As she came out, drying her hands on her jeans, she was stopped by a man of late middle age who was vaguely familiar. 'Hello! You're the young lady living in the cottage above the stream?'

Beth considered. 'That's right.'

'I've seen you round and about. How are you getting on up there?'

'Very well, thank you.' She smiled.

Encouraged, the man went on, 'Well, I'm Bob. I've got the garage on the Cheltenham road. It's nice to see a new young face about the place.'

Beth nodded, wondering how she felt about everyone knowing where she lived and that she was new to the area, but she decided it was part of village life, like excellent sausage rolls and home-made wine.

'A lot of the new people are second-home owners,' Bob went on. 'We need young people who'll settle down here.'

For a second Beth wondered if the village had suffered a Pied Piper of Hamelin type incident. Then she realised it would be that most of the local young people had moved away because they couldn't afford property in the area. Or there were no jobs. 'It's a gorgeous area. Even in winter it's pretty.'

'It is that.' Bob laughed loudly, then he said, 'And they're just about to draw the lucky programmes. Have you got yours there? It's like a raffle, see?'

Beth, who had worked this out herself, produced

her programme from the pocket of her parka as they both moved nearer the stage at one end of the hall. Bob waited expectantly while the announcements went on. He seemed to take Beth's good fortune personally and wanted to see her win something.

Of course she didn't until almost the last number. Looking over her shoulder Bob called out, 'We've a winner here!'

Beth checked her number. She was indeed a winner. Slightly hoping it wasn't the home-made parsnip liqueur that was on the list of prizes, she waited for developments.

'It seems there's some confusion,' said the man behind the microphone. 'We've got two programmes with that number.'

Beth began to say she didn't mind not winning and was happy to resign but her champion wouldn't let her. 'Well, how's that happened?' Bob demanded.

'We'll have to sort that out later,' said the man with the microphone, which he continued to use although people were now clustering round and he didn't need the extra volume. 'Who else has got the lucky programme?'

Lindy appeared with Rachel. 'Here!'

Beth sighed with relief. 'Oh, phew, that's OK.

You can have whatever it is, Rachel. I'm sure I won't mind not having it.' Then she worried that she'd sounded rude.

'Do you know what it is?' said Rachel.

'No. Do you?' said Beth.

Rachel nodded. 'It's a really lovely vintage tea set. You probably will mind not having it.' She looked wistful as she said this. 'I have two plates in the same pattern at home. It's Shelley.'

'Then you must have it,' insisted Beth. 'Really.'

'That wouldn't be right,' said Rachel.

'No, really—'

Possibly sensing this could go on some time, Lindy broke in. 'If it were my boys I'd say you had to share it.'

Rachel turned to her. 'What, a timeshare tea set?'

Lindy nodded. 'Take it in turns to own it.'

Beth had now had time to inspect the tea set displayed in a pretty wicker hamper, and discovered that it was indeed extremely pretty. And as she did so she visualised lots and lots of pretty tea sets filled with cake and sandwiches. A vintage wedding: that would suit Helena far better than the glittering champagne affair their mother had wanted for her, and would be much more affordable too. She suddenly suffered a stab of panic when she realised what she'd taken on with this wedding. Really, she hadn't a clue what was involved. She'd have to trawl the internet and find out. One thing she had learnt at uni that was how useful eBay and Gumtree and Freecycle were.

'Why don't we go to the pub to discuss it?' suggested Lindy. 'I could ring my gran – she's got the boys – and tell her I'll be a bit later than I said and then we can miss the speeches.'

A short time later the three young women were entering the pub.

Beth looked about her. It wasn't quite what she was expecting from a country pub. There was no thick patterned carpet, horse brasses and leather seating areas. It was much more shabby chic, like someone's larger than average sitting room. There was a glamorous black-haired woman behind the bar who seemed to be in charge.

Suddenly Beth remembered how little money she had with her. 'Um, can I suggest, unless we want three drinks, we just pay for ourselves?'

Lindy seemed relieved. 'Good idea. I can't stay for three drinks, anyway.'

They went up to the bar. 'Hi, Sukey,' said Lindy. 'I've brought new people with me.'

Sukey smiled. 'Cool. What are you all having?'

'Red wine,' the three chorused.

'Coming up. And what's that you've got under your arm?' She pointed to the tea set that Rachel was carrying in the basket.

'It's one of the prizes from the lucky programmes. Beth and Rachel both won it,' Lindy explained. 'There was a mistake in the printing on the programmes.'

'Tricky!' said Sukey and placed two glasses of wine on the counter. Then she reached for another glass.

They carried their drinks to a vacant sofa next to a fire that crackled and spat behind a fireguard. Stretched out in front of the fire was a greyhound, who lifted the last inch of his tail in acknowledgement of the young women.

'Sorry, I wasn't really listening before, but remind why you're organising your sister's wedding?' asked Rachel.

'Basically my mother feels it's her absolute right to plan my sister's wedding and have it as she wants it. If she's paying she gets to decide on everything.'

'A Mumzilla,' said Lindy. 'Heard about them. Go on.'

'Well, my sister doesn't want to get married in a cathedral she's never stepped foot inside before and then go to a massive hotel and invite a whole lot of people she's never met.' She paused. 'So I said I'd sort it out for her.'

'I'm assuming there's a good reason why she can't do it herself?' said Rachel. 'I can't imagine letting anyone else organise something so important.'

Beth nodded. 'She and her fiancé have gone travelling. They felt they'd never have the opportunity otherwise. Jeff has got a new job starting in September, so it was now or never. They didn't have gap years to go travelling in.' Beth realised she sounded as if she was apologising for them. 'Anyway, you can imagine how that went down with our mother. Just appalled,' she added, in case her new friends couldn't imagine this. 'And I'm in a new place, currently with no job, so I offered.'

'Goodness,' said Lindy. 'My mum was great about my wedding. She was great about the divorce, too.'

'And is there a reason why your mother thinks it's her right to plan your sister's wedding?' asked Rachel. She seemed a woman who liked to get to the bottom of things.

'I think her mother totally told her what to do

and so now it's her chance to have control. She thinks my sister is being totally unreasonable not letting her.'

'What about your dad?' asked Lindy.

'Bless him, he did give my sister money towards the wedding but she spent it on her trip of a lifetime.'

'Didn't he mind?' Rachel gave a little shake of her head. 'Sorry, I seem to be asking questions all the time.'

'It's OK. And he didn't really mind but he was surprised. But Helena said that Mum would still try to control the wedding and she'd rather spend the money on seeing the world.'

'So what's your budget?' asked Lindy. 'If you'd like me to help, I am very good at doing things for almost nothing.'

'Well, that's great!' said Beth, laughing. 'Because that is exactly what my budget is. Almost nothing.'

'I think that sounds a brilliant challenge,' said Rachel. 'I was married – for a short time – and we had a very smart, very upmarket wedding for a very few upmarket friends. I think a budget wedding sounds much more fun.'

'My wedding was fairly small too,' said Lindy. 'But I was pregnant so I didn't really care.' She gave an embarrassed little laugh. 'It only lasted long enough for me to get pregnant again.'

'Don't tell me if you don't want to,' said Beth, 'but how did you get pregnant when you seem so sensible? And then do it again?'

'That is a bit personal,' said Rachel, frowning at Beth.

'No, it's OK. My trouble was, I slept with the wrong brother.'

'Ooh. Big mistake,' said Beth.

Lindy pushed her and grinned. Beth stopped feeling guilty for asking the question. Lindy seemed happy to talk about it. 'I was madly in love – well, of course it wasn't love, it was a crush, but a massive one – with this boy who was much older. Five years older.'

'That's nothing when you're grown up,' said Rachel. 'But it's massive when you're – how old?'

'Sixteen,' said Lindy. 'The brother left to go abroad to study or work or maybe both, I can't remember now. Anyway, his younger brother and I were both upset and got a bit drunk. It turned out he'd had a crush on me but I never noticed because of Angus, his brother. We turned to each other for comfort.'

'That's a word for it I hadn't heard,' said Beth, anxious to keep things light.

'Beth!' said Rachel.

'Sorry,' muttered Beth.

'I got pregnant and – massive disapproval from his parents of course. I had ruined his life—'

'He ruined yours,' said Rachel indignantly.

'Anyway, we rubbed along until I got pregnant again. He got over his crush and we parted.'

'Did you get over yours?' asked Beth.

'Beth! It was a crush. They don't last forever,' said Lindy, but something about the way she said it made Beth wonder.

She sighed, slightly deflated by Lindy's story. 'So you two are great examples of how marriages can go wrong,' she said. 'Maybe I'd better tell my sister not to bother.'

Rachel and Lindy both protested. 'No! I was only seventeen when we got married,' said Lindy. 'It was bound to fail.'

'And I got married . . .' Rachel paused. 'Well, I did love him. And I think he loved me. But not quite enough. We drifted apart.' She paused. 'And maybe I wasn't exactly perfect, wife-wise.'

'I'd hate to put anyone off marriage because mine failed,' said Lindy.

'Me too,' said Rachel. She smiled. 'Besides, if you tell your sister not to get married I can't help with the wedding.'

'Do you want to? Are you a wedding planner?'

Rachel shook her head. 'I'm an accountant – freelance – but I'd love to be more creative.'

Lindy nodded. 'I have heard that creative accountants don't have a great reputation.'

Because of her solemn expression it took the others a second to realise she was joking.

'That's why I've had to find other outlets for my creativity,' said Rachel. 'I'd love to have a go at the village hall, for instance.'

'In what way?' said Lindy. 'I'm sure my mother would love to hear your ideas.'

'I haven't had time for ideas yet but I just think it's a lovely building and if it was done up, it could earn its keep. So perfect for a wedding. It's only a short walk from the church. Imagine the bridal party processing across the village green—'

'Dragging their dresses in the mud,' said Lindy.

'—to an old-fashioned feast spread out on trestle tables,' Rachel finished, and then added, 'With bunting.'

Beth looked at her. 'That does sound wonderful.

And the sort of thing my mother would absolutely hate. I'll suggest it to Helena.'

'I do think you should do what Helena wants, not what your mother would hate,' said Lindy.

Beth nodded. 'So do I, but I do think Hels would love that. I'll suggest it to her next time we can Skype. What with her being on the move all the time we can't always,' she added.

'But would she want to get married here?' asked Lindy.

'I think she might. Jeff's parents have connections here. The cottage where I'm living at the moment is their pension. They want to retire somewhere down here.'

'But the village hall is hardly fit for a wedding,' said Lindy. 'You were only in it for a short time while it was full of people. It looks at its best then. It needs a lot of work.'

'Remind me when the wedding is, Beth?' Rachel asked.

Beth shrugged. 'We haven't got a specific date yet. The end of August sometime.'

'Will you still be here then?' asked Lindy. 'Won't your house be rented out?'

'It might be. I'm there now because their insurance isn't valid if it isn't occupied or something.

When and if I find a job, I'll be on the lookout for something else. I don't suppose there are many jobs round here.'

'No,' said Lindy. 'You might have to work for yourself in some way, like I do.'

Beth sighed. 'The trouble is, I don't have any skills,' she said.

'Well, look for a job for now and concentrate on your sister's wedding,' said Lindy.

'That'll certainly keep me busy until August,' said Beth.

'Plenty of time to arrange a wedding, if you focus,' said Rachel.

'Not if we've got to do the village hall first,' said Lindy.

'We'll work better with something to aim towards,' said Rachel. 'A big wedding at the end of the summer could be just the incentive.'

Lindy looked at her doubtfully. 'I think you'd better go on Mum's committee,' she said. 'She'll be thrilled. It'll need a lot of enthusiasm.'

'That would be great for me,' said Rachel. 'I'm doing a bit of work in Letterby but it's quite a long commute. I'm hoping to get some work round here. I know there aren't that many businesses but some of them might need me to sort out their finances. Being on a committee might give me good contacts.'

'Of course. Mum will die of joy. An accountant? On the committee? Can I tell her you'll do it?'

Rachel took a breath. 'Only if you two will let me buy you another glass of wine. I'm not sure one is enough for this sort of thing.'

'Well, I think we should have a toast,' said Lindy when Rachel had returned with more wine. 'Meeting you two has been lovely!'

'I think I should toast moving into my own house after months of work,' said Rachel. 'I didn't want to do it on my own.'

'And I think we should all toast new beginnings,' said Beth. 'I know it's not the same for Lindy, who's always been here, but me and Rachel are starting a new life in the country.'

'You know what? I think if we thought hard we'd find some sort of project to do together,' said Lindy. 'Not just the village hall,' she added.

'I'll drink to that!' said Rachel.

'So will I! New beginnings—'

'And new friends!' said Lindy, raising her glass.

'Hooray!' said Beth, as she clinked glasses with her two new friends. Life was looking up.

A
Vintage
Wedding

Katie Fforde

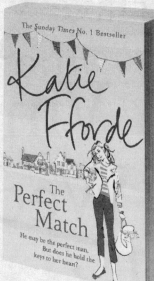

Have **you** read them all?

Find the whole list at...

www.katiefforde.com/books

Step into the world of

Katie Fforde

Hear direct from Katie by signing up to her newsletter, be the first to hear about her forthcoming books, enter competitions and much more at Katie's dedicated website

www.katiefforde.com

Connect with other fans and stay up to date with Katie's news by following her social media channels

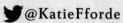